ALL THE LITTLE LIARS

Also by Victoria Selman

Truly, Darkly, Deeply

ALL THE LITTLE LIARS

VICTORIA SELMAN

QUERCUS

First published in Great Britain in 2023 by

QUERCUS

Quercus Editions Ltd
Carmelite House
50 Victoria Embankment
London EC4Y 0DZ

An Hachette UK company

A CIP catalogue record for this book is available
from the British Library

HB ISBN 978 1 52943 034 9
TPB ISBN 978 1 52943 035 6
EB ISBN 978 1 52943 037 0

10 9 8 7 6 5 4 3 2 1

Typeset by CC Book Production
Printed and bound in Great Britain by Clays Ltd, Elcograf S.p.A.

Papers used by Quercus are from well-managed forests and other responsible sources.

To my son Max,
one of my favourite people in the whole wide world,
and in memory of Maggie.
We will miss you always, baby girl.

'... *it all [came] from such a simple thing as just wanting to be loved*'

Patricia Krenwinkel

This book was inspired by various true crime cases. However, the characters in the novel, their actions and motivations, are all entirely the product of the author's imagination and are wholly fictitious.

From the *California Tribune*

July 21, 2003

FEARS MOUNT FOR TURTLE LAKE TEEN

Fears mount for a thirteen-year-old girl who disappeared from a party at Carlsbad's Turtle Lake four days ago — *Maya Hopkins reports.*

What We Know
The missing girl was last seen at around midnight on July 17. She told friends she was leaving because she'd 'had enough'. They offered to go with her but she told them to stay and have fun. That she would be fine on her own.

No one has seen or heard from her since.

Chilling . . .
Then yesterday, hikers made a grisly discovery: the word 'LIAR' on a tree trunk near the lake – scrawled in blood.

Police are yet to confirm whether the blood is a match for the missing teen, though a source told the *Tribune* the development is 'troubling'.

Latest

Investigators have now issued an AMBER Alert and are urging partygoers to call 911 if they have any information.

'Someone will have seen something, even if they didn't realize what it was at the time,' Lieutenant Owen King told reporters. 'People don't just vanish into thin air. Nobody disappears without a trace.'

Yet there is still no trace of the missing girl.

NOW

It was a case that shocked the nation, rocked our town to its roots. Put it on the map for all the wrong reasons.

As the details emerged, strangers hashed over the particulars waiting in line at supermarkets and Starbucks. Shook their heads at the horror of it all. At the terrible tragedy. On each of their faces, the same expressions of slack-jawed disbelief. And perhaps a certain ghoulish delight too.

How could such a thing happen? they asked. *Here in our neighbourhood? A neighbourhood like this?*

It's always the quiet ones, they said. *Shows you can never really know anybody . . .*

In time, of course, the conversation shifted. Obama was elected president. Michael Jackson suffered a cardiac arrest. The financial markets crashed.

Izzy's fate became just another true crime curiosity for people to puzzle over. They didn't forget about her, but they did move on.

It's different for me. I'm Izzy Jackman's sister. I don't get to forget or move on.

3

Especially given my role in what happened to her. The shameful part I played.

My iPhone rings as I'm rummaging in my handbag for a paracetamol. Shoulders hunched against the driving rain. Converse soaked; socks sodden.

The water is cold between my toes. March already but still no sign of spring.

I should have brought an umbrella, should have drunk less last night. Could have at least knocked back a glass of water before I hit the hay. That would have been good, would have made a change.

Story of my life: should've, could've, would've . . .

When will I learn?

The phone trills again, a nail through my skull.

I thought the point of vodka was it didn't give you a hangover. Or maybe I'm just getting old. Less tolerant in more ways than one. Knocking on thirty and already ancient.

Maybe if I drank less . . .

Should. Could. Won't.

I bypass the pill packet, pull out the phone, check the screen. It's not often I get calls. Or make them.

Backlit, three words: No Caller ID.

A telemarketer, I expect.

I could have some fun here. Say I've got my hands full, don't have time to speak. Unless do they perhaps know where I can get hold of some strong acid on the down-low? And a human-size barrel?

Or how about requesting their home number so I can call

them back at a more convenient time. Refuse to take 'no' for an answer, like that scene in *Curb Your Enthusiasm*. I do a pretty good Larry David impression. '*Prett-ay, prett-ay good . . .*'

Or perhaps just a sharp whistle down the line? Simple but effective. Though I'm not sure my thumping brain could take it today.

I answer.

'Yes?'

Always braver in my head . . .

There's a pause and a click as the line connects. The wail of a police siren in the background, different to the type you get on the limey side of the pond.

My physical response is immediate. A prickle down my spine. Hairs rising on my forearms.

Muscle memory. They say the mind forgets but the body never does.

'Finn?' says the voice on the other end.

Californian. Female. A faint lisp.

'Finn Jackman?'

Finn?

Blood crashes in my ears, the sudden onslaught of waves. My grip tightens around the phone, fingers unconsciously searching for solidity. In my chest cavity, a hollowing.

Finn Jackman . . .

It's been twenty years since I've heard that name.

Twenty years, I've been wearing a mask.

BEFORE

I changed my name after I lost my sister. All anybody saw when they saw me was Izzy Jackman even though she was a good foot taller and we looked absolutely nothing alike.

Izzy with her turned-in knees and knobbly elbows. Wide-set eyes and coltish limbs. Sprawled sideways on a chair, legs flung over the arm. Chewing the tip of a pen or a hangnail. Always chewing something.

Versus me of the stocky legs and dust-covered feet. Scabs from climbing trees. Easily bored and hair invariably awry.

Branded cattle after I lost my sister. A flashing sign above my head.

Going to the grocery store, walking down the street – wherever I went, strangers would gawk. Whisper behind their hands—

'Isn't that Finn? Izzy Jackman's sister?'

'God, that family . . . What must it be like?'

'Only thirteen. Just awful . . .'

It was three years before *Hannah Montana* hit the Disney Channel, yet even then most ten-year-olds dreamed of fame. But I wasn't most girls. Not after Turtle Lake.

After Izzy was taken from us, I craved anonymity. Longed to blend into the background. To become invisible.

Instead, I was an exhibit. Everyone wanted a piece of me. The reporters who'd holler after me as I walked to school, wanting to know how I was doing. How it felt to be related to Izzy.

People I knew, people I'd never met. They all had an opinion, all wanted to be part of the story.

Vultures, my father called them, pushing the slats in the blinds apart with his thumb and forefinger. Tutting as he took in the hounds and their news vans before ducking back into his study . . . His sanctuary. His escape room.

I longed to escape what had happened. Not that you ever get to escape something like that. Murder is a stone cast into a pond. The ripples fan wide, a disturbance beneath the surface that never goes away.

Carlsbad was haunted. My sister was everywhere I looked and yet nowhere she should have been. Her ghost was down by the lagoon where we clambered on rocks and caught the frog that day. In the potato-chips aisle at Vons, badgering Dita for Fritos back before she started dieting and checking the calorie count on everything. In the yard reading Judy Blume, swaying gently in our old string hammock.

If only I could stop seeing her, stop thinking about her. Remembering was agony. Every cloud carried her face, every crack in the sidewalk brought back her smile. It was as if the whole world were conspiring to remind me what I'd had and what I'd lost.

As if it would never let me alone.

My father was haunted, too. He forgot to eat, would go days without sleeping. I'd come down in the morning to find him sitting in yesterday's clothes, eyes made of marble.

He spoke in monosyllables. Got thinner by the week.

'Goddamn internet,' he'd mutter. 'Are they ever going to stop?'

The web had given him a rough ride. People he'd never even met, blaming him for what had happened with Izzy.

They called him a 'bad parent', reckoned if he'd been working fewer hours and paying closer attention, things wouldn't have wound up the way they had. That she would never have got involved with a man like Ryder Grady. That her friendship with Plum and Lu would never have turned so deadly.

Maybe the naysayers were right.

Maybe I was a bad sister too. There are things I should have done differently as well. Things that might have changed what came to pass.

He was aloof, folk said when my father ignored their questions. Cold, when he kept his eyes directed at the ground.

'I've never once seen him cry,' I heard one of our dumbass neighbours tell the mailman.

Mothers at the school gates pondered whether he was 'taking anything'. Our pastor suggested he started coming to services. *Jesus loves you . . .*

Jesus had a funny way of showing it.

My father was a judge, one of the youngest ever elected to the Californian bench, though he never seemed very young to me with his plodding walk and the way he squinted at the Olive Garden menu when he forgot to bring his reading glasses.

Not that he needed them. He always ordered the same thing.

Let me guess. Parmigiana for you, Judge?

I used to think he was famous. Everyone seemed to know who he was. Used to have a 'Hi, Judge' for him when he came into their shops. Asked his opinion on everything from fishing to football, although he was interested in neither (but polite enough not to show it).

Or maybe he was just smart. He needed folk to like him. Needed them to put a cross by his name each time fresh ballot papers came out.

My sister and I didn't see that side of it. We were just two girls proud of our dad.

'People really look up to him,' Izzy said. 'Imagine what that must feel like . . .'

It all changed after Turtle Lake. The judge found himself judged, which was tough, not least because of how hard he was already judging himself. The town's criticisms amplifying his own:

How did I miss the signs?

Where did it all go wrong?

How could I have been so blind?

I've spent my adult life asking the same questions, reading whatever I could lay my hands on about Turtle Lake.

I must have listened to every podcast, scoured every Reddit thread. Studied all the books and police reports. Even watched that stupid movie that came out on cable a couple of years ago. *Inside the Circle*, it was called. The shout line: *She thought they were her friends . . .* Yet despite all my searching, I still don't understand how it could have happened. How things could have gone so far.

Gone so wrong.

BEFORE

We left California and moved to London at the end of '03. Three months after the sentencing, three days after the capture of Saddam Hussein. The dictator's dishevelled hair and scraggy beard were on all the front pages but all anyone in our town was talking about was Izzy.

'Fresh start will be good for us,' my father said, sealing yet another box shut.

BOOKS, he wrote on the side in black marker pen. Added: *FINN* in brackets.

'Not Finn,' I whined. 'You have to call me Kat now.'

As if a new name would change what had happened. As if it would make everything okay.

'What's that?' he asked in an absent way, breaking off another piece of tape with his teeth.

'My name's Kat. Not Finn anymore.'

How many times had I told him?

'Sorry, yes,' he mumbled. 'Takes a bit of getting used to . . .'

The idea of moving took some getting used to as well.

The house was filled with cardboard boxes. Rooms stripped

bare, back to their bones. A carcass when the birds have done picking at it.

I was on the couch, sorting the contents of a drawer. The couch that had been in our living room my whole life. There was now a photo of it on eBay: *L-shaped sectional, 100% brown leather* . . .

'Are you ready for me to do that one up?' my father asked, coming over to inspect how far I'd got. (Not very far.)

He pulled out a pink shell, grains of sand embedded in the whorls. Let out an exasperated sigh.

'I'm tired of saying the same thing, Finn. You need to be selective. We can't take every little doodad.'

'Kat, not Finn!'

I snatched the shell back, traced my finger along the spiral lines.

'It's special.'

'So is everything, apparently. Put it in the "chuck" pile, please.'

I don't know why I didn't tell him I'd found the shell at South Beach with my mother. He might have let me keep it if I had.

She had died six years earlier. June 1997, a few short months after our housekeeper, Dita, moved in with us. A collision coming home from the supermarket. On the passenger seat beside her, a cooler bag containing the rum raisin Häagen-Dazs I'd nagged her to get because we were all out and it was my favourite. The reason she'd gone out that day. The reason she hadn't made it home.

'You can't think like that, chick,' Dita told me. 'It wasn't your fault.'

'Whose fault was it, then?'

She kissed the top of my head, said God must have needed another angel in heaven.

'He only chooses the best people.'

I was mad at God for a long time. Why couldn't he have picked someone else's mom?

I liked to hold the things that reminded me of her. A penny she'd given to me for luck. The perfectly round pebble we'd discovered together on a walk up in the hills. The pink shell my father was now demanding I leave behind.

He could demand all he liked . . .

I told him I was going to the bathroom and snuck into Dita's room, planning to secrete the shell in one of her boxes. No way my father would go through our housekeeper's things.

'Place would fall apart without Dita,' he used to say.

The year my mother died, my father was elected to the Superior Court bench. I'm not sure which of the two events was the real reason he started working longer hours. Shutting himself in his study more. Telling us silence was golden and he wasn't to be disturbed.

Dita was the boss, he said.

'Make sure you do what she tells you.'

'You pay her. Doesn't that make *you* the boss?'

He said that was a terrible way to talk about a person who loved me like her own. It occurred to me that he hadn't answered my question, and also that it was probably wise not to say so. My father liked to encourage what he called 'independent thinking', but he also didn't like backchat.

A tricky tightrope.

Plus, it was true. Dita did love Izzy and me. And we loved her right back. Even when she was lecturing us about our attitudes and the state of our hair or fingernails.

You trying to start a garden under those? Go clean them before you get worms . . .

I opened the door to her room now, a room that always smelled of cinnamon and vanilla. The smell of baking and of her.

It took me a beat to realise what was wrong.

We were moving to England in two days and yet there wasn't a single box or suitcase in sight. Her hairbrushes and pots of face cream were still laid out on top of her dresser. The closet still full of her clothes. Her cardigans and smocks and the polka-dot two-piece she kept special for church. A size twenty and too tight on her.

Dita's clothes were always big and always tight.

On the shelves, the collection of porcelain kittens that had belonged to her mother, whom she'd stayed in Green River to nurse before moving in with us, because 'Family's all you got. You do everything you can to take care of them, chick'.

On the nightstand, one of her Barbara Cartland paperbacks with two people in Victorian costume kissing on the jacket. A box of Kleenex. A half-empty box of See's Candies. (I checked, helped myself to a Scotchmallow.)

I looked around, chewing. Understanding slowly seeping in.

'Dita!' I yelled. 'Dita!'

She came hurrying into the room, wiping floury hands on her apron. Put one of them to my forehead.

'What's wrong? Are you feeling okay?'

I pushed her off, made a sweeping gesture with my arm.

'All your stuff . . . None of it's packed.'

She exhaled, rubbed her lips together. Then in a soft voice –

'I'm not coming with you, chick.'

I examined her face, searching for the joke. But her expression was serious.

'What are you talking about?'

Dita had practically raised me after my mother passed. It was Dita who tucked me in at night and got me up for school in the morning. Dita who knew without me needing to say a word if something was wrong. Who always knew what to say to make it better.

Of course, she was coming. We couldn't move without her!

I love you girls to heaven and back, she'd tell Izzy and me.

I was three and a half when she arrived on our doorstep with her big carpetbag and Mary Poppins umbrella. It was the year Madeleine Albright became the first female secretary of state and *The Lion King* debuted on Broadway. An omen in that, my father would joke once we'd got to know her better. *Nothing Miss Dita wouldn't do for her cubs!*

My mother introduced us carefully, explained this was our new housekeeper and she was coming to live with us. To help look after us and take care of the place.

'Can you say "hello" nicely, Finn?'

I stuck out my lip, told her, 'I wouldn't say it meanly.'

Dita laughed a booming laugh that matched her big bouncy curls. A laugh from the belly with her head tipped back and all her teeth on display. I'd never seen such white teeth. Asked, 'Are you a dentist?'

She crouched down so we were level, took my hands in hers. Swung my arms open and closed.

'Afraid I like cookies too much to be a dentist,' she said, chuckling, and straight away I knew we'd be friends.

I loved her immediately. Loved her scent of snickerdoodles, which it turned out she was rather good at making, though peach cobbler was her real speciality.

'How old are you?' I asked.

She winked, tapped the side of her nose.

'Old enough not to share.'

I never did find out her age, though she wasn't exactly what she'd have called a 'spring lamb'. Mrs Malaprop, my father nicknamed her. For a long time, I thought that was her actual last name.

The idea she wasn't coming with us to London was ridiculous. I must have misunderstood.

'You mean you're getting a different flight?'

Maybe she was staying back to close up the house? To tidy away the last bits? If so, perhaps she could help me out with that shell . . .

She shook her head.

'No, honey. I'm not taking a different flight.'

'Then what? I don't get it.'

She breathed in deep, said my father would explain.

'But—'

'Talk to Daddy, chick . . .'

'Fine, I will,' I replied as if it were a threat.

I marched into the living room where my father was closing up another box.

'Dita says she's not coming to London. You need to tell her she is.'

He set down the tape, squeezed his temples.

I took in the set of his shoulders, the downturn at the corners of his mouth.

'Daddy?' I said, stomach tightening. Then, in a quieter tone – 'What's going on?'

'I can't get her a visa,' he said.

'What are you talking about? You got them for us.'

'It's different. I'm sorry. I've tried everything, Finn.'

I folded my arms, told him to try harder.

You can achieve anything you want if you just put your mind to it, he used to tell my sister and me. One of his 'life lessons'.

Hard work is all it takes. A bit of elbow grease.

Clearly, he wasn't giving it his all. I said as much.

He shook his head slowly from side to side, told me he was sorry.

'I've done everything I can, sweetheart.'

But he wouldn't look at me as he said it.

I started to cry.

'She's got to come. She's family.'

All we have left hung unspoken like so much else.

At last, he met my eyes. Told me:

'I'm your family, Finn.'

'So is Dita,' I shouted. 'And I've told you. My name's Kat!'

NOW

The woman at the end of the phone speaks again.

'Are you still there, Finn?'

Finn . . .

Down the line, her voice splinters. Shards sticking in my veins.

How does she know who I am?

How has she found me?

How has she got my number?

After we moved to England, my father finally stopped calling me Finn. He slipped now and then, but each time I put him straight and gradually he became used to my new name. Or maybe he just didn't care anymore about who I used to be.

I know I didn't.

I stopped caring about anything. Worked hard at it, realising not caring was the only way not to feel. And what wouldn't I sacrifice to not feel? What wouldn't I do?

I craved numbness the same way girls my age craved adventure. If only I could block out what had happened.

If only I could kid myself I'd had nothing to do with it. That it wasn't my fault.

At school we learned about the Buddhist Wheel of Life. The hungry ghosts with empty stomachs they can't fill because their necks are too thin for food. My father and I were hungry ghosts, unable to connect with the world. Empty inside.

'I don't know how to move past it,' he admitted one time.

'Me neither,' I told him.

A rare moment of openness on both our parts. After Izzy, after the move to England, we both turned inwards. Clammed up.

I kept my bedroom door shut, Coldplay's 'Fix You' crying through the walls as I took my first experimental nips of vodka and painted my nails black.

It was only at night, when the house was still, that I let the tears come. Silent tears leaking into my pillow.

Words uttered like a mantra to keep me safe—

'My name is Kat. My name is Kat . . .'

I whispered the words over and over until the sobs began to fade and I finally drifted off to sleep.

My name is Kat . . .

I've been saying it so long, I almost believe it. Yet the woman at the end of the phone knows it's a lie.

Knows my name isn't Kat. It's Finn Jackman.

BEFORE

I chose my new name on a whim. I was eating a KitKat, nib-
bling the chocolate off the fingers in a way my father said
always put him in mind of a hamster.

'Your mother used to eat them the same way . . .'

'Sure you don't want to give it some more thought?' Dita
asked as I filled in the name change form later on.

I shook my head, told her no. Kat would do.

All I wanted was to be someone else. I didn't care who, so
long as it wasn't Finn Jackman anymore.

It was a far cry from the first time I'd changed my name.

My mother was a voracious reader. She called me and my
sister after her favourite literary characters, though neither
moniker stuck.

Izzy was christened Elizabeth after Elizabeth Bennet in *Pride
and Prejudice*. My father wasn't sure about it, felt it was a bit
formal for such a 'little one' and promptly shortened it to 'Lizzie',
which in time got cut down to Izzy, and that one clung fast, no
matter how much my mother kept up with her Elizabeth-ing.

She tried and failed again with me. I was never going to be

an Anne, just as I'd never be persuaded out of my overalls or down from the trees. *Would you get out of there? You're a girl, not a gorilla . . .*

'I hate the name Anne.'

Hated Anne of Green Gables too. What a priss!

'Anne's a lovely, sensible name. Everyone should be called Anne.'

My father laughed.

'That'd work . . .'

He rented *The Adventures of Huck Finn* from the Blockbuster over on El Camino Real.

DVDs make such a difference. When you compare the picture quality to cassettes . . .

We watched it together one rainy afternoon, the two of us curled up on the couch with Twizzlers and a big bowl of buttered popcorn.

'Huck's brilliant,' I said between mouthfuls.

A kindred spirit as against 'sivilizing' as I was. No one ever managed to force that guy into fancy clothes or shouted at him for snapping up their cigarettes to stop them getting lung cancer.

My mother came into the den as the credits were rolling. She perched on the arm of the couch and helped herself to a handful of corn. One piece at a time in her mouth like a baby bird.

'What have you two been watching?'

My father told her. I told her I wanted to change my name. That Huck was my new hero and that's what I wanted to be called from now on.

'I'm not calling you Huckleberry,' she replied, face steely like the day she'd discovered what I'd done to her Marlboros.

'Finn, then.'

And that was that.

NOW

'Finn . . . ?'

The woman on the end of the phone isn't giving up.

'It's Kat now,' I say, immediately kicking myself. I haven't got by all these years by spilling the beans on the first 'hello'.

'I know who you are,' she replies.

The animal part of my brain is screaming, but when I respond, my voice is steady. A pitch higher than usual, maybe, but not so high as to draw attention to my creeping panic. I've been wearing a mask for twenty years, hiding who I am. I've got good at it.

Good at deflecting too.

'Who are you?'

I hear the click of a lighter. A deep draw.

'Elsa Stone. I'm working on a TV documentary about your sister's case. An exposé.'

'What sort of exposé?'

I inject a note of disdain into the last word. There have been a number of programme-makers over the years claiming to have new details about what has become known as the 'Turtle

Lake Case'. So far, the only thing that's ever been new is the person narrating.

'I've uncovered some information,' Elsa Stone says. 'Raises some questions . . .'

'Oh yeah? What sort of questions?'

'If we got the whole picture.'

I scoff.

'Seems every day there's some new conspiracy theory.'

It's true and yet, despite what I tell myself about not expecting anything, I live in hope that one of them will hit the mark. Because, although I have no intention of admitting it to Elsa Stone, I've spent the last twenty years wondering if there's more to what happened at Turtle Lake than we've been led to believe.

The confessions wrapped things up nicely for the District Attorney, but for me, the ribbon was loosely tied. Questions nag all this time later, questions I've never been quite able to resolve.

Elsa Stone seems to read my mind, not a mean feat from five and a half thousand miles away. Or what must be the early hours in Cali.

'The DA got his scalps,' she says. 'But there are parts of the story that don't make sense. Especially given what I've discovered.'

'And what have you discovered?'

I try to sound dismissive. I never was much good at poker though. Elsa Stone, it seems, is rather better at it than me.

She injects a teasing note – 'I'll show you mine if you show me yours . . .'

I feign ignorance, keep my voice neutral despite my scudding heart.

'I was ten years old,' I say. 'I don't know what you think I know.'

'I expect you know more than you think you do,' she answers, echoing the way Lieutenant King implored the Turtle Lake partygoers to come forward as the days wore on with no results.

We're more interested in what you know than what you did . . .

'Don't you want to know what really happened out there?' Stone asks.

More than anything, I think but don't say.

Again, she reads my mind. Asks:

'What if I could help you fill in the blanks?'

BEFORE

I can't help thinking that what happened at Turtle Lake was in some way born out of our mother's car accident back when my sister was in the second grade learning her multiplication tables – and I was still at home watching *Sesame Street*.

If our mother had been around, would Izzy have become so shy? Such an introvert? Would she have struggled quite so hard to fit in? Wanted to, so much?

Would she have been such an easy target for Ryder Grady? Or Plum and Lu, who were in many ways just as predatory. Plum in particular was a master manipulator. A skilled puppeteer.

Grady's pimp, I suspect. Bringing him girls so desperate to belong, they'd fall for his charm and false promises.

Though perhaps that's unfair. Grady was good-looking and charismatic enough to lure his own girls, from what I've read since.

I don't know if our mother's death paved the way to Turtle Lake, but I do know it exploded our world. Nothing could be counted on anymore, nothing taken for granted.

'I thought death was something that happened to other

people,' I told my father one night, as he sat by my bed stroking my hair while I fought sleep and the terrors that came with it.

'Everyone dies, sweetheart,' he said, voice thick.

'Not like *that*.'

He kissed the top of my head, lips resting there an extra second.

'No,' he agreed. 'Not like that.'

In an instant, the friendly existence we'd known had become unsafe. Threats lurked in every crevice, monsters under the bed all too real.

I bawled each time my father got in the car, started shaking whenever the doorbell rang.

Was there a police officer on the stoop? What fresh horror were they waiting to relay?

Who had died now?

The way we found out about the car accident wasn't dissimilar to the way we found out about Izzy. The police showing up at the door. The terrible pronouncement.

The aftershock.

The shock of our mother's sudden death affected Izzy and me differently. For my part, I reacted with panic attacks and nightmares.

My sister stopped talking.

She became completely mute, although inside, she was screaming.

A screaming that left no space for words, Dr Ableman, our family doctor, explained. When pain becomes too much to bear, we shut down.

'It's the brain's way of protecting itself.'

The only time I heard Izzy speak was in her sleep as I tiptoed to the bathroom in the night. She was garrulous then, even if what she said was nonsense: *Where's my cape . . . Try harder . . . Stand back!*

I'd curl up on the floor beside her bed to listen. To remind myself of how her voice sounded. Of the way things used to be.

I have a memory of her elementary school principal, Mrs Langley, phoning up my father to say she was worried about her.

'It's not only that Izzy's not speaking. I'm concerned she's cutting herself off from the other kids, Judge. She sits by herself in the corner, refusing to join everyone else on the mat at circle time. At recess, she just kicks a pebble about. At lunchtime, she hardly eats.'

There was a moment's pause and then when my father didn't fill it, Mrs Langley suggested that perhaps it might be worth taking her to a therapist.

I was listening in on the phone in the living room. A habit I'd recently acquired in the fervent hope that any day now we were going to get a call telling us there had been a huge mistake and my mother hadn't died after all.

If that call came, I wanted to be the first to hear it.

'When traumas are left unprocessed, they metastasize,' the principal told my father. 'Talking is the only way to heal.'

He made a scoffing sound.

'I think that's what you call a Catch-22, Mrs Langley.'

I wasn't sure what playing ball had to do with anything.

Dr Ableman came to the house again. The man who gave

us all our childhood illness vaccinations and lemon sherbets afterwards. *What a brave girl. I told you it wouldn't hurt!*

He took Izzy's pulse. Flattened her tongue with a popsicle stick and looked down her throat. Checked her heart with a stethoscope that he rubbed on his jacket first to warm it up.

'Friction,' he explained to my sister, who responded with a robot stare and steely silence.

He said he was going to check her heart rate if that was okay with her.

She said nothing to that either.

'Do you know what your heart's for, Izzy?'

I glanced at Dita. He knew she's stopped talking, right?

'I know what your heart's for,' I said, wondering if the right answer would earn me a candy. 'It's where you keep your love.'

Dr Ableman smiled at my father, said something about wasn't that precious? But nothing about lemon sherbets.

'It's been two months, Doc,' he responded, throwing his hands up. 'The child hasn't said a word. Not one.'

Ableman wound up his stethoscope. Put it away in his black leather bag that magically snapped shut without a single zip or clasp.

'There's nothing wrong with her. She's simply processing the trauma, Judge. She'll speak when she's ready.'

'Two months,' my father repeated, exasperated. 'It's not right.'

'You can't expect her to understand the permanence of death, to come to terms immediately with her mother's loss. To be honest, Nathaniel, even I struggle to understand death sometimes.'

My father rubbed his chin. The bristles made a sandpaper sound. It had been a while since he'd shaved.

'How long will it last? This ... mutism.'

He was a man who liked certainty, who dealt in facts.

Dr Ableman shrugged. Moved his pudgy palms up and down like he was weighing the air.

'It's hard to say. Every case is different.'

'What can I do, doctor?' Dita asked. *Doc-tor.* 'I'd do anything for these girls. But nothing's working. Bribes. Cuddles. Washington Beach. Nothing ...'

Washington Beach was a fair old ways away from our house, but Dita's favourite place ever since my father had first introduced it to us all one Labor Day weekend.

She'd take us to the pier. *Look, girls! Do you see the seals?* Treat us to ice cream sundaes at Moo Town, the parlour 'your daddy's folks used to take him when he was a kid ...'

She shook her head now. Tutted.

'Poor little worm.'

Ableman's bushy eyebrows shot up.

'Worm?'

'A term of endearment,' my father explained.

He didn't explain 'Mrs Malaprop'.

'Of course, it's an endearment,' Dita said, clearly horrified the doctor could possibly think anything different. 'Izzy is my whole world. Both those girls are. Please, how to get my baby talking again?'

Her grammar aways got screwy when she was anxious or stressed.

The doctor picked up his leather bag that I'd been playing with, stole my nose.

'Give her time,' he answered, and then he was gone.

Weeks went by, maybe longer. Izzy kept her lips sealed shut, communicated only with nods and head shakes.

'She'll come round,' my father reassured Dita, his tone hopeful more than confident. 'You heard what the doc said. Just needs time, that's all.'

'Doctor's barking at the wrong dog,' Dita muttered. 'That child don't need time. She needs to speak. You remember what her principal told you? That Mrs Langley. You can't heal without talking.'

I wasn't sure if Dita knew about the conversation with Mrs Langley because my father had told her, or because she'd been listening in on his phone call as I had.

'Dita's like Santa Claus,' my mother used to say. 'She knows everything.

'So, you'd better behave yourselves . . .'

'Dr Ableman's a professional,' my father said now. 'We need to trust him. He knows best.'

She made the little harrumphing noise Izzy reckoned made her sound like the seals she took us to watch at the beach. *Their cute little whiskery faces . . .*

When he'd left for court, she did things her way. And as usual, her way involved food.

'What you need is an incentive, chick. Am I right? Doctor knows best?' Another harrumph. 'Not better than Dita.'

There followed a series of bribes.

'Say my name, chick. Just my name, that's all, and you can have a Tootsie Roll.'

Izzy sat under the table picking at her cuffs as if wondering how far she could stretch them. Whether they'd make her disappear.

'Or a piece of apple pie? You like apple pie, don't you, baby?'

'I like apple pie,' I said, pulling at Dita's apron. 'I'll say your name . . .'

Izzy tugged harder at her cuffs, couldn't quite get them over her wrists.

Dita swatted me away (*Not now, chick* . . .) crouched down to Izzy's level.

'With ice cream. You want ice cream? Just my name, baby. Or yours. Can you say your name for me?'

My sister looked up at Dita, like all she could hear was white noise.

Then she went back to her sleeves.

BEFORE

It turned out there was one person Izzy was prepared to speak to, as I discovered on a rainy evening in early fall, three months exactly since our mother's car accident. I know the date because every day I'd make a tally mark on the wall behind my headboard. My secret place.

I'm not sure why I was keeping track of the time, only that it seemed important to mark the days between 'Before' and 'After'.

When we lost Izzy, I delineated time in the same way. Though I didn't mark it off on my wall.

Dita told me so long as my mother was in my heart, she'd always be with me. But already I felt she was slipping away. As the weeks passed, I found it harder to conjure the way she felt when I hugged her. The sound of her laugh. How she smelled.

I'd open her closet sometimes, take out a sweater. Bury my nose in it trying to catch her scent. Though too often, all I caught was Yardley's Lavender rather than the true tang of her.

Dita found me crying once, my mother's pink angora cardigan balled up in my lap.

'What's wrong?' she asked and I told her.

'Your mother smelled of sunshine,' she said. 'And toast and vanilla. Her smell is here. The smell of home. Breathe it in. You couldn't lose it if you tried.'

She pulled me on to her lap. Kissed my hair, rubbed my back in circles the way she did when I'd had a bad dream.

Dita smelled of home, too.

Gradually my tears dried up.

Izzy didn't cry after our mother died. But she did speak to her, even though she was unable to speak to us.

Dita had sent me upstairs to tidy my room. *Like a grenade's hit it . . .*

Izzy's bedroom was next to mine. Her door was open, rain pattering against the windowpane.

From inside, the sound of someone talking.

It took me a beat to realise that someone was Izzy.

I peered in.

Who was she speaking to? There was no one else there, just Izzy lying on her back, staring at the ceiling with her knees tented. Deep in one-sided conversation with the air while she fiddled with her charm bracelet. A Christmas present from my mother. Our last Christmas together.

She wore it all the time in those days, only taking it off at night. 'You don't want the chain catching and snapping while you're asleep,' Dita said.

So, Izzy tucked it under her pillow, the same place she used to leave her teeth for the tooth fairy, until she decided fairies were babyish and not real and it was just Dita anyway.

How can it be Dita? She doesn't have wings . . .

I watched now, holding my breath in case it gave me away and broke the spell.

'I miss you,' Izzy was saying. 'Why did you have to leave us?'

There was a pause, a moment's silence punctuated only by the tick of her elephant clock on the nightstand. Its trunk was the minute hand. Its tail marked the seconds.

Dita said when I learned to tell time, I could get one too.

'I know you're always with us but not *everywhere*, right?' Izzy asked. 'Not the bathroom, I mean . . .'

There was another pause, then she said okay, good. Followed by: 'Have you met God yet?'

I couldn't contain myself any longer. Not because of the excitement at hearing Izzy speaking again after months of silence, but rather because I'd figured out who she was speaking to.

'Where is she?' I asked, bursting in.

My head went this way and that searching.

'Mommy?' I got down on the floor to look under the bed. Opened Izzy's closet. 'Where are you?'

'Don't be a dum-dum,' Izzy said rolling her eyes. 'You can't see her.'

'Can *you*?' I asked.

She shook her head, told me of course not.

'But you can hear her?'

Izzy just shrugged.

My stomach fluttered. A whole flock of butterflies, or whatever the collective noun is, landing at once.

'What did she say? When is she coming back?'

'She's not coming back, Finn. That's what dying means.'

'But you're talking to her?'

She stroked her bracelet, said, 'Yes.'

The butterflies gave way to something heavier.

'Why is she talking to you and not me? Why can't I hear her?'

I was so jealous of Izzy right then, but now a different feeling strikes me. How desperately sad it was that the only person she could communicate with was a ghost.

'I can pass a message on if you like?'

I sniffled. Told her, 'Okay.'

'What do you want me to say?'

'That I miss her,' I said. 'And that I'm sorry.'

She didn't ask why I was sorry. Just repeated what I'd said to the air. Then she reported back:

'Mom says she misses you too. And that you need to brush your hair more.'

I laughed. That sounded exactly like my mother. Like Dita too.

After that, Izzy started talking to the rest of us as well, although she wasn't as chatty as she used to be. Her voice stilted as though it had gone rusty from lack of use.

There was nothing stilted about Dita though. She got terribly overexcited when Izzy came into the kitchen and asked what was for dinner that evening.

'Oh, sweet Lord! She's speaking! My baby's speaking again. Thank you, Jesus. Thank you!'

My father had to take her aside and suggest – in what I thought of as his 'court voice' – not to make too big a deal out of it.

'We don't want her reacting the wrong way and clamming up again.'

He never was very good with big displays of emotion.

It was as though things were back to normal, or as normal as they could be without my mother there. But they weren't as normal as we might have liked.

Mrs Langley phoned up again one evening just as my father was taking off his work shoes and pouring a glass of port. A nightly tradition. Always sipped in silence in his easy chair by the fireplace with his eyes closed. We were only allowed to talk to him when the glass was drained. *'A person needs a moment to decompress . . .'*

'I'm still a little concerned about Izzy,' Mrs Langley said.

I was listening in to the call. Heard the sigh that I knew signified my father's irritation.

'My daughter doesn't need a shrink, if that's what you're suggesting again,' he said curtly. 'She just needs time.'

'Of course,' the principal agreed in an appeasing tone. 'And everybody grieves in different ways. What concerns me is how Izzy is coping.'

'What about how she's coping?' my father asked.

Mrs Langley sucked her teeth, spoke in a softer tone.

'Some of the things she's been saying. She's clearly anxious. Hyperfocused on death.'

My father laughed bitterly.

'Well, of course she is.'

'I think we might be looking at a form of PTSD,' the principal continued quickly. 'The other day, she burst into tears because she couldn't feel her heart beating. We're concerned, Judge Jackman.'

He said nothing. She tried a different tack.

'Have you noticed anything unusual in her behaviour at home?'

He said no, he hadn't. Didn't mention that she was wetting the bed. Or that she'd started sleepwalking.

Nor did he mention the conversations she was having with our dead mother, though there was a different reason for that.

He didn't know about them.

I sat with Izzy every evening while she communed with the other side. Bedtime is when she's listening most, she claimed.

'How do you know?' I asked.

'Because that's when we say our prayers, of course.'

She was wise, my sister. Or rather, I thought so then. The decisions she made later suggest otherwise.

The movie strapline: *She thought they were her friends . . .*

That night, I asked Izzy if I could sleep in her room.

'Why?'

'Mommy might have a message for me while I'm asleep.'

She considered the request, clucked her tongue on the roof of her mouth the way Dita did when she was trying to work out how long to stick a pot roast in the oven.

'Okay,' she agreed. 'But only if you give me your snow globe.'

The snow globe was my last Christmas present from our mother, the soundtrack from *The English Patient* playing in the background while we tore off wrapping paper.

Izzy had been jealous when I opened my gift, wanted to know why she hadn't got a globe too.

My parents exchanged amused glances.

'For the last year you've been driving me mad for a charm bracelet!' my mother told her.

She laughed, called Izzy a silly bunny. Said she only wanted the globe because I'd got one. Then, turning to me – 'See, Finny, it's Carlsbad inside. There's the church and the golf course and the lagoon.'

A tiny glass world. I loved it.

I kept it by my bed. We shook it together every night before I went to sleep. After my mother died, I pretended she was sitting beside me watching the flakes fall on our town.

'I'll give you anything else you want,' I told Izzy now. 'Just not that.'

She shook her head. Said, 'The snow globe's the only thing I want.'

I tried to bargain.

'What if I get you your own one? Reese's Pieces too. One of the big bags.'

Izzy shook her head, *no.*

'I want yours. Not some stupid one from a shop.'

I asked her why it made any difference, though of course I knew. I could have got her an identical globe but it wouldn't have been as good as mine because my mother wouldn't have touched it.

Izzy shrugged, played a good hand.

'I mean, if you don't want to talk to Mommy . . .'

I gritted my teeth. What choice did I have?

So, I relented, and in return Izzy continued to pass on celestial messages that were usually to do with how I should share better with my sister and let her hold the TV remote when we watched Cartoon Network.

It wasn't the best trade-off. And then a few weeks later, I found the globe in her wastepaper basket. The glass was cracked as if it had been smashed against something hard. A three-inch scar running across its surface.

'You broke it!' I shouted, eyes welling. 'How could you?'

I'd been holding on to a secret hope of getting it back. Honestly or otherwise.

'You had no right snooping through my things,' Izzy answered with absolutely no apology.

Neither of us were much good at saying sorry or owning up.

I told her she needn't think she was so special, I snooped through everyone's things. And then I spent the rest of the day pointedly avoiding her. Exiting a room when she entered it. Saying no when she suggested a game. A hundred tiny cuts until she came grovelling as I knew she would. Though she still didn't say the S-word.

'It was an accident. Trust me.'

My father always said when a person asks you to trust them, it's a sure sign you should do the reverse. But Izzy was my sister.

'If you can't trust family, who can you trust?' Dita said.

Two days later, Izzy gave me another snow globe she'd bought in Rite Aid. *Me and Dita went there specially.* It didn't have the same association. But I said thank you and that I forgave her, and in time I did.

I never thought to ask her *why* she'd broken the one I'd given her. It's only now, with the benefit of hindsight, that I think I understand.

Izzy hadn't been careless, or vindictive, as I'd been convinced at the time. Rather she'd smashed the glass world because her world was broken. And it was easier to express her pain with actions than words.

NOW

'Hindsight is an amazing thing . . .'

Elsa Stone is trying to prise me open the way Dita would shuck clams with the little rounded knife she kept specially. *You want something, you got to work at it, chick . . .*

Elsa Stone is working at it, that's for sure.

'I'd like to share this new information with you, get your take. And some other details about the case that don't add up. Maybe you can help shed some light.'

I wonder for a moment if she's thinking of the particular detail that's always troubled me. But how can she possibly be? She wasn't even there.

'What's this information, then?' I ask as nonchalantly as I can.

A voice that promises nothing in return.

She misunderstands. Or perhaps she just answers as if she has.

Wily bastards, journalists, my father used to say.

After Turtle Lake, after the newshounds tried every move in the playbook to get him to talk. Tried them on Dita and me too.

Wily bastards . . .

He never cursed before we lost Izzy, and the only beef he had with reporters was that they might prejudice a trial. Afterwards, 'bastards' was one of the milder expressions he used about the media. And his 'beef' with them went way beyond their potential impact on a jury.

Instead of divulging this so-called 'new information', Elsa Stone starts listing some of the facts she says don't chime.

'Like where she was found. Doesn't it strike you as strange?'

Her words conjure the image ADA Madden showed the court. *Exhibit C. The victim's body . . .*

Bloated and marshmallow white from being in the water so long. A life reduced to marine debris.

I shake my head to dispel the mental picture, ask Elsa Stone what's strange about the discovery site.

Discovery site. Such a clinical term, though it does help to think that way. The language of pathology is designed to keep emotion in check.

'It was thirty miles away from Turtle Lake,' Elsa Stone says.

I tell her I don't follow.

'So, how did it get there?' she clarifies.

I rub the back of my neck. If only she'd called this evening, I could be uncapping a screw top. Taking the edge off.

'Grady?' I suggest. 'He had wheels.'

A VW Bug, as I've since learned. The windows painted black.

I sense Elsa Stone shake her head. Hear the click of her lighter again.

'Grady didn't get his hands dirty. You know that.'

She's right. But it doesn't mean he didn't have blood on them.

'Either way, it doesn't change anything,' I say.

I'd let in a sliver of hope that maybe this woman had something. You'd think I'd have learned by now, hope never helped anyone.

I'm about to end the call when Elsa Stone speaks again.

'Maybe where she was found doesn't change anything,' she says. 'But what I've uncovered might . . .'

From the *True Crime Stories* blog

True Crimes Uncovered: Case #23 – Turtle Lake

July 17, 2003: Three friends went to a party. Only two came back.

The 'Turtle Lake Case' shocked the world in a way few other crimes ever have. Twenty years on, people are still talking about what happened that night – and how it could have happened.

Still asking: 'Why?'

As a mother of a thirteen-year-old girl, the case has a particular resonance for me.

With teens governed by their perpetual need for peer approval and exposed to predators on a near daily basis, the dangers facing them are rife.

'Stranger Danger' no longer means a dirty old man trying to lure your kid into his car with a bag of candy. These days, the 'stranger' is most likely someone they have befriended online. Someone they think understands them in a way no one else can.

But as Turtle Lake shows, it's not just strangers and the internet our children have to worry about. The real threat can lie much closer to home.

As so, I tell my daughter:

'Be careful who you trust. Salt and sugar look the same.'

BEFORE

'Just think of all the new friends you'll make,' Dita told me in the same cajoling tone she used to get me to sample some new food or other.

You can't say you don't like it if you haven't even tried it. Go on, just one bite . . .

She couldn't get me to bite this time though.

I was starting grade school and wasn't the least bit happy about it. Izzy didn't seem overly keen on the place and from what she'd told me, I couldn't see why I would be either.

Every morning she had to be up at seven-thirty and out the door by eight with Dita nagging at her all the while to hustle or she'd be late. She never got to play outside after breakfast and had to do homework when she got in. Spelling bees, math quizzes, it was never-ending.

Plus, the other kids were dopes, she said. Just plain mean.

'They judge you on everything,' she warned me. 'If you don't wear the right clothes, nobody speaks to you the whole day.'

I glanced down at my grubby overalls, at the new rip on the knee.

'What are the right clothes?'

Izzy gave an exaggerated shrug, shoulders all the way up to her ears.

'Don't ask me!'

There were plenty of good trees to climb in our backyard and a rope swing we'd rigged up at the edge of the Eucalyptus Grove Trail. Not to mention fresh cookies in the pantry and as much TV as I could persuade Dita to let me watch.

'Maybe I'll go to school next year,' I told my father.

'Yes, you'll go then too,' he said and then chuckled as though he'd made a good joke.

I gave him the stink eye, tried a different tack.

'I don't feel well. I think I've got a bug.'

I clutched my belly, pulled a face.

'Back-to-school-itis, I expect,' he said, chuckling again.

The chuckling was annoying. I let him know. Asked why he couldn't just teach me himself.

'I have a job, Finn,' he replied. 'Who's going to bang the gavel if I don't show up at court?'

'You taught me to read, what's the difference?'

He ding-donged my pigtail.

'You want to end up as bad at math as your old man?'

So, we were negotiating . . .

'Okay, forget math. We can just read.'

He shook his head and turned the page of his newspaper to indicate the subject was closed.

'I'm afraid it doesn't operate that way, sweetheart. School starts tomorrow. Now run along and have your bath, please.'

The radio was on. He turned up the volume. Smiled as the anchor announced: *Gore leads Bush in six polls.*

The next day, Izzy and I walked through the school gates together. I'd moaned and bitched all the way there but now we'd actually arrived, I felt a little fizz of excitement. This was Izzy's domain and I was about to get the keys.

'You sure you don't want me to come with you? Help you settle in,' Dita asked.

I shook my head, told her Izzy would take me to my room. Reminded her my father had said that was fine.

'But it's your first day . . .'

'I've got Izzy,' I repeated, not picking up on the hurt note in her voice.

My sister was a skinny little thing who wouldn't say boo to a barn owl (one of Dita's sayings) but I felt brave with her around, like no one could hurt me. It didn't occur to me that she could be the one getting hurt.

Dita said, 'Alrighty then, if you're sure.' Gave me a hard kiss on the top of my head, a hand pressed to each cheek. 'Can't believe how big you're getting.'

I stood on my tippy toes.

'Nearly as tall as you.'

'Will be soon . . .'

'Stop it,' Izzy hissed. 'People are looking.'

I couldn't see anyone looking and didn't give a hoot if they were, but I did what my sister told me and scampered through the gates after her.

So, this is what it felt like to go to school!

The courtyard was buzzing with people. A cacophony of

voices that Izzy said gave her a headache, though really it wasn't so loud.

There were kids playing tag. Others chatting in groups, breaking off to welcome this or that one into the circle with excited heys. Stray fathers looking at their watches. Mothers standing around in gaggles swapping recipes and vacation stories.

I watched them a moment, a sudden sharp sting in my chest. My mother used to swap recipes and vacation stories too. Was always at the centre of any gaggle.

'You make friends wherever you go,' my father used to tell her.

She'd laugh, tell him he might make some too if he was less of an old curmudgeon.

I'm not that old . . .

Izzy was watching the moms too. I knew instinctively that she was feeling the same way as me. I slipped a hand in hers. She shook me off, cheeks flushing pink.

'What's wrong?' I asked.

'School's different,' she whispered, even though there was no one around to hear.

'Why?'

She just shuffled her feet, told me not to embarrass her.

I scowled, turned my back on her.

'I hate seeing them all with their mommies,' she admitted after a moment.

I knew it was her way of saying sorry and forgave her. Told her:

'Me too.'

A gang of girls all with the same perfectly straight blonde hair and pink high-tops were whispering in a huddle. One of them glanced over at where Izzy and I were standing. Izzy hesitated then gave a shy wave. The girl smirked, turned back to her posse. Said something that made them look as one at Izzy then start snickering.

'Are they laughing at you?' I asked my sister.

'Of course not,' she answered, face flaming. Then – 'Let's go wait someplace else.'

I spotted a kid who lived down our street. We'd run into each other down by the lagoon a few times over the summer. Built a dam together in the shallows, caught ourselves a little minnow.

'Hey Tucker,' I called, galloping over. 'Wait up!'

When the bell rang and his mother told him it was time to go in, I went back to find Izzy. She was right where I'd left her, kicking at the dirt with the toe of her sneaker, concentrating very hard on her feet.

'So, you've made a friend already,' she said, tone almost accusing. 'You were gone ages. What d'you talk about?'

I shrugged. What had we talked about?

Izzy fiddled with the charms on her bracelet, bit down on her lip.

'Well, I'm pleased for you,' she told me.

She didn't sound pleased.

The knot of blonde girls from before sauntered past, arms draped round each other. Whispering and giggling.

My sister stared after them longingly.

Extract from *Inside Ryder Grady's Ring*
(an NDC documentary)

Detective Albert Arnold (Carlsbad PD)

Izzy Jackman struggled to fit in socially. In grade school she was a loner. An outsider who ate lunch by herself and spent recess holed up in the library reading.

Her report cards from this time talk about a child who tried to interact with her peers but never quite 'got it right'.

In 2000, her homeroom teacher wrote: 'My sense is that Izzy wants to make friends, but doesn't quite know how.'

I believe we need to view what happened at Turtle Lake through this lens. A kid desperate to be accepted. Whatever the cost . . .

BEFORE

We had no way of knowing back then the cost of Izzy's pain. Where her desperation to be accepted would lead.

Anyone with eyes could see she was struggling though. How badly she wanted to fit in. To have friends to pass notes to in class. Someone to save her a place in the cafeteria. To call her by a silly nickname.

Daddy calls you Smelly Socks . . .

It's not the same.

It must have been excruciating to always have her nose pressed up to the glass. To watch the other kids running about inside the candy store but never be let through the door.

'Just ask to join in,' I told her one time.

She scuffed at the dirt, mumbled that she didn't know how. I tossed a balding tennis ball from one hand to the other. Said it was easy.

'There's always a game of tag or jump rope going on. It's no big deal.'

'Who do I ask?' she said. 'What do I say?'

I shrugged, said it didn't matter. And frankly, she didn't have to ask anyone.

'Just join in,' I repeated. 'No one cares who plays.'

'But what if they do?'

I made an exasperated noise like I was the big sister.

'You don't need to make such a matzo pudding out of it!'

Dita would have said 'palaver'. Matzo pudding was an expression of my father's. A number of his colleagues were Jewish. We were Episcopalians, not that you'd have guessed it from the Yiddish sayings he picked up on the bench. Or his obsession with Jackie Mason. *Hands down the funniest man in America . . .*

'You wouldn't understand,' Izzy snapped back. 'People like you. You don't even have to try.'

A line came back to me from a recent episode of *Everybody Loves Raymond*.

'People would like you too if you gave them a chance to get to know you. Just join in, Izzy.'

She shrugged, kicked at the dirt some more. Stirred up orange clouds of dust.

'Maybe . . .'

If I'd known what was round the corner, I'd have given her rather different advice:

Stay in your room until you're eighteen.

Switch to home-schooling.

Don't join in. Ever.

It wasn't long after this conversation that Izzy decided to take matters into her own hands. Quite literally.

*

It was a Saturday morning. We were down by the lagoon. Grey May and on the chilly side. I was climbing a jacaranda. Dita had her back propped against a rock, eating clementines and reading one of her precious Barbara Cartlands. She glanced over the top of the book, warned me I'd fall if I went any higher.

'You heard of Humpty Dumpty, right?'

I was about to retort that Humpty fell off a wall, not out of a tree, when I noticed Izzy at the water's edge. She'd rolled her jeans up to her knees and was standing in the shallows like an egret, skinny legs disappearing beneath the surface. Hands fishing about.

The light caught the down on her forearms. Lit the golden strands in her hair. She made a grab for something in the water, body darting down. Came up straight. Darted again.

What was she doing?

I shimmied down the trunk – ignoring Dita's entreaties to 'Take it slow, I don't have time to take you to the emergency room' – and wandered over to my sister.

'Can I play?'

She let out a frustrated 'dammit!'.

'I can't keep a hold of them.'

'Keep a hold of what?'

'These frogs. I've caught four so far, but each time they've got away.'

I scratched the back of my calf with the toe of my shoe.

'What do you want with a frog?'

Tadpoles I understood. We caught those all the time, kept them in jam jars until they grew legs. 'Metamorphosis', my father called it. *Amazing the way they transform . . .*

'I want a pet,' Izzy explained, brushing the hair out of her eyes with the back of her knobbly wrist.

'Ugly sort of pet.' I pulled a face. 'Imagine cuddling a frog! Horrid, slimy thing!'

I affected a shudder.

'Urgh!'

She said she thought they were 'kind of cute actually' and I shouldn't speak so loud, I might hurt their feelings.

'You've got a funny idea of cute,' I told her. 'And they can't hear me underwater.'

She shrugged again, scanning the lagoon for a tell-tale ripple.

'I just want something I can look after.'

'So, get a cat.'

A cat, I could get behind. Heather M from school had a cat. It slept on the end of her bed and let her brush its fur like a My Little Pony.

I said so to Izzy.

'Much better than a stupid frog.'

She shook her head and counted off on her fingers all the reasons why a cat wouldn't work, in the overly logical black and white way that was so typical of her.

'A. Daddy's allergic. B. Cats are always running away. C. They scratch. D—'

She broke off, pounced as a dark shadow moved through the water.

'Not again! They're too quick.'

I laughed.

'Guess frogs get away too, huh?'

'Will you help me?' she asked. 'Maybe if there are two of us . . .'

I wasn't too sure about the prize but I was keen on the game. I peeled off my socks and sneakers and waded in to join her.

It took us the rest of the morning but we got Izzy her frog in the end.

'What are you going to call it?' I asked.

'Abigail,' she said immediately.

It was our mother's name.

I can't help wondering now if Izzy wanted a pet because she wanted to control something, since she couldn't control anything else in her life. What the kids at school thought of her. Our mother dying . . .

My father used to accuse her of controlling me too, though I never minded. Being controlled by Izzy meant being wanted by her. She might not have had friends, but there was never a time I didn't want her to be mine.

She carried the Kermit home in her jacket pocket (and refused to call it that, no matter how much more appropriate a name it was than Abigail).

I'm not sure Mom would have liked a nasty frog named after her . . .

It's not nasty. And it's my frog. I can call it what I want.

The frog croaked as if in reply, squirmed about inside her jacket. She stroked it, whispered, 'Shh, it's okay' and 'Mama's here, Abigail' in soothing tones that didn't seem to soothe the frog one bit.

'Gives me the heebie-hobies,' Dita said. 'Whatever will you do with it?'

'Make it a house out of my old Heelys box,' Izzy answered.

'I'm going to fill it with leaves and wet grass. And it can swim about with me when I take a bath.'

'Wish I hadn't asked,' Dita muttered, looking a little queasy.

'What'll you feed it?' I said.

'They like flies.'

'You can't buy flies at PetSmart.'

Izzy thought about it, said maybe fishing tackle would work.

'Dita, can we go to Mr Hooper's store this afternoon?'

'You couldn't have just asked your daddy for a cat?'

'That's what I said!' I exclaimed triumphantly.

Izzy rolled her eyes and grumbled something about not going over all this again.

All through lunch, we heard the frog screaming inside its new house. A high-pitched wail that Dita said sounded like a human 'bean' being tortured.

'You need to let it out. Put it in a pond where it belongs.'

'She's just getting used to being here. She'll be okay when I go and play with her.'

'How do you know it's a her?' I asked.

'It wouldn't be called Abigail if it was a boy.'

The frog screeched again.

Dita set down her knife and fork, pursed her lips.

'Either you let it go, or I will.'

Izzy's eyes pooled. Eyes the exact same brown as Hershey's chocolate sauce.

'Give her a few more minutes. Please. She'll settle down. I promise.'

The frog screamed again. The sort of noise that cuts right through you.

'Dita's right,' I told Izzy. 'It's upset.'

'She's not an "it" and she's not upset. She's just lonesome, that's all.' Then calling up to the frog—

'Mama will be there in a minute, Abigail!'

Dita pushed her chair back.

'I'm not telling you again, Izzy. It's cruel . . .'

There was a moment's stand-off, the two of them glaring at each other across the cornbread, both their hands squared on the table. One second, two . . . and then Izzy's shoulders slumped.

'Fine. But you do it, I can't . . .'

Dita gave a little nod, told Izzy she was proud of her for doing the right thing. Went off to put 'Abigail' out of her misery.

'I'll set it in the Robertsons' pond. I'm sure they'll be happy for you to go visit.'

In the kitchen, Izzy blinked back tears. Whispered—

'She was my friend . . .'

NOW

I hang up with Elsa Stone as I reach my father's care home, a twice-weekly visit on my way into work. Unable to talk or even feed himself, he's unrecognisable as the man I once knew.

A man who was always immaculately dressed: a three-piece suit and pocket watch on court days, a button-down shirt and navy-blue sweater vest on weekends. Who quoted Jackie Mason like they were old friends and who believed in fairness above all else.

'It's why I went into the law,' he told my sister and me once. 'The world's full of folk who think the only way to pull themselves up is by pulling others down. That they're better than everyone else on account of how much is in their pockets. But in a court of law, everyone has to abide by the same rules. I like that.'

He was pretty keen on table manners too, going by how many times I got told to please hold my knife and fork properly and kindly chew with my mouth closed:

'This is not a laundromat, Finn. Nobody wants to see your food going round and round.'

'You don't put food in the laundry.'

He told me to take my elbows off the table and just eat nicely, please.

'Stupid rules,' I muttered, to which he responded that without rules, society would fall apart.

I didn't see how the way I ate kept society going, but Izzy got there before I could.

'Not all rules are good, Daddy.'

'Go on . . .'

My father liked it when she debated with him, reckoned a mind that challenged what it heard couldn't be corrupted.

Cue the irony . . .

'Like African Americans not being allowed at the front of buses,' she said. 'That wasn't a good rule.'

He nodded, agreed no, it certainly wasn't.

'And Jewish people not being allowed to join country clubs. And women not being allowed to vote . . .'

I expect she could have gone on a while.

'Ever thought of being a lawyer when you're older?' he asked. 'Something tells me you'd make a rather good one.'

Izzy lowered her eyes, played with her meatloaf.

'But then I'd have to make speeches. Talk in front of everyone.'

'You might find you liked it if you gave it a go . . .'

She just shrugged, didn't answer.

Izzy was so self-conscious she couldn't even recite the Pledge of Allegiance with the rest of her classmates.

After we lost her, my father stopped speaking too. He had a stroke just before I was due to sit my A levels. Eight years after we moved to the UK. Eight years after Turtle Lake. Everything he'd wanted for us turned to dust. Izzy in the mud.

I ride the elevator up to his floor now, catch sight of my reflection in the mirror and wish I'd thought to put on concealer. The shadows under my eyes are the colour of crows. Can't remember when I last had a decent night's sleep.

The doors open. I walk up the corridor. Knock when I get to his room.

'Hello, Dad.'

He looks up as I come in, recognition in his eyes but nothing more.

I kiss his cheek, the skin paper thin and cold. His hands are marbled with purple blotches. I make a mental note to bring him an electric blanket next time.

To anyone observing, I'm a dutiful daughter visiting regularly, making sure he's got everything he needs. But really, I'm a robot. Dead inside. Doing 'the right thing' while feeling nothing.

After we moved to England, a ravine opened up between us. I was mad at him for ripping me away from the only home I'd ever known. For bringing me to a miserable country where it was always raining and I was always cold.

But most of all, I was mad at him for leaving Dita behind.

I wrote her all the time, but she never wrote back and in the end, I gave up.

Better that way, my father said. *We need to move on.*

We didn't move on though, just stayed stuck. Unable to get past Turtle Lake despite the thousands of miles separating us from it. Ghosts have a way of following you. Doesn't matter how far you flee. You can't outrun the past.

These days, I plump up his pillows, make sure he's being looked after. *Family's all you got. You do everything you can to take care of them, chick.* But the distance between us is still there; our shared pain pushing us apart rather than bringing us closer together.

Maybe if we talked, it would be different, not that that's going to happen any time soon.

I pour him a glass of water, hold it to his lips so he can drink. Out in the corridor, a mobile phone trills – the ringtone the same as mine: Tubular Bells.

'A journalist phoned about Izzy,' I say. Pavlov's dog. 'Some woman called Elsa Stone.'

I'm not sure why I tell him; it's not like I'm in the habit of using this place as a confessional. And he's hardly in a position to give advice.

My father is as out of it as I am after a few drinks.

Yet on hearing Elsa Stone's name, his dead eyes come to life. His cheeks flush. He chokes on his water.

'Do you know her?' I ask, the hairs rising on the back of my neck.

But of course, he can't say.

Extract from Izzy Jackman's diary

August 29 2002

Well, you are never going to believe this but I've finally made a friend!! I still can't believe it's happened!!! I'm so happy I could just burst! Is that a thing, do you think? Can people burst with happiness?

For a whole week I didn't speak to a single soul at Heritage Elm (my new middle school). Or should I say, not a single soul spoke to me?

Daddy was so sure it was going to be 'the making' of me and kept telling me what a great place it was and how lucky I was going to a wonderful school like this. And I pretended to be positive, because obviously that's what he wanted and the last thing I needed was yet another lecture about my 'poor attitude' and how I need to 'try more' and 'just be friendly, it's not that hard, Izzy'.

Only it IS that hard when no one wants to be friendly back and even if they did, I wouldn't know what to say to them because I never know what to say to anybody. Though

I didn't say any of that either. With Daddy it's just easier to agree and tell him I'm sorry and I'll try harder.

The first week was every bit as miserable as I thought it would be. I don't know what's wrong with me. I'm like this misfit who just doesn't know how to BE with people. I wish it was easy for me like it is for Finn. First day at grade school, she already had a ton of friends. All she has to do is say 'Hey!' to a person and then bam, they're best buddies.

I'd do anything to be like that. Switch places with someone popular and pretty just for a day like that movie Freaky Friday with Jodie Foster.

Except now I have a friend too!! Lu Nox. She's shy and awkward like me and so she gets me perfectly!! She even likes animals more than people too and when we're older, we're going to have a farm with horses and dogs and maybe even alpacas.

I'm not sure what an alpaca is. Guess I'd better look it up if I'm going to be farming them!!

September 2 2002

I swear my life is turning around!! I made friends with ANOTHER girl today!!! Her name is Plum. Isn't that the coolest? She knows Lu from her last school and her dad (who is a tool, that's her word, isn't it great?!) ran off to Florida with a dumb waitress so it's just her and her mom now.

I told her I don't have a mom and Lu said her mom's sick and her dad's always busy so it's kind of like she doesn't have ANY parents and we just kind of bonded over that.

How we're all missing someone from our lives. And I know it sounds a bit morbid but it was actually sort of nice.

Does that make sense? I hope so!

Plum says she and Lu are going to see Men in Black 2 on the weekend and she'll call me tonight once she's checked the movie times in case I want to come along.

In case I want to?!!! Haha!

I haven't seen the first Men in Black but I didn't tell them that. I don't want them to think I'm lame and stop wanting to be my friends.

Instead, I tried to act cool and sophisticated and pretended I wasn't sure what else I had on but if I could make it, that would be great, meanwhile I was just floating with elation!

I've been sitting by the phone for like an hour now sending telepathic messages to get it to ring. Though so far, nothing . . .

Oh I really, really hope she calls . . . !

BEFORE

When the phone rang, I was sitting up at the kitchen counter drinking fruit punch and kicking my heels against the stool in a way Dita claimed was driving her to distraction.

There was a pot of marinara sauce bubbling on the stove, firing occasional tomatoey splashes at the tiles. The warm smell of cooking.

My father was in his study, 'not to be disturbed'. Izzy was upstairs taking a bath.

'I'm not going to tell you again,' Dita had said, shooing her off the couch and out the living room. 'And don't forget to wash your hair.'

Funny, I remember everything about that evening as if even then, a part of me sensed it was a turning point. The moment everything started to change.

I heard once that reading about an event after you've experienced it can change your memory. Distort what you recall into something that never happened.

I've read so much about Turtle Lake and the build-up to it that I can't be certain anymore what is real and what is imagined.

Even so, I'm sure I felt things tip that fateful Friday when Dita picked up the phone, and first spoke to Plum Underwood.

The weather was skewy, I remember that too. Rain pelting the windows. Sky dark as bullets. The beginning of September and only sixty degrees. Pathetic fallacy, if this were a Victorian novel.

I was in the fourth grade. Izzy had just started middle school at Heritage Elm. An all-girls private establishment with neckties and chequered skirts and a mission statement about expanding pupils' minds and helping them develop their passions.

'I'm hoping she might find her niche there,' I heard my father tell Dita. 'The smaller classes should help her feel less lost.'

I don't know if the class sizes made any difference but Izzy certainly found her niche at Heritage Elm. It was not a good thing.

As Dita answered the phone, she managed to knock over my drink, a sticky red puddle spreading across the white countertop.

Blood on snow.

An omen perhaps.

Dita ran a cloth under the faucet, wiped up the spillage.

'Jackman residence . . .'

She always answered the phone that way.

'It's not the White House,' I used to tell her.

My sister was worse though. She'd just pick up the phone and wait for whoever was at the other end to start speaking. Oftentimes the caller simply hung up thinking there was no one there.

Fragments of a voice pulsed through the receiver now.

'Hang on a sec,' Dita said. She put the phone on speaker, shut off the water. 'That's better. Who did you say you are?'

A girl's voice answered. Well spoken. Used to getting what she wanted. (Though maybe I'm imagining that last bit. Hindsight changing the shape of things.)

'Plum Underwood. I'm a friend of Izzy's.'

'A friend of Izzy's?' Dita repeated, brows rocketing up.

No one had ever phoned for my sister before, let alone described themselves as her friend.

'From Heritage,' Plum clarified.

She'd only just started at the school and already she was abbreviating the name. There was something possessive about it. Arrogant.

'We're going to see *Men in Black 2*,' Plum continued. 'Can Izzy come with?'

'Who's "we"?' Dita asked, as if they were speaking different languages.

Plum laughed a tinkly laugh. The sort of laugh I'd heard women in coffee shops use. The sort that always sounded a bit phoney.

Silly you! the laugh said. *Aren't you droll?*

It was precocious on a twelve-year-old girl. Put on.

A kid playing a part.

'Me and Lu, of course,' Plum said.

'Of course,' Dita said.

The sarcasm was wasted on Plum Underwood though, washed right over her.

'So, can she come?'

I'd find out later why it was 'me and Lu, of course'. That Lu trailed everywhere after Plum. A Peter Pan shadow stitched to her heels since grade school.

It wouldn't be long before Izzy was doing the exact same thing.

BEFORE

'Izzy has friends now?' I asked Dita as she hung up the phone.

She stood there staring at the receiver as if wondering whether she'd imagined the whole exchange. I wondered the same thing.

Izzy hadn't been on a single play date since our mother died and despite Dita's urgings, she'd never be persuaded to ask anyone over either. And she only got invited to birthday parties if the rest of her class had been asked given it would be unkind to leave just one kid out (as she overheard her teacher inform Missy Tyfield when Missy tried to leave Izzy off the list 'because she's weird and no one likes her').

'You needn't sound so surprised,' Dita said now, putting the phone back in its cradle, a pleased smile cruising her lips. 'Your sister's wonderful. The sweetest soul. Who wouldn't want to be her friend?'

'Just about everybody at her last school,' I replied. 'And she's not that sweet.'

Dita narrowed her eyes at me. Told me if I had nothing nice to say, don't bother saying anything at all.

She was always so quick to defend Izzy. Because she was her favourite, I reckoned.

'She just had to find her feet, that's all . . .'

I rolled my eyes, told her being popular had nothing to do with feet.

Though Hallie Reuben had said she liked my sneakers at lunch that day and did I want to partner with her for gymnastics? So maybe feet did have something to do with it.

It all changed later, but in those days, I was pretty popular. Had at least six friendship bracelets up and down my arm.

'I can teach you how to make them if you want one,' I told my sister.

She called me a blockhead. I couldn't understand why. I was only being nice.

And if anyone was the blockhead, it was her. She never got my friends' jokes when I repeated them at the dinner table, clutching my sides at the punchlines.

'Why's that funny?' she'd say.

Even after I explained them, she said she still didn't understand.

'Can you teach me?' she asked, coming into my room one time.

I looked up from my comic book, rubbed a mosquito bite.

'Teach you what?'

'How to talk to people. I never know what to say.'

I'd have told her if I could, but how do you explain something you do without thinking?

Clearly, she'd figured it out since starting at Heritage Elm though.

'Are you going to let her go with that girl?' I asked Dita now.

'To the movies with her friends? Why wouldn't I?'

I shrugged.

Why wouldn't she, indeed?

What unconscious detail was I picking up on to make me ask that question? Was it the off-note in Plum's laugh? The strangeness of someone asking my sister to go out with them that made me distrust the invitation?

Or something else?

A premonition maybe?

If Dita had known what would come to pass, would she have asked herself the same question?

Should I let her go?

Would she have told Izzy to give Plum and Lu a wide berth? Warned her to stay away from those girls, they're trouble?

Would it have made any difference if she had?

Article from *San Diego News Channel* – SDNC.com

Children With Social Anxiety Are More Likely To Be Victims

(California SDNC.com) A recent study carried out by the Children's Center has shown that children who suffer from social anxiety and low self-esteem are most likely to be the victims of predators.

These children tend to have a poor self-image. They struggle to make friends and often believe themselves to be unlikeable. As a result, they feel disconnected from their peers and constantly compare themselves in a negative way.

They are lonely, isolated and needy.

These characteristics make them easy targets for predators, who play on their feelings of low self-worth by accepting them and making them feel special.

Recent headlines show that the very places where we expect our children to be safe – schools, churches, even friends' houses – can become grooming grounds for predators.

The Children's Center has this advice for parents:

'Ask questions. Make sure you know who your child is spending time with. Trust your gut. And if you think something seems off, it probably is.'

BEFORE

There was something off about Plum though it was hard to pinpoint exactly what. All I know is I got an uncomfortable feeling in my belly whenever she came over. A nagging worry I couldn't quite explain.

I didn't like Lu either, but for whatever reason, it was Plum I focused my distrust on. I didn't like the way Izzy was around her. Her voice became different, the way she laughed. Not just as though she was trying to be cool, but rather as though she were trying to be Plum.

She started copying Plum's look. The way she parted her hair. The cotton candy pink she painted her nails. Her little denim skirts with flower embroidery, the sort of design you'd find in a little kid's colouring book.

Lu paid homage to Plum in the same way, so the three of them gradually became clones. Same clothes, same laugh, same coltish legs and skinny little arms.

'She's a show-off,' I told Dita. 'Always trying to be the centre of attention. Doesn't like it when you're not looking at her. Have you noticed that?'

Dita told me no, she had not, and that I should be nice to Izzy's friends. But she can't have missed it. Plum was only happy if the world was revolving around her.

'Thinks she's the sun,' I said.

Dita scoffed.

'The sun indeed!'

I was right though. Why couldn't Dita see it?

'Like the other night,' I said.

My father had been working late. The girls had stayed for dinner after doing their homework together. Plum had insisted on standing up at the table to eat.

'It's much better for your digestion,' she said, tossing back her hair, when Dita asked her to kindly sit back down like everyone else.

No way she'd have pulled that crap if my father had been there. She was always as charming as the Cheshire cat (a Dita-ism) when he was around. Batted her thick eyelashes at him, called him 'sir'. Smiled fake shyness when he told Izzy what lovely, polite friends she had.

But without him around, her true colours came out.

She smirked, told Izzy and Lu that they should try standing up too.

'So much healthier. Burns loads more calories.'

Straight away they got to their feet. All Plum had to do was whistle and the two of them would start dancing.

Dita glowered, told Izzy to set her hiney down right now. But Izzy refused.

'It's better for your digestion,' she said, with a quick glance at Plum who smiled her approval.

'Are you learning parrot at your new school?' I asked, which earned me a sharp look from ungrateful Dita.

Why did I bother?

The week before, Plum had turned my sister into a vegetarian. Quite a feat given no one loved burgers more than Izzy.

'I don't eat fear,' Plum had said, pushing her plate away when Dita set it in front of her.

Another meal without my father. He and Judge Reynolds were working on a women's prison reform campaign. I didn't know the details only that the current practice – whatever it was – was 'inhumane'.

Dita's eyes narrowed but she didn't respond. Just took the meat off Plum's plate and put it on Izzy's.

'I don't want it,' Izzy announced, pushing it away the same way Plum had. 'I don't eat fear.'

'Izzy Jackman, you are not wasting perfectly good food. Now eat up.'

Izzy went to pick up her fork and would in all likelihood have done what she was told had Plum not piped up:

'No one has the right to tell you what to put in your body, Iz.'

My sister lowered her fork. Looked Dita dead in the eye: 'You don't get to tell me what I do and don't eat.'

Plum rewarded her with a little nod. *Good doggie . . .*

I rolled my eyes to show Dita I was on her side. That I thought Plum was a bozo too.

When they were done with their meal, Izzy and Lu brought their dishes to the side but Plum just left hers on the table. Sauntered out the kitchen asking, 'You guys coming?' as if it were her house.

'What did your last servant die of?' Dita called after her.

Plum turned to the others who'd come trotting after her, said in a stage whisper, 'What does she think she gets paid for?'

Dita's features tightened with hurt.

'Entitled little madam,' she muttered under her breath.

I brought my dishes over, made a big point about helping her with the washing-up. Told her for the umpteenth time I didn't like Plum.

Dita ran her hands down her sides, inhaled deeply.

'She likes your sister though. That's what counts.'

'You mean, Izzy likes her?'

She frowned then said, yes, that's what she'd meant.

Did Plum like Izzy though? A short time ago, I'd overheard her being mean about my sister to Lu.

'I'm going to phone her up on a three-way but I won't say you're on the call. I'll get her talking shit about you and then I'll be like, "Oh by the way, you know Lu's here too!"' She laughed. 'Wicked, right?'

'Wicked,' Lu agreed, laughing too.

Little Polly Pocket, the other kids used to call Lu at grade school. They had a song too. *Little Polly Pocket, see what I can do. Whatever dumb thing Plum wants me to* . . .

Lu was tiny. Legs like twigs and always covered in mosquito bites. Nails bitten to the quick, and blue eyes with a ring of brown around the pupils that my father said was called heterochromia and was extremely rare. She had a lisp too that I was sure she put on but that he said was also probably hereditary.

Turned out, her mother was very sick. Cancer, Izzy wrote in

her diary. Mrs Nox had been bedridden for years. It made her father preoccupied and distant, apparently.

'Doesn't know I'm around half the time,' she said to my sister and Plum one time.

'You've got me though,' Plum told her. 'That's what matters.'

Lu looked pleased.

'Yes,' she agreed, fiddling with her hair. 'But I wish he'd notice me occasionally. Tell me he's proud I got an A or whatever.'

Plum's set-up was different. When she was in the third grade, her father had run off to Florida to live with a woman Plum had never met. A waitress from Hooters, apparently. *They have a baby now. He's over fifty. It's disgusting.*

He sent Plum a Minnie Mouse T-shirt for her birthday.

'Like I'm a little kid. And it doesn't even fit.'

She told Izzy and Lu all the ways she'd tried to punish him. Phoning his house in the middle of the night and just breathing down the line. Sending death threats in the mail made up of letters cut out of *CosmoGirl*. Calling up his 'stupid dumb wife' claiming to be an intern he was sleeping with.

'Just thought you should know, I said. Would hate for you to get your heart broken. By the way, he's planning on leaving you.'

'Bit harsh,' Izzy responded.

She made it sound like a question.

'Not fucking harsh enough,' Plum laughed.

It was just her and her mom now, she said, and that was fine by her.

'Mainly because she's always strung out on Xanax and lets me do whatever I want.'

She laughed again like she'd got a great deal, but looking back, I wonder if there was some sadness in it. Though it's more likely I'm searching for a humanity that was never there.

I've read up on psychopaths since Turtle Lake. The consensus amongst professionals is that you can't be diagnosed with psychopathy until you're an adult. Even so, Plum ticked all the boxes on the Hare Checklist I came across a few years ago: Narcissistic. Manipulative. Lack of empathy. No remorse.

Creepy too.

She invented a game called 'How Do You Want To Die?' Got the girls playing it all the time.

'Your go, Izzy. Drowning in hot lava or being stabbed through with a spear?'

My sister considered, settled on the spear.

'Be over quicker that way.'

Plum smiled. Told her good answer, followed up with: 'Poker up the ass or hung, drawn and quartered?'

Izzy gnawed her lip, blinked several times.

'Um . . . I don't know. You answer, Lu.'

Plum smirked.

'Uh-uh. It's still your turn.'

She flipped her hair.

'How do you want to die, Izzy Jackman?'

Extract from Izzy Jackman's diary

December 18 2002

Just a couple more days and then school is out for a whole two weeks. I'm excited for Christmas obviously but I'm a bit worried too.

I'm having such a good time with Plum and Lu. You have no idea what it feels like to have friends after wanting them for so long. But what if they forget about me over the holidays? What if they go off me when we're away from each other? Start to think I'm boring or whatever?

I think it might be happening already. Things are changing. I can feel it. They've started being kind of secretive. Whispering and giggling and then clamming up as soon as I come over. When I ask what they've been talking about, they just say: 'Oh, nothing,' which makes me think maybe they've been talking about me.

I wish I was pretty like Plum. Then maybe she'd like me better. She's always telling me to watch what I eat – that I need to lay off fries and carbs – and that my posture is bad and I should condition my hair with eggs to make it shiny.

Only when I did that, the eggs scrambled so badly I thought I was going to have to cut all my hair off.

Dita asked me where I got the idea to do something crazy like that ('some-at' she says) and I just said a magazine because I didn't want her to think badly of Plum.

I wish I could talk to Dita the way I used to but it's like we're from different planets these days. She doesn't get me at all. No one does.

When I ask Dita why can't she stop preaching and leave me alone? She says: 'I'm only looking out for you.'

But how is telling me to tidy my room looking out for me?

It would be so nice to find someone who understood me completely and liked me anyway. Imagine that!

I know it sounds dumb since you're a BOOK but sometimes I think you're the only one who gets me – even more than Plum and Lu who are my best friends in the world. I can be myself with you and you don't judge. I don't have to worry if I'm saying the right thing or being boring. I can just BE.

Does that exist in real life, do you think?

Can you ever just be you? Is that ever good enough?

BEFORE

My sister's friendship with Plum and Lu was the death of the relationship between her and me. A cancer silently spreading. I don't know who I hated more: them for taking her from me, or her for letting them.

Before they came along, she let me in. Told me snippets about her life. That she'd been picked last *again* for dodgeball. That there was yet another birthday party she hadn't been asked to. That the kids in her grade were 'dumb and stupid'.

But that all changed once Plum and Lu came on the scene. From then on, it was: 'Stop bugging me.' Or: 'You're so annoying!' – often this was when the girls were over at our house, as though being mean to me was a way of scoring points with them.

It wasn't only the way she spoke to me – or didn't speak to me – that was different. She started pretending not to like things I happened to know she liked plenty too. Climbing trees. Building forts. Whittling sticks . . .

Only recently those had been our favourite activities to do together. I didn't even know what she liked doing anymore.

In increments, she became a person I didn't know. When I snooped in her room, I found it foreign. Posters of bands I'd never heard her mention. Floaty scarves draped over lamps. Incense sticks in jam jars, their burned tips like the lava stones we'd collected together on a long-ago trip to Arizona.

Later, I'd notice other things, too, without understanding what they meant. A foreign smell on her skin. A half-asleep look in her eyes.

They were clues, I see now, but back then all they meant was my sister was drifting out to sea and I had no idea how to pull her back.

One time, I found her on the swing set in the backyard with Plum and Lu, gossiping about whatever tweens gossip about. How unfair their parents were. Why they hated this or that teacher. That so-and-so had got to second base.

What was so special about second base? I scored home runs all the time.

I climbed up the slide, sat at the top sucking a cherry popsicle. Watching my sister and her friends while pretending not to.

Plum whispered something to Izzy, nodded in my direction. My sister flushed, told me to bug off.

'You don't own the yard, Izzy Jackman,' I said.

'We were here first. Go away.'

I sucked my popsicle. Told her I had as much right as she had to be here as you have.

'It's a free country.'

Izzy sent me a look of pure hate, suggested to Plum and Lu that they go to her room where they'd have some privacy.

'My sister's so pathetic.'

I held in the tears until she'd disappeared inside, then ran off to find Dita.

'Give her space, chicken,' Dita advised. 'You can't expect her to hang around her baby sister all the time no more.'

I stamped my foot, said I wasn't a baby.

She shot me one of her infuriating *Is that so?* looks.

'And I'm not a chicken either.'

'These peas aren't going to shell themselves. How about giving me a hand?'

I told her I didn't need her charity, thank you.

'Is it charity when I ask you to help with the dishes too?'

I snarled at her. She set aside the bowl of peas, opened her arms.

'Come here,' she said. Told me she was sorry. 'I know it's hard . . .'

I sniffled, wiped my nose on her apron.

'What did I even do?' I asked.

'You didn't do nothing. Your sister's growing up, is all.'

My father's radio carried through the wall. President Bush's voice: *We cannot know every turn this battle will take* . . .

A war in Iraq. A war at home . . .

'Plum's the stupidest name I've ever heard, ' I said. 'What're her parents called? Mr and Mrs Banana?'

Dita laughed, kissed the top of my head. Followed it up with a rude remark about how maybe I should wash my hair more often.

'We're talking about Izzy, not my hair,' I snapped, pulling

away. 'No one will listen to me about those girls! It's like I'm Cassandra.'

'That a kid from your grade?'

I scoffed, enjoyed a moment of superiority (even though I'd only just learned about Cassandra myself) .

'She's a priestess from Troy. You know, as in the Trojan Horse.'

'Oh, right,' Dita said although it was clear she didn't know what I was talking about.

'She was cursed to see the future and never be believed,' I explained. 'Same as me.'

Dita sighed, pulled me in for another hug.

'I know it's hard, chick. But it's good your sister's finally got some friends.'

'Not friends like that, it's not . . .'

She wouldn't listen though, and nor would my father – the two of them singing from the same lousy hymn book.

'Give it time, honey,' he said when I went grumbling to him later. 'She'll come back to you when she's ready.'

'What if she doesn't?'

He put on his slippers. Reached for the *Times*.

'Your sister's nearly a teenager now. Growing apart from us is part of growing up. It'll all come out right in the end though, I promise.'

Does it count as a lie if you don't know you're telling it?

NOW

Has Elsa Stone lied to me? Is she really who she says she is?

I've left my father's care home and am heading to the library where I work. The whole walk over, his reaction to her name has been playing in my head. The way his eyes widened, the involuntary parting of his lips.

What was his face trying to convey?

Shock? Fear? Concern?

How does he know that woman?

I walk up the steps of Hogarth Hill Library, push open the heavy wooden door. Immediately, I'm wrapped in the warm smell of much-loved books. The smell of smoke and earth and vanilla.

I breathe it in. Feel my shoulders loosen.

I've been working here for five years. A haven, where conversation is actively discouraged.

There's no need to charm your way up the career ladder, to engage in small talk by the water cooler. A nod and a 'Hope you enjoy it' suffices nicely.

I like the rules, the order. *No talking . . . No mobile phones.* And a personal favourite of my boss, a moany-faced cardigan-wearer called Mrs Bostock: *No eating while reading* . . .

What I like most though is that none of the people who come in here have a clue who I am. Who my sister is. What happened to her. And if they have heard of Turtle Lake – which to be fair, most folk have – they don't connect it in any way with me.

The library is a place I can switch off: stamping books, reading when there's a lull. Getting first dibs on the new releases.

Perk of the job, Mrs Bostock says. Crime is her favourite. *I do enjoy a good whodunnit* . . .

Personally, I've had enough crime to last me a lifetime.

She glances up from her crossword as I come in. Scowls.

'Late again, Kate.'

Five years we've worked together. Five years she's been getting my name wrong.

I've given up correcting her.

Instead, I tell her I'm sorry, even though we both know I'm not and I'll likely be late tomorrow too.

'I'll get cracking on the catalogues,' I say.

Though what I really want to be doing is jumping online and doing a search for Elsa Stone.

What did my father's expression mean? Has he got her mixed up with someone else? The stroke has made him confused . . .

Or does he know something I don't? That maybe I should?

Bostock gives me the once-over, takes in my wet clothes and dripping hair. It started properly bucketing after I left the care home. Great day to leave my umbrella at home.

'You'll need a towel,' she says.

Uncharacteristically thoughtful.

I put on a smile. Shrug. Tell her don't worry. I'll dry.

The heating's always cranked way up, even in the summer. Mrs Bostock suffers from poor circulation. Runs in her family apparently. *My poor cold feet . . .*

'You're making puddles all over the floor,' she says, going back to the crossword it will take her all day to complete. 'On second thoughts, grab a mop.'

There she is, the woman I know and would rather I didn't.

I clean up then take a ring binder from the trolley and head over to my desk in the corner, ready to crack on. Except there's someone sitting there. A beanpole of a woman with hair that looks like it's never seen a brush. Dita would not approve. *Must have been some knothole . . .*

'Public computers are over there,' I say, indicating the bank of outdated monitors along the far wall.

She'll have made my seat warm, sticky fingers all over the keyboard.

The beanpole doesn't budge though. Doesn't even do me the courtesy of looking up.

'It's okay. I work here,' she says.

I fold my arms, ask since when.

Bostock hasn't mentioned anything about hiring someone else. But then again, that's not terribly surprising. The woman doesn't tell me much beyond the state of her health. *Rheumatism's playing up again. Must be rain on the way . . .*

The beanpole finally deigns to raise her head. As she does, her eyes widen rather like my father's did earlier.

'Oh my God! Kat?' she says. 'Is that you?'

I consider saying no. Opt to say nothing.

'You don't remember me, do you?'

I shake my head. Don't add the obligatory 'sorry'. Or make out her name is on the tip of my tongue.

She responds with a shy smile, winds a lock of tangled hair round her finger.

'I'm Willow Rowling. We were at Brentwood High School together.' Then when I still don't answer – 'You really don't remember me?'

I tell her no.

It's a lie though. I do remember Willow Rowling.

Weeping Willow, the other kids called her. Moaning Myrtle sometimes too. Everyone was reading *Harry Potter*. No one was terribly original.

I came across Willow crying in the school bathroom one lunchtime. She was examining some sores on her shoulder, covered them quickly as I entered.

Looking back, they might have been cigarette burns; they were the right size and shape for that. Maybe she would have opened up if I'd said something. But I didn't. Just went into a cubicle and locked the door.

'Don't tell,' she said in a way that could have meant: please ask.

'Whatever,' I said, taking a compass out of my pencil case and began scratching an expletive on the stall wall.

After Turtle Lake, the only person I was interested in comforting was myself. Acts of petty vandalism to begin with. Then, in time, drink and pills and whatever else helped me forget. I wasn't fussy so long as it did the trick.

I may not have helped her, but Willow helped me, albeit inadvertently. With her around to gossip about, no one bothered themselves about me. No one wondered who Kat really was and what she was running away from.

'I used to sit behind you in English lit,' she persists now. 'You were really smart. Remember Mrs Morgan? That way she read *Macbeth*?'

She does an impression. *Is this a dagger . . . ?*

It's not bad.

'Don't think she ever got over not being on the stage. Remember?'

It strikes me that this persistence is new about Willow. So too the chattiness and the way she holds my gaze. The Willow I knew was mouse quiet. Only ever looked at the floor.

I tell her I need to get on with cataloguing the returns, wait pointedly for her to take the hint and give me my desk back. Instead, she asks if I want a hand.

I tell her no thanks. I don't need help.

She raises a teasing brow.

'Everyone needs help, Kat.'

'Not me,' I say.

School was a long time ago. And I'm not looking for friends.

Extract from *Inside Ryder Grady's Ring*
(an NDC documentary)

Detective Albert Arnold (Carlsbad PD)

'You're with friends,' we now know Grady would tell the girls. 'You don't have to be someone you're not with me.'

It always started that way. From the moment a new girl was brought into the group, he began working on her, making her feel loved and special and understood. Grooming her.

Izzy Jackman is believed to have been twelve years old when she first became involved with Ryder Grady at a party at his apartment in the San Paulo Hills. Grady is thought to have been twenty-nine at the time, though some sources suggest he may have been older.

BEFORE

The girls were hanging out in our backyard, sipping cans of Diet Coke. Reclining on their elbows. Long skinny legs stretched out in the sun.

Plum stroked Izzy's calf with her fingertips, made a disapproving noise.

'You should wax,' she said. 'Leaves your skin much smoother than shaving.'

Izzy tucked her legs under her, pulled at the hem of her shorts the way she'd done with her cuffs that day under the table.

'Or an epilator,' Plum continued.

'Hurts like fuck though,' Lu muttered, taking another swig of Coke.

Plum ran her hands down her sides.

'You have to suffer to be beautiful, Lu.'

'Why do you think I've eaten nothing but peanut butter and a banana today?' Lu answered in a braggy tone.

Plum scoffed.

'Do you know how many calories there are in a banana?'

I was in my room spying on them from the window, ready to duck if they chanced to glance up. Plum was sitting on the grass between Izzy and Lu. She always sat between them. And they were always watching her. Each time she touched her hair, they'd touch theirs.

I wondered if they even knew they were doing it.

'So, there's this party tonight,' Plum told Izzy. 'Up in the hills. You want to come?'

She was sprawled out on the grass, eyes closed, but there was a nervous energy in her voice. Like Izzy's answer mattered to her.

'Yeah, maybe,' Izzy said.

'Why only "maybe"?' Plum asked.

She sounded cross. Izzy must have sensed that, too. She backtracked quickly.

'I just mean I'll need to check with Dita.'

'Dita's just the help. What do you need to check with her for? It's your life, Izzy.'

Izzy stroked her charm bracelet in an absent sort of way. Stuttered a little.

'I'll have to ask her for a lift. That's all I meant. I want to go, obviously.'

'Oh,' Plum said. *Ohhh.* 'You don't need to worry about a lift.' She laughed the phoney laugh I remembered from the first phone call. 'We'll all go together. Sleep over at mine after. Sound good, Lu?'

'Sounds good! It's going to be groovy.'

Groo-veeeey . . .

She had a Marilyn voice. Like a lispy little girl. I wondered if she put it on.

And who said groovy?

'Ryder's parties are the best.' She wound a strand of hair round her finger. 'He's such an amazing person.'

'Amazing,' Plum agreed.

There should have been a thunderclap at that moment. A lightning bolt. A wolf howl from the east. Some sort of warning. An omen that this was the instant everything changed.

Stop all the clocks. Dismantle the sun . . .

But there was nothing. Not even a ripple in the air. How could a name that would come to mean so much not raise a single hair?

'Ryder?' Izzy asked. 'As in, Ryder Grady?'

'He knows this model scout,' Lu answered, draining the last of her Diet Coke. 'He's going to introduce me.'

Plum picked a daisy from the grass, plucked off its petals one by one. *He loves me, he loves me not . . .*

'We've told him all about you, Izzy. He specifically said to bring you tonight.'

Izzy dipped her head, trying to hide her smile.

'He did?'

'You're going to love him,' Lu said.

'And he's going to love *you!*' Plum added.

Izzy beamed.

'You think so?'

Plum nodded. *Of course!* Then her tone changed, became serious.

'It's a big deal, him inviting you. You get that, right?'

'He doesn't ask just anyone,' Lu added.

Plum shifted position, lay her head in Lu's lap. Lu braided her hair.

'Ryder's very selective.'

Izzy was practically beaming now.

'He really asked *specifically* for you to bring me?'

Plum reached over, started playing with the fringe on Izzy's cut-offs.

'Specifically asked for you.'

They started discussing what they were going to wear. What Izzy should wear.

'I've got this dress you can borrow,' Plum told her. 'Strapless denim. Beyoncé has one just the same. Knocks off like ten pounds.'

'I'll bring my body glitter,' Lu said.

'Glitterati ferrati!' Plum replied, which made them both start laughing.

After a second's hesitation, Izzy began laughing too. Put on, I could tell.

I didn't get the joke either.

'You really think he'll like me?' she asked after a bit.

Her neediness made me cringe. Lit up the lizard part of my brain. I was only nine but I'd been around the block enough by then to know neediness equals vulnerability.

Ryder Grady knew the same thing.

Extract from Izzy Jackman's diary

January 25 2003

Dad and Dita would definitely tell me I should be 'ashamed' of myself if they knew what I did last night – and the old me might have felt that way. But I'm not ashamed. I'm flying and I can't WAIT to do it again!!

It was the most amazing experience of my life. I was secretly a bit nervous about going to Ryder's party. The only people I knew there were Plum and Lu. What if they just disappeared off and left me on my own? What if I didn't know what to say to the other kids? What if they didn't like me?

I don't even know why I worried! It's like Dita always says, half the things you worry about don't come true anyway so what's the point of wasting emotional energy on something that might not even happen?

It was such a great crowd of girls who just welcomed me like I was 'supposed' to be there. Like we were all already old friends. They were so chill. Lolling around on cushions in Ryder's big apartment. Or else sprawled out on the beige couches and just 'hanging'.

Everything was beige! Beige walls, beige furniture, beige shaggy rugs my feet just sank into like sand on a beach!

'Welcome, new girl,' they said. And, 'Hey there, you.'

At first it was just them and then there was this sort of crackle of electricity in the air and Ryder appeared carrying a tray of cupcakes and everyone just sort of sat up a little taller and somebody said, 'Groovy . . .' and they all started laughing.

I laughed too even though I didn't get it because I didn't want to look like a loser who's no fun.

Ryder didn't laugh though. He just stood there quietly, looking at me like I was the most precious thing he'd ever seen. And then everyone else stopped laughing and started looking at me too. But not in a way I minded.

'Be proud to be you,' Ryder said. Then – 'You're with friends now.'

He has this soft, kind voice. The sort of voice you can't imagine ever shouting or getting mad.

I didn't know what to say so I just said hi and then straight away realised it was a dumb thing to say. Like completely unsophisticated or whatever. But Ryder was smiling at me, the kindest, warmest smile I've ever seen. The absolute bluest eyes. Like actual crystal blue.

He gave his tray to one of the girls, came over and knelt at my feet. Took my hands in his, his thumbs rubbing circles on the inside of my wrists.

'You're perfect just the way you are,' he said in this quiet voice as if it was just me and him in the room even though it wasn't and everybody else was watching.

'Don't ever let anyone tell you differently.'

And oh God, I started crying. Fat sloppy tears running down my cheeks because how did he know me so well? How did he get me so completely in a way I never thought anyone ever would?

I bit the inside of my cheek to stop the tears, tried to pull it together. What must Plum and Lu be thinking? I thought. They're going to cut me, wish they'd never brought me here.

'Let it out,' he said, looking so deep into my eyes it was as if he was looking into my actual soul. 'You can't be truly free until you surrender your ego. You want to be free, don't you, Izzy?'

I nodded, told him yes. Because I really did. I really do.

He squeezed my hands.

'You're safe here, Izzy,' he said. 'You're home now.'

And this snug feeling came over me. Like it was true, I was home.

Ryder told the girl with the tray to hand out the cakes.

'Who wants to play?' he asked in a teasing voice and everyone started saying, 'Me!' and 'I do!'

We all took a cupcake. I ate mine, watching the other girls out the corner of my eye to make sure I was playing the game right. But what was the game?

'You remember Golden Ticket from grade school?' Lu said and I said yes, even though I didn't.

'Well, it's like that,' she told me. 'Except more of a trip.'

Plum laughed and I did too even though I didn't get it. But this time I wasn't laughing because I didn't want to look lame, I was laughing because ... well, I don't know why. Just that I liked it.

I began to sweat. Beads of moisture pricking all over my body.

'I feel funny,' I said. 'I feel . . .'

But I couldn't get the rest of the words out. The room was breathing, Ryder's beige walls moving in and out. His black picture frames dripping, the only things in the room that weren't beige.

What if they stained his beautiful carpet? Made everything dirty. I staggered up to catch the spills but my legs were made of lead and I fell back down.

I felt heat on my shoulder, spreading butter yellow down the back of my neck.

'Welcome to the chocolate factory,' Ryder said, close to my ear so that I felt his voice melt into my body and become one with me. 'It's okay,' he said, stroking my face. His fingertips moving across my neck, my throat. Such warm fingers. 'Let yourself go. I'm here, Izzy. You're safe.'

Someone put on some music. Elton John, I think. And the couch cushions got up and started dancing and the music smelled like caramel. I got up and started dancing too. Me dancing, in front of everyone! Like I WAS the music. Like I was playing for them.

I smelled Dita's chicken pot pie all the way back home in Aviara. I could hear Plum blinking on the other side of the room and my mother saying my name up in heaven.

I felt free in a way I've never felt before. Completely relaxed, and when somebody told me to take off my dress, I did.

'Twirl!'

'Dance for us, Izzy!'

I moved my arms above my head, swirled my hips the way they said to. Shy me dancing in circles in my underwear without a care in the world. Light as a bird. Free, free, free . . .

Afterwards, Plum said the Golden Ticket is acid and that I was tripping.

'Lucky you! Isn't Ryder great?'

I told her yes. Asked when could we play again? Said I really, really liked tripping.

My life is finally changing. I can feel it. Anything's possible now!

BEFORE

It's hard to pinpoint the exact moment Izzy changed.

I want to say I sensed she was in trouble, some sisterly tele-pathy that told me she was in over her head. But any telepathy is after the fact. After the confessions and the autopsy report and the sentences were handed out.

Knowledge of what would come to pass painted over my memory of what actually happened.

I was on the window seat in my bedroom reading an Archie comic book. The girls were outside in the yard, their voices drifting up like smoke.

'If only I could shift these last sloppy pounds,' Lu was saying.

'I cut out fries last week,' Izzy replied. 'It's so hard!'

'Can't remember when I last ate fries,' Plum announced. 'It's all about self-discipline.'

I closed my comic book, rattled without knowing why.

In the weeks that followed, Dita would get rattled too.

'It'll be your birthday soon, Iz. How about we go to Fashion Valley, catch a movie?' she suggested. 'I've heard *My Big Fat*

Greek Wedding is hilarious. How about that? Maybe P.F. Chang's after? Get the sesame chicken and lettuce rolls you like.'

Izzy gave a contemptuous snort. Asked if she had any idea how much sugar was in sesame chicken and said she had absolutely zero interest in Hollywood hegemony.

Dita waggled her eyebrows.

'Hollywood what now?'

'Movies are basically mind control.'

'You like Derren Brown,' I said.

'God, you're so plastic, Finn,' my sister retorted with a contemptuous snort before flouncing off to her room.

'What did I say?' I asked Dita.

She shrugged, opened her hands.

'Wish I knew, chick.'

We ended up not celebrating Izzy's birthday at all.

'I live in the now,' she informed us. 'Marking time is part of the patriarchal plot.'

Dita widened her eyes.

'Someone been feeding you the Kool-Aid.'

She was more on the money than she realised.

NOW

A library user is jangling loose coins in his trouser pocket while he reads the paper. Making horrible squelching noises with his Juicy Fruit gum. I glower at him but he doesn't notice.

Or doesn't care.

The noise grates like a car alarm that won't quit. I have a sudden urge to pop out my eyeballs just for something to flick at him.

The new girl, Willow Rowling, is grating on me too. She's over in the stacks yakking away to one of the regulars, no regard for the *Keep Quiet* signs.

'Chekhov opened a whole world for me . . .'

What a pretentious asshole! I bet Willow Rowling is one of those people who has a complete set of Shakespeare on their bookcase so people think they're 'serious'.

Mrs Bostock wants to be seen as serious, too. She's at the front desk hunched over the *Times*, beavering away at the crossword. She's been at it all morning. I wonder if she's got to 'Down' yet.

They're both occupied though, that's what matters.

I throw a quick glance over my shoulder in case anyone can see my computer screen, then open up that new search engine. The one that doesn't track your entries. Not Duck Duck Goose, but something like that . . .

In the query box, I input: *Elsa Stone.*

My father's reaction to her name has been playing on me all day. I expect that's why I've been so pissy. I never was good with mysteries. You'd have thought I'd have gotten better over the years. But if anything, I'm worse.

'Always want to know everything,' Dita used to say.

Elsa Stone.

Twenty-nine million results pop up in less than half a second. Facebook profiles. A jewellery store. A porcelain tile that is apparently ideal for paths and patios.

There are images too. Kardashian-type posers – heads down, eyes up. A woman in a choker necklace. And a pebble illustrated with some character from *Frozen.*

None of them seem like 'my' Elsa Stone though.

I try again. Add the word 'journalist' to the search this time. Hit return.

Fewer results pop up. None of them relevant.

I check over my shoulder again. I feel a thousand eyes on me even though no one's watching.

Alcohol paranoia, says a voice in my head.

I add Izzy's name to the other search terms. The woman is making a documentary about her. There must be something online about it.

Except there's not.

There are plenty of results containing 'Izzy Jackman' – Wikipedia pages, articles from the *Guardian*, *Sky News* and other news sites, blog posts, fan pages . . . (Fan pages? Christ's sake!)

I spot my name (my old name) in one or two of them, but at the bottom of every listing is the same thing:

Missing: ~~elsa stone~~ | Must include: elsa stone

Must, but doesn't . . .

I don't understand. Surely a journalist would have an internet presence. Even back in 2003 – pre-Facebook and Instagram – Izzy left a mark online.

So why hasn't Elsa?

Extract from *'You're Perfect Just as You Are'*:
Ryder Grady, a Biography

Grady groomed 'his' girls by tapping into their insecurities and need to be loved. He might tell a shy girl she was beautiful. A girl in need of guidance, to think of him as a father.

'You're home now,' he'd say. 'You're perfect just as you are.'

He had a talent for honing in on what they needed to hear and capitalising on it. For taking a truth and turning it into a lie.

'Love isn't possessive,' he'd say before going on to possess each and every one of them completely.

As what happened at Turtle Lake in July 2003 shows . . .

Extract from Izzy Jackman's diary

February 15 2003

I can hardly believe I'm writing this . . . It actually happened. I had SEX!!!! Little mousy me who no one ever glanced at twice – can you actually believe it??!!!

I wonder if I look different. If anybody will be able to tell.

Lucky I got that lockbox for you, isn't it?! I couldn't take the chance Dita or Finn might read you and find out my secrets. Sweet, sweet secrets!!! I never thought I'd be the kind of girl who had so many!!!

After that first party, I made sure to tell Plum what a brilliant, brilliant time I'd had. She got the hint, Diary (of course she did, she's my best friend!) and she told me there was another party next week and did I want to come?

Did I??!!

Since then, I must have been back to Ryder's place six or seven times at least and each time is more thrilling than the last!

The world used to feel so scary but it doesn't feel that way anymore. When I'm at Ryder's, I feel like I can do anything.

That this whole time, life has just been waiting for me to notice it's there and explore it.

How is it possible that each trip is better than the last? That I can feel so powerful and alive when I've never felt powerful about anything?!

That's how it was last night. No inhibitions. Just free! The walls were melting and Ryder was sitting there holding my hand telling me it was okay, that he wouldn't let anything hurt me.

'You don't have to do anything you're not ready for,' he whispered.

That sweet soft voice. Those blue eyes.

I don't remember how it happened, only that one minute I was resting my head on his shoulder. Tasting the cedar scent of his skin, hearing his pulse tick-tocking like it was the loudest thing in the room. And the next I was touching him. Becoming him, my skin melting into his skin. My face fusing with his face.

I could see the blood vessels moving in his cheeks, fluttering like butterflies. Saw each of his hair's DNA spiralling and helixing out of his head. I knew without knowing that we were making love and that it was magnificent and I'd never wanted anything more than I wanted him.

There was a Kylie track playing – 'Can't Get You Out of My Head' – and I could see the words dancing in the air. Flashes of white light. Noises like the clickety-click sound you can make with your tongue.

'Smile,' someone said and I smiled. So wide I thought my face was splitting.

Then Ryder kissed me and my smile became his smile and dissolved into him.

The other girls have sex with him too. You'd think I'd feel jealous but there's something special about us all loving the same man. This man. Ryder Grady.

Ryder. Ryder. Ryder . . .

God, I love him!

BEFORE

I saw Ryder Grady three times.

Three seemingly insignificant moments. Three chances to change the future.

Three opportunities I failed to take.

The first time was a Sunday afternoon in early April 2003. I was on a play date in the hills with a kid from my grade. Marnie Wilkes had red hair and bright pink cheeks like a Raggedy Ann doll and parents who were going through a messy divorce.

'My mom does Weight Watchers and Keep Fit videos in a leotard in the living room.' Marnie pulled a face. 'She's so sad.'

'Poor her,' I said. 'If your dad's sad too, maybe they'll get back together.'

Mrs Wilkes seemed more interested in my father than her ex-husband though.

'Is he seeing anyone?' she'd ask, smoothing down her freshly bleached hair. 'What sort of hobbies is he into?'

She'd send me home with apple pies, tell me to be sure to tell him she'd baked them herself.

'We could be sisters,' Marnie said.

After Turtle Lake, Mrs Wilkes backed right off. Like what happened was a disease she was afraid of catching. A lot of people were that way.

That particular Sunday in April, Marnie and I were up in her room giving each other glitter tattoos, when we heard the unmistakable tinkle of an ice cream truck coming along the street and ran galloping down the stairs.

'Can we get popsicles, Mom?' Marnie asked, hand opening for money.

Mrs Wilkes set aside the *Entertainment Weekly* she'd been reading – an article about Britney and Justin Timberlake's recent split (*Such a shame. They were the cutest couple*) – and fished a couple of dollars out of her purse.

'I miss eating ice cream,' she said wistfully as we hightailed it out the door.

There was already a long line outside the truck by the time we got there. We inched forward, grumbling about how long it was taking and would we ever get served.

My eyes wandered. And that's when I saw her. Him too, not that I knew who he was then.

A group of girls was coming down the dirt track that snaked between the pine trees. Some of them were holding hands, others were linking arms. Girls in denim cut-offs with spotty scarves tied around their chests. Laughing with their heads thrown back. Sticking out their tongues and making licking motions as if tasting the air.

'I need ice cream!' one of them called out.

'I scream, you scream,' another started singing, which made the rest of them laugh.

'Was the sky always this high?' a third girl asked.

She twirled around, hair cloaking around her.

'The moon is a banana! Man, I'm hungry!'

I couldn't take my eyes off them; the way they were laughing. Their aura of otherliness, not of this world somehow.

Water nymphs trying out the land.

They all had their long hair loose and feet bare. The same frail skinny shoulders and honeyed skin.

And then, there in the midst of them, was Izzy, walking in step with a shaggy-haired man. Hair the colour of wet sand; wavy and unruly and cut to a chiselled jawline. Wide-set eyes. A knowing smile.

He had the look of Heath Ledger from *A Knight's Tale*, I thought. Minus the armour obviously.

Plum was on the other side of him. Her hand in his, chin angled up. Mooning.

He dropped it as they reached the curb. Took a roll of bank notes out of his back pocket and peeled off a couple of bills. Gave them to Plum. Slapped her bottom. Hung back, watching as the girls ran giggling towards the truck.

Giggling and tripping over their feet. Izzy giggling and tripping too. Relaxed and happy in a way that made her a stranger.

Marnie nudged me. We'd reached the front of the line.

'Hurry up, honey,' the ice cream seller said. 'There's folks waiting.'

On autopilot, I asked for a sundae cone. When I turned back round, Izzy had disappeared.

So had the beautiful man.

'Who was that guy you were with?' I asked my sister later at home, the two of us setting the table for dinner while Dita put the finishing touches on a lasagne in the kitchen.

The tips of her ears lit up. She concentrated very hard on where she was placing the silverware.

'What guy?'

'In the hills. With the ice cream truck.'

'Don't know what you're talking about,' she said, shaking her head, lower lip ski-jumping an inch.

She wouldn't look at me though.

'I saw you,' I persisted. 'Plum was there too. He gave her money.'

'Plum?'

The worry lines on Izzy's forehead cleared.

'Oh, *that* guy! Yeah, that was Plum's dad. He's here visiting.'

I didn't know then that Plum's father never visited.

Or why a grown man would have been cavorting with a gang of teenage girls.

NOW

I'm walking home from the library when I see him.

He's leaning against a wall, tapping at his phone. His hair skims his jawline, blonde and wavy. He's wearing a black leather jacket, a dark grey tee.

I feel the heat rush to my face, blood filling my cheeks. My breath comes out as a pant. Short and rasping. Like I'm trying to gulp the air and can't get it down fast enough.

I'm sweating. Shaking. My vision on a carousel.

Heart thump-thumping. Stars dancing in front of my eyes. Legs tingling.

The number thirteen bus trundles past, belching fumes.

A spaniel tied up outside Tesco barks indignantly at having to wait in the cold.

My chest is tight as though squeezed. So tight it makes me choke.

I put my hand to my throat, feel the tears come right there in the middle of the sidewalk for the world to see. Can't stop them.

'Are you okay, love?'

It takes me a moment to register the hand on my shoulder, the elderly lady with the tartan shopping caddy inclining her head towards mine.

'Are you okay?'

Something in the warmth of her touch, the concerned timbre in her voice, brings me back to earth.

The man leaning against the wall is still there but he's not Ryder Grady. Of course he's not.

I feel stupid and relieved at the same time.

It would be easy to blame Elsa Stone for the panic attack, for bringing everything to the fore. Though truth is, Grady has been haunting me for years.

A shape glimpsed in my peripheral vision. Footsteps behind me late at night. I see him everywhere.

The man puts his phone away, brushes the hair out of his eyes. Ducks into Le Pain Quotidien.

He's taller than Ryder Grady. Thinner. Features less chiselled.

Izzy's voice in my head: *You're such a bonehead.*

Feeling returns to my hands. The tingling in my legs subsides. So too my racing heartbeat.

'I'm okay,' I tell the old woman.

'Are you sure?' she asks, hand still on my shoulder, and for the craziest second, I imagine her enveloping me in her grandmotherly arms. Telling her everything.

Unloading it all.

Who I am. Who my sister is. What I did.

How freeing it would be to cast off my mask. To speak openly. To be listened to without being judged.

But instead, I simply thank her. Tell her I'm fine.

She gives me one last look, right in my eyes as if she knows the truth. As if she cares.

Then she says: 'Look after yourself, dear.'

And walks away.

BEFORE

'Okay, fine. I give up! You can have one!'

After a lengthy campaign (*Everyone else has got one, why can't I?*) my father relented and bought Izzy a mobile phone.

'Make sure you look after it. I'm not getting you another one if you lose it,' he said, handing her the Nokia box. 'All this *mishigas* over a phone!'

She threw her arms round his neck, made loud kissing noises.

'Thank you, thank you, Daddy! I love you!'

'I think that's what they call cupboard love,' he answered, but he was smiling.

'Nice she's got kids to call these days,' he told Dita as Izzy bounded upstairs to programme her numbers in.

You can send pictures from it too . . .

Dita took a pie from the oven, cherry filling oozing out the sides.

'It's a relief, Judge,' she agreed. 'Can kill a person to have no friends.'

He nodded, murmured, 'Very true.'

It didn't occur to either of them that having friends can sometimes kill a person, too . . .

I got the plates and muttered something about how frankly it was better when she didn't have any friends.

My father chuckled.

'Better for whom, Miss Priss?'

'Better for Izzy, obviously,' I said in a tone that implied: *What else could you possibly mean?* Though I knew perfectly well what he was insinuating.

'She's turned into a total idiot since she started hanging around with stupid Plum and Lu. It's all their fault. She was fine before those losers came along.'

He pinched my cheek, made a clickety-click noise with his mouth that sounded like a camera. Told me my sister was happy and that's what mattered.

'And don't call her names, please. Or her friends.'

Was Izzy happy though?

She'd become so quiet, so distracted. I'd ask her a question or try out a new insult and she wouldn't react. Just sat on the couch with her legs hooked over the arm staring at her hands.

Other times, she lashed out over nothing. Accused me of reading her diary although I hadn't done that for ages. Not since she'd shut it away in some stupid box that needed a combination code to open it.

'You think I don't know?' she hissed. Jabbed her pointy finger in my face. 'Leave my stuff alone.'

Another time, I came across her looking clearly upset. But when I asked what was wrong she just said she wasn't sure.

'Going cuckoo,' I told Dita, making corkscrew motions at the side of my head.

Dita told me to cut it out and give my sister some space.

'On at her all the time. It's not nice.'

She could say what she liked but I could tell Dita was concerned too, even if she wouldn't admit it to me. Over spring break, she tried to lure Izzy on picnics and trips to the zoo and the beach. My sister wasn't interested though.

'You think the beach is a trip?'

She smirked as though she'd told a clever joke, but if she had, I didn't get it.

The only thing she was interested in was her phone. She was on it all the time. Texting every two seconds.

'Don't you ever run out of things to say?' my father asked.

My brain flashed on my first day at grade school, Izzy asking me what I talked to people about. How the rabbit had turned, as Dita would have said.

What did Izzy talk about? What was so special about her phone?

I was determined to find out, and then finally one evening, I got my chance.

Izzy was in the shower. Her Nokia on her nightstand.

I could hear the sound of water running in the bathroom. Dita clunking about in the kitchen downstairs. My father in his study listening to the radio announcing US troops had captured Baghdad.

Bush tells Iraqis: 'Freedom is near . . .'

Checking over my shoulder, I tiptoed into Izzy's room and picked up her phone. There was an image of an adult hand reaching for a child's on the screen. The generic Nokia screen-saver, but somewhat creepy looking back.

I hit the menu key and the image disappeared. In its place, a grainy video that Izzy must have just been watching.

The film was shaky like one of those old home movies. It showed a blonde man in a grey T-shirt playing the guitar, his fingers gently strumming the strings. His head was bowed so I couldn't make out his face, though I could see the ring of girls sitting on the floor around him. Arms circling each other's shoulders. Swaying to the beat.

And a lone guy standing on the edge of the frame with a camera round his neck. Denim jacket. Jeans. Thumbs hooked in his belt.

The man with the guitar started singing, the sound tinny through the phone speakers:

Come to me and cease to worry,

Shake off your chains, be anybody . . .

Other voices began to join in. All female, all singing with gusto.

I am your everything if you love me.

I am your father and your brother,

Your friend and your lover . . .

Was that Izzy's voice? Louder than the others (because she was holding the phone, I suppose) and out of tune. She always was tone-deaf. Never would sing in public either. Not even in church. Yet here she was, singing away without a care.

Come to me and cease to worry,

Shake off your chains, be anybody . . .

The man strummed a final chord and then he looked up. Directly at the camera.

My skin tingled, my brain lighting up.

Wavy hair cut to his chin. Chiselled jawline. A knowing smile.

Why was Izzy filming Plum's dad? Why was he beckoning to her?

His finger was crooked. He stirred the air with it. *You. Come here.*

The picture shifted, the camera trained now on Izzy's feet as she walked towards him, wobbling slightly. Her feet were bare like that day at the ice cream truck. Her toenails painted pink. The polish chipped.

The camera didn't show Plum but it did capture her voice. Her plaintive tone as she complained:

'But it's supposed to be my turn . . .'

BEFORE

A discord was seeping in between Izzy and her friends. A worm in the apple.

I couldn't have been more delighted.

My father had helped me build a tree house one May weekend. It wasn't anything grand, just some boards nailed together to form a makeshift box that Dita kept kibbitzing was going to collapse at any moment. But I loved it. My own private hidey-hole.

I was up there one afternoon, lying on my stomach in a sunbeam and sucking on Red Vines.

Izzy was tanning down below with Plum and Lu. They didn't know I was in my nest and I didn't see any reason to tell them.

'Jesus, Izzy! Do you have to lay so close?' Plum snapped. 'You're practically on top of me!'

'Shift over if you don't like it,' Izzy spat back.

It was the first time I'd ever heard her answer back to Plum, ever heard her so bold.

I put my eye to a crack in the boards. Kept super still so they wouldn't creak and give me away.

Plum was lying on her back, knees bent up, arms folded over her chest. Izzy was lolling on her stomach watching a ladybug crawl between her fingers. Lu sitting beside her, chowing on a Snickers bar.

I'd never seen her eat chocolate before. She always seemed to be watching her weight and boasting how few calories she'd had that day, which would invariably prompt a pissing competition between the three girls as to who'd consumed least.

Plum eyed her disapprovingly.

'You really going to eat all that?'

Lu lowered the candy bar, touched her hair.

'I don't know what's wrong with me,' she said sadly. 'I can't stop guzzling chocolate.'

Izzy blew on her finger. The ladybug flew away. *Your house is on fire, your children all gone . . .*

'I'm that way after . . . you know . . .' she said. 'All I want is sugar.'

'It's a matter of self-control,' Plum announced pompously. 'A moment on the lips . . .'

Lu touched her stomach, eyes cast down. Then she took another bite.

Plum shook her head, tutted softly.

'The camera adds ten pounds, you know.'

'You want some, don't you?' Izzy said in a teasing voice. 'You just have to ask, Plum . . .'

Lu proffered the bar. Plum shoved her hand away.

'We shouldn't always have to share.'

'I don't mind sharing,' my sister said.

Plum scoffed.

'Course you don't.'

'God, you're such a bitch!'

I felt my jaw slacken. Did Izzy really just say that?

Plum sat up, narrowed her eyes.

'I wish I'd never—'

'Never what?' Izzy asked, like she knew exactly what nasty thing was on Plum's mind and was daring her to come out with it.

'Forget it,' Plum said in a *you're not worth it* tone, and it was then that I noticed she wasn't in her usual spot. That my sister was now the one occupying the middle 'seat'.

There was a short silence. It looked like Izzy had won whatever battle this was, but then Plum rallied.

She stood up, brushed off her clothes.

'It's boring here. Let's go do something.'

Dooooo something . . .

'Like what?' Izzy asked.

Plum smirked.

'Not you. Just Lu. Come on, Lu, let's get out of here.'

Lu stood up, stuffed the now empty Snickers wrapper in her pocket.

'What's wrong with me? Why can't I stop eating these?'

'You know what you have to do?' Plum said.

Lu nodded, looked at her feet.

'I know.'

'It's okay. You'll feel so much better after.'

What on earth were they talking about? I shifted position, put my eye back to the crack.

Plum slipped an arm through Lu's.

'Come on.'

'I've got *Hitman* on my computer,' Lu told her.

'The only way to live is to die, right?'

Lu giggled.

'Right,' she agreed.

Izzy watched them go, blinking rapidly. Her legs were pink from lying in the sun, a criss-cross pattern on her legs from the grass. Like someone had taken a knife to them.

I should have felt bad for her but I didn't. What I saw was an opportunity.

'You don't need them,' I said, poking my head out of my hiding place. 'Want to hang out in my tree house?'

Her eyes narrowed the way Plum's had after Izzy called her a bitch.

'You've been spying on us? What the fuck's wrong with you?'

'Dita!' I yelled. 'Izzy said the F-word . . .'

My sister shot me a look of pure disdain. Asked if I had any idea how pathetic I was.

'A sad, pathetic little worm. Like I'd want to hang out with a loser like you!'

My stomach tightened. I wanted to fight back but for once I had no words.

That evening, there was a hullabaloo. Izzy couldn't find her charm bracelet.

'It was on my nightstand. Now it's gone.'

She was hysterical, yelling the place down. Her most precious belonging. Where was it?

'You've got to help me find it!'

Dita took her room apart, my father coming out of his study to help as soon as he'd wound up his conference call.

126

'It's got to be here somewhere. Where did you put it?'

'On my nightstand. I already told you! '

'Are you sure that's where you left it?'

She stamped her foot, fists clenched into hard little rocks.

'Yes, I'm sure. It's just . . . disappeared.'

'Things don't just vanish, chick,' Dita said, trying to inject some calm into the situation.

But it seemed the bracelet had.

I observed the chaos from a distance, then went downstairs to watch *SpongeBob*. Izzy stormed into the living room, face ablaze.

'You're just sitting there?'

I shrugged, told her it was up to me where I sat.

Her eyes brimmed over.

'If you lost something Mommy gave you . . . The last thing she gave you . . .'

She broke off, couldn't finish the sentence.

I muted the TV, folded my arms. Prepared to ask whether she was sorry for calling me pathetic and all the other lousy things she'd said.

But she got there first.

'God, you're such a loser.'

I felt my features stiffen. Eyeballed her.

'A loser who knows where your charm bracelet is.'

Her shoulders dropped. She took a step towards me.

'What? Where?'

'Plum took it. I saw her,' I answered and turned the TV back up.

NOW

Elsa Stone calls again that evening as I'm topping up my vodka glass and watching *Frasier* re-runs on TV. The number is withheld but I know it's her.

What I don't immediately know is whether I'm going to pick up.

She still hasn't told me what this new information she's uncovered is, preferring instead to dangle it as bait. 'Quid pro quo' goes unsaid. If she talks, so do I.

It's been twenty years but am I ready to tell my story, to reveal my part in Izzy's? And if so, do I really want to tell it to this woman?

What does my father know about her that I don't? What ghost did her name raise?

Who is she?

According to the internet, Elsa Stone the journalist doesn't exist.

For the past decade, my father has been little more than a vegetable. He recognised her name though. I didn't imagine that look in his eyes. Didn't dream up the way they widened when I brought her up.

My finger oscillates between Accept and Decline. Curiosity wins out. Good thing I'm not a cat, I suppose . . .

'Hello?' I say in a voice that hopefully says, *I'm busy. This better be good.*

'Have you thought about what we discussed?' Elsa Stone asks, straight to the point. A woman who means business.

'Who is this?' I ask, just to be a dick.

She tells me. Then says, 'My bosses are keen for us to sort out an interview. Do you have any time this week?'

She's smart but I'm not going to be rushed into anything. I do want to know what she knows though.

Rock and hard place . . .

I take a slug of Smirnoff, feel the burn. The liquid hug.

'I looked you up,' I tell her. 'There's nothing about you online.'

'You looked me up?' she repeats, tone rising a pitch.

I say, 'Yes.' Add: 'There's not a single mention of you.'

'Ah well, to tell the truth, that's not really surprising.'

I hear her click her lighter on and off. A creak as though she's adjusting her position.

'I'm more what you call "behind the scenes",' she explains. 'On the investigative side, you see?'

Then before I can say anything to that, she's launching in.

Getting down to *tachlis*, my father would have said. Yiddish, apparently, for talking turkey.

'Must say, I'm surprised you don't seem more interested in what I've found.'

'You're not the first person claiming to have new information,' I retort.

'No one's uncovered this though,' she counters.

We're playing poker again. It's a delicate game.

'And what's "this"?' I ask, heavy emphasis on the last word.

She smiles; I hear it in her voice.

'So, you'll talk to me?'

I tilt forward, put my elbows on my knees. Cradle my glass.

'Depends what you've got.'

There's a pause. Down the line I hear Elsa Stone suck her teeth. Something tells me they're sharp.

'How about a little amuse-bouche?' she says in a perfect French accent.

'An amuse what now?'

She clicks her lighter, takes a drag.

'A titbit to whet your appetite.'

I wet my whistle.

'Go on,' I say. Then channelling Frasier Crane: 'I'm listening.'

'She kept a diary,' Elsa Stone tells me.

I frown, ask who did.

'Lu.'

I make a snorting noise to show I'm not impressed.

'That's hardly news, Ms Stone.'

She's unperturbed.

'This one's from afterwards . . .'

A tickle traces my spine. When I lift my glass to my lips, my hand is trembling.

'So?'

The bluff would fall flat if she could see my face.

Elsa Stone raises the stakes.

'Lu was convinced someone else was there that night,' she says. 'That they were being watched.'

BEFORE

The third time I saw Ryder Grady, Dita and I were at the gates of Izzy's school watching for her to come out. She'd been complaining of a toothache – a cavity, Dita suspected. We were taking her to the dentist.

'Too much candy, if you ask me,' I said while we waited.

'Says the skillet to the toaster.'

'Huh?'

'It's an expression. Means worry about yourself.'

A balding man with a ginger combover skipped down the front steps. He was wearing a black professorial gown over beige chinos, a bow tie and stripy sweater vest. A Homer Simpson stomach strained against his waistband.

His name was George Smorgasbord and he was principal of Heritage Elm School for Girls.

'Good afternoon, ladies,' he said, stopping to shake our hands.

They were big on handshakes at that school, I remember. Izzy didn't like it, used to carry a little bottle of Germ-X in her bag. *If you don't look them in the eye while you're doing it, they make you do it all over again.*

'You're a bit early for pick-up,' Mr Smorgasbord said with a smile that showed a wide row of tiny teeth.

What he meant was: *what are you doing here?*

'Izzy's been eating too much candy,' I told him. 'She might need a filling.'

Dita gave me a hard dig in the ribs.

'I called the office,' she said. 'They said it was okay to come and get her early.'

She sounded nervous. I wasn't used to hearing her sound that way.

Mr Smorgasbord held up a hand, told her it was no problem.

'But if you have time for a quick word . . .'

She stiffened, asked what was wrong.

'Nothing to worry about, I'm sure. Only Izzy's grades have been slipping a bit recently and she's becoming rather a day-dreamer. Spends much of her classes staring out the window, I hear . . .'

'I see,' Dita said. 'Thank you for telling me. I'll speak to her.'

The principal smiled again, all those little teeth on display. Then told her that might be a good idea, as if Dita had been the one to call Izzy's grades to his attention.

'It's because of Plum and Lu,' I piped up.

Mr Smorgasbord looked confused, asked what was because of them?

Dita shot me a warning look which I happily ignored.

'They're not nice girls,' I said in a confidential tone, the sort my father used on the phone sometimes. 'She always used to work hard at school. Until they came along and ruined everything.'

The principal looked even more flummoxed than before.

'Ruined what?' he asked.

Dita pinched my arm, bent close to my ear.

'That's quite enough,' she hissed, meaning 'I'll deal with you later, missy' and that's when I saw Ryder Grady for the third time.

He walked into the quad looking so different from the video on Izzy's phone that it took me a moment to recognise him.

Gone was the guitar and grey tee. In their place, a black suit, pale blue necktie and polished brogues. His shaggy hair was gelled and brushed back, his face freshly shaved.

He was holding a sheaf of papers under his arm and walking alongside a waifish student whose coltish legs and big round eyes put me in mind of Bambi.

She couldn't seem to take them off him.

His head was tipped towards her, nodding every so often. Listening carefully to whatever she was saying. Giving her his full attention.

They came closer.

'What do you think?' I heard her ask, in a hopeful tone.

'I think it's brilliant, Marsha. You should believe in yourself more.'

She blushed, looked up at him through fluttering eyelashes.

'You really think so?'

'Yes, Marsha,' he said. His voice cocoa warm. 'I really do.'

I watched as he adjusted his papers under his arm. Touched her shoulder momentarily.

'It's brilliant and so are you.'

Suddenly, it clicked.

'What's Plum's dad doing here?' I asked Mr Smorgasbord.

The principal frowned.

'Plum's father?' he repeated in a confused voice.

'Yes,' I said, pointing. 'Over there.'

He followed my gaze and laughed in that indulgent way adults do when they're being particularly patronising.

'That's not Plum's father,' he said. *Silly girl!* 'That's our new biology teacher. Mr Grady.'

Then, turning to Dita, 'We're terribly lucky to have him. He's such a hit with the girls . . .'

Extract from Izzy Jackman's diary

July 2 2003

I'm so lucky to know Ryder. When I'm with him I feel like
I'm dancing on rainbows, colour-dripping rainbows that sing
and smell like cotton candy. I love the drugs but I love, love,
love that man. I'd do anything for him. That's what love is,
right? You'll do anything for the other person.

I told him as much and he said in that deep way of his:
'Anything is a lot of something, buttercup.' And I said I
meant it. I'd die for him. And I wasn't just saying it because I
was baked.

He kissed me full on the lips, his beautiful hands up in my
hair. Told me I was perfect, made me say it back to him.

'I'm perfect.'

'Yes, you are, buttercup. Say it again.'

'I'm perfect.'

'You're perfect, buttercup.'

He has names for all of us. But I like my name best.

He picked up his camera, ran his lips lightly over my
shoulder. Made my skin tremble.

'Let me take a picture of you, buttercup. Do you have any idea how beautiful you are?'

Plum was lounging on the other side of him. She stretched a leg over his lap, began moving it about in a way that made me wish she'd stop even though we're supposed to share and love isn't possessive.

'I wouldn't just die for you. I'd kill for you,' she said in this husky voice, all sleepy from the pot.

It was good pot, although acid is my favourite. I felt both heavy and light at the same time. Does that make sense? Maybe not. I think I'm still a little buzzed, haha!

Ryder started stroking Plum's leg and clicking his camera at her. Told her to tip her head back, open her mouth a bit.

'The magazines are going to just love you, daisy chain . . .'

Lu watched. Proper couch-locked stoned.

'I'd kill for you too,' she said, slurring her words a bit.

'Kill for me, huh?' he said and laughed and we all laughed with him. 'Well, just remember what I always say, girls. If you're going to do something, make sure you do it well! Okay?'

And we all laughed at that too because it's what he says in class.

God, I love that man!

BEFORE

A night in early July, just weeks before Turtle Lake, I woke to the sound of Izzy crying. Her sobs travelling through our shared wall. I lay very still, listening.

What was wrong? Was she still upset about her charm bracelet?

That was ages ago though, and after I told her it was Plum who'd taken it, she hadn't mentioned it again.

Why hadn't she confronted her? Why were they still friends?

Or were they?

I thought back to what I'd seen on the bathroom mirror this evening: the words she'd written in the condensation reappearing when I took a shower.

I could barely contain my delight at the time.

And yet when I'd come downstairs afterwards, Izzy was in the kitchen asking if she could go to the outlet mall with Plum on the weekend as Dita set up the new coffee table my father had ordered from IKEA.

She's just texted. There's a big sale on at Guess . . .

I was disappointed but also not all that surprised. Even at grade school, you could tell a person they were your best friend and that you hated them in practically the same breath. Friendships were always up and down. Break up one minute, make up the next.

The crying continued now.

Should I go see if she was okay? Or would I just get yelled at for sticking my beak in?

Butt out, Finn. It's none of your beeswax . . .

Izzy never cried, not even after our mother died. I remember Dita going on about it at the time.

'Not talking, not crying,' she told my father. 'It's no good for her. She needs to let it out.'

He looked up from his paper, sighed. Told her everyone grieves in different ways.

'It can lead to emotional problems down the line,' Dita persisted, never one to back down. 'I read about it in *Good Housekeeping*. You don't cry when someone dies, you get depression later in life. Addictions. All sorts.'

My father shook the paper to straighten it out, turned the page.

'You can't force a person to cry if they don't want to, Dita.'

Yet here she was now, bawling her eyes out.

What had happened?

What could possibly be more devastating than losing our mother?

When I look back on that night, a different question strikes me:

What had unlocked inside Izzy that she was *able* to cry? And how had it been released?

I was just pushing back the covers – I couldn't simply ignore her – when I heard the muffled sound of her voice. For a stupid second, I thought she was talking to herself, before realising she must be on her phone. I put my ear to the wall.

'But I never said that . . .'

'I promise. He's got to believe me . . .'

It made no sense and in the end I lost interest and fell back asleep. If only I'd listened for longer.

A world of *if onlys* . . .

In my mind, the days merge together after that. I have a vague memory of Dita and I dropping Izzy off at the Cheesecake Factory to meet Plum and Lu. Another hazy recollection of the three of them painting their nails in the backyard, a big beach towel spread on the grass that would later be covered with dark red splatters.

What I do remember clearly is how Izzy was sucking up to Plum. Gone was the snappishness I'd overheard that day in the tree house. So too the fighting talk about where she was sitting. Instead, she simpered at all stupid Plum's jokes. Told her how pretty her hair was. How much she liked her new ballet shoes.

What a doormat!

'Worried about tipping the canoe, I expect,' Dita said when I went to report back.

I screwed up my face, asked: 'What canoe?'

She added a splash of milk to the cheese sauce she was making. A grind of nutmeg.

'It's an expression. Means your sister doesn't want to find herself with no friends again.'

'Has she even asked about her charm bracelet?' I grumbled. Then – 'Why does she love Plum so much anyway?'

Dita shrugged, whisked the sauce.

'Flattered to be chosen by her, I suppose. First time she's ever been chosen by anybody.'

A few days after that, Lu called. Izzy was waxing her legs, the bathroom door ajar. She put her mobile on speaker phone. Peeled the strip off her thigh.

Lu's voice carried to where I was doing headstands in the corridor. 'There's this big party happening at Turtle Lake tonight,' I heard her say.

'Turtle Lake?' Izzy repeated.

'It's all over Friendster. Last blowout before everyone goes away for the summer. Bunch of sophomores are organising it. It'll be perfect.

'You're going to just die, Izzy Jackman . . .'

The date was July 17, 2003.

From the *Carlsbad Recorder*

Girl Disappears From Party at Turtle Lake

A thirteen-year-old girl has gone missing following a party at Carlsbad's Turtle Lake.

Between 100 and 150 minors are believed to have attended the party, which is where she was last seen. The last known ping from her cell phone was around midnight near the lake.

The teen was 'troubled', according to school friends. Her disappearance is currently being treated as a runaway by police.

Police have urged her to call her family to let them know she's okay.

Or better still, return home.

NOW

We had no idea Izzy had snuck off to Turtle Lake that night. As far as we were concerned, she was stuffing her face with gummy worms and watching *Sweet Home Alabama* at Plum's house.

It's a sleepover. Can I go?

Occasionally, I wake up with a glorious split second of amnesia until the memory comes crashing back. Suffocating me the way they suffocated her.

Some days I can pull myself through. Get out of bed, down a coffee, go to work. Others, I'm sunk before the day has even started. The smallest tasks a massive effort.

I used to fantasise about doing a Michael J. Fox, going back in time and putting the future right. But even if I had a time machine, where would I start?

Would I tell Dita and my father about the video on Izzy's phone? Would I warn my sister not to make friends with Plum and Lu? Would I take back what I said?

Would changing any of those things make a difference? Were they even the pivotal moments? Or was the tipping point something else entirely? Something I didn't even see?

We learned about the butterfly effect in the second grade.

'Seemingly trivial events can have huge consequences,' Miss Bowman told the class. 'They say a butterfly flapping its wings in Calcutta can cause a tornado in Carlsbad.'

How many butterflies flapped their wings that summer?

I talk to my sister in my head, hold whole conversations with her ghost. The Izzy from before Plum and Lu. The Izzy who still talked to me.

God, I miss her!

'We'd get a coffee this morning, if you were here.'

'Panera?'

'Or the Coffee Bean at Solana Beach.'

'The blueberry muffins there were always our favourite.'

'Remember how you always used to pick the fruit out first, Iz?'

'Dita said I had the table manners of a pig.'

'And you said, "What kind of pig eats blueberry muffins?"'

I swallow away the lump in my throat. Damn the parallel universe and how easy it is to picture.

If it hadn't been for Turtle Lake, I don't suppose we'd have left California.

My father would have worked his way up to the appellate court, maybe beyond.

Izzy would have had a family and a career (though nothing to do with frogs, one hopes).

And I would have graduated high school instead of flunking my A levels and winding up with a boss who I'm fairly sure gets my name wrong on purpose and keeps a box's worth of used Kleenex up her sleeve.

'You've got to move on,' says Izzy's voice inside my head.

But how can I possibly move on without knowing what really happened that night?

AFTER

When I look back on my childhood, I see it divided into two parts: before and after Turtle Lake. Even though immediately after the disappearance there was still hope everything would turn out okay. That she really had just run away like everybody was saying.

Because although there was hope right then, I know now that's the point everything changed. That from Turtle Lake onwards, our lives would never be the same.

That it was just a matter of time before it became official. That we'd lost Izzy. That my worst fears had been realised.

July 18, 2003:

The house phone rang as Dita was flipping pancakes and I was hunting in the pantry for maple syrup.

Dita answered the way she had the afternoon Plum had first called the house. Receiver crooked against her ear and shoulder. Dish towel flung over her shoulder.

'Jackman residence . . .'

Under my breath:

'You've reached the White House.'

Dita waggled her eyebrows at me, then her face turned serious.

'I'm afraid the judge isn't home, Mrs Underwood. Is everything okay?'

A flush crept up her neck. Her eyes flitted in my direction then settled on her hands. She turned off the stove.

'The girls haven't come home? I didn't realise they were going out . . . I see . . . Have you tried Plum's cell?' A pause. 'Right. Okay . . . I'll ring Izzy and call you straight back. Can you let me have your number again?'

She rummaged about in a drawer for a pen, scribbled the Underwoods' number on the side of a Kleenex box.

'– 3141, okay. I'll call her now. And Mrs Underwood, don't worry. They'll be alright. You know what kids are like . . .'

For weeks afterwards the digits stared at us from the box like a taunt.

You thought it was all going to be fine. You idiots . . .

Twelve hours later, only two had returned.

'I think it's time to call the police,' my father said.

Suddenly everyone was talking about the 'missing Carlsbad teen', as she was branded by the press. The *Ledger* needed two print runs those first weeks. The *Recorder* too.

'Schadenfreude,' my father called it.

'I don't see what Freud has to do with it,' Dita said. 'Sadists, that's what they are. Getting off on other people's pain.'

My father pressed his lips together, didn't bother putting her straight. I didn't say anything either, just sat up in my room with the drapes shut, chewing my nails. Spinning out.

I think on some level I already knew.

I couldn't eat. A hard knot in my throat made it impossible to swallow. A permanent sickness in my stomach.

At night I didn't sleep. Just lay there in a tight foetal ball, tears running down my face without realising I was crying. When I did drift off, I was seized by nightmares. Frequently waking Dita with my screams.

She'd come hurrying into my room, tying her robe. Kneel by my bed, stroke my hair.

'Hush, chick. You had a bad dream, that's all.'

But what if it wasn't a dream? What if it was real?

What if she had . . . ?

Everyone had an opinion.

Something going on at home, I expect . . .

Having a difficult time, I heard.

Always was a funny one . . .

Folk feigning concern but secretly revelling in the biggest drama to hit the town since sewage spills closed South Beach five years before.

Teenagers run away all the time.

Not without their phone chargers, they don't.

She didn't take her charger?

Not according to the Herald, *she didn't . . .*

Whereas before, our screentime had been strictly limited so we didn't get square eyes, the television was suddenly on in our house the whole time.

The first seventy-two hours are the most critical in a missing persons case. After this time, the number of leads tends to drop off, and with every hour that passes, the likelihood of finding the subject alive decreases . . .

My father paused in the doorway, came to sit beside me on the couch.

I looked at him, waiting for the words that would take away my fear without me having to articulate what that fear was. A fear I could hardly admit to myself.

He opened his mouth to speak then closed it again. Patted my hand.

'My tummy hurts,' I told him.

'You want some Pepto Bismol?'

I shook my head, said it wasn't that sort of hurting.

He nodded, said, 'Okay.' Patted my hand again.

I thought about what I'd done and what I'd seen.

'She's dead, isn't she?' I whispered.

My father didn't answer.

The first seventy-two hours shivered to a close.

From the *San Diego Sun*

TURTLE LAKE PARTYGOERS STAY SILENT

Authorities have expressed frustration that their investigation has been stalled by partygoers refusing to speak to them.

There have been reports of illegal activity – including underage drinking and drug-taking – at the now infamous party that took place at Turtle Lake three nights days ago. Police believe this is preventing partygoers from speaking up, because they are worried about getting in trouble.

'Someone will have seen something that night. Somebody knows more than they might realise. We need that person – or persons – to come forward.

'A girl's life depends on it.'

AFTER

I kept thinking about those last weeks leading up to Turtle Lake. Raking over them in a desperate search for clues, trying to convince myself that my fears were unfounded. That there was another reason she'd gone missing.

That she would be found safe and sound.

That it wasn't my fault.

Searching for clues. Sifting through the past. Not much has changed in that department, I guess.

It was different then though. Back then, there was still hope. Even if it was just a sliver.

She could still come walking through the door at any moment. Full of sass and eye-rolls as always.

Full of life.

And although I'd hated her so hard at times, I'd have burst with delight if she had come back then. Because it would have meant everything was okay and the nagging worry that kept me awake at night was for nothing.

But she didn't return and the worry kept growing until I

didn't have headspace for anything else. What ifs? crowding out any other thoughts.

The papers were saying she was 'troubled', that there were possibly drugs involved. But I didn't believe that. We'd learned about narcotics at school. Watched the film about what your brain would look like if it were an egg on drugs. How it sizzled and spat on the heat.

Drugs were for bums. They made your teeth fall out. Turned you into a person that crouched in doorways shaking and dribbling.

Izzy and her friends could be a little nuts sometimes – all that rubbish they spouted about capitalism and hegemony (whatever that meant). But they weren't *crazy* And they had all their teeth.

No, the papers had it wrong.

Except I was the one who had it wrong. Even when rumours about an older man began to surface, I didn't connect the flags and think of Ryder Grady. The man who'd given Plum and those other kids money for ice cream. Who'd beckoned to Izzy on the video. Who taught biology at her school.

Such a hit . . .

I'd heard the girls talking about him but it had all seemed like silly chatter to me.

Izzy and her friends might have had a crush but what did that have to do with Turtle Lake?

Plus, everyone knows you can trust teachers. They're the people you talk to when you have a problem. The ones who'd know how to fix it.

*

After the first three days, the number of potential leads drops off dramatically. Four days have passed since the now notorious party at Turtle Lake . . .

I was watching TV in the living room, kneeling right up close to the set as though I might miss something by sitting further back. There was a shot of Turtle Lake, a yellow crime scene tape flapping in the breeze. And along the bottom of the screen, a ticker tape:

Breaking: Lucia Nox speaks to police

It took me a moment to realise 'Lucia' was Lu. I'd never heard her called that before.

I turned up the volume. An anchorwoman began to speak.

Our reporter Rekah Malik caught up with Miss Nox for San Diego News . . .

The camera flipped to a dark-haired woman in a crisp white shirt holding a microphone. Opposite her was Lu, her face perfectly made up.

'What can you tell us?' the reporter asked, pointing the microphone in her direction.

'She was depressed. Really down. Said no one understood her and she just needed space.'

'Do you have any idea what might have happened to her?'

'She must have run away. It's the only thing that makes sense.'

Dita blew out loudly through her nose. I startled, hadn't noticed her come into the room.

'That girl should . . .'

'Should what?' I asked.

But she just shook her head.

'Never mind.'

The anchorwoman was back on the screen:

Lucia Nox has told police she believes the missing teen is simply playing hooky. But if that's true, where does the mysterious graffiti fit in . . . ?

From the *Carlsbad Ledger*

Grisly Graffiti Discovered at Turtle Lake

Police today announced the word 'LIAR' has been discovered on the trunk of a cottonwood tree at Turtle Lake.

Chillingly, the graffiti was scrawled in blood.

Lieutenant Owen King told reporters:

'We would urge anyone who was at the party to think carefully in case they remember seeing anything unusual. And for the public to remain vigilant.'

AFTER

It was Lu's idea to hold a vigil.

'Could be useful,' the officer heading up the investigation told my father. 'If there has been foul play, there's a strong possibility the offender will turn up.'

The officer's name was Detective Arnold; a great bear of a man with a penchant for cookies and who let me try out his walkie the first time he stopped by the house 'to ask you all a few questions'.

It took me a while to work out whether Arnold was his first or last name. I thought a name that could be either was pretty cool.

'It'd be a risk for them to show their face, surely?' my father said.

Arnold shrugged, told him he'd be surprised.

'Risk is what these types live for, Judge. They get off on the idea they know something we don't.'

'You think there's an offender? That there *has* been foul play?' Dita asked, pouring him a tall glass of lemonade. *I made it myself, Detective.*

She offered him a brownie to go with it. *Fresh out the oven this morning . . .*

He'd been round to the house several times by this point and he always accepted a brownie from Dita when he came. Often two.

'Important thing is to keep an open mind,' he said now. 'We're working with an FBI profiler. We'll be on the lookout for anyone behaving suspiciously.'

I felt a wormy sensation in my belly. So they *did* think something had happened to her.

'Suspicious how so?' Dita asked, topping up his glass even though it was still half full.

I leaned forward in my seat, ears pricked.

How did guilty people act? What kind of things gave them away?

Arnold wet his lips, told her it was complicated. I may not be able to read guilt, but I could spot an evasion from a mile off, as I told Dita afterwards.

'Keeping something back,' I said.

She tutted, told me I was so sure I knew everything all the time.

'You're in a nice mood,' I replied, for which I got to spend the rest of the morning in my room thinking about my attitude.

It seemed as though the whole of Carlsbad was at the vigil. The beach so full of people you could hardly see the sand.

'Most of them don't even know her,' I whispered to my father.

'That's what makes it even more special they came.'

Plum's mom and Lu's dad were standing with us. Lu's mother

was at home in bed with her bottles of medicine and a carer her father had brought in specially for the evening.

'Can't even go to the bathroom by herself anymore,' Lu told Plum and my sister not so long ago.

'I don't think it's special,' I said to my father. 'It's that sharder thing like you said.'

Dita nudged me in the ribs. Told me to behave myself.

'That chocolate on your sleeve?' I asked, pleased to have a chance to get my own back for earlier. 'I thought you were dieting.'

Dita always said she was big-boned, but the truth is, she liked dessert a bit too much. Had a thing about cleanliness too.

'How'd that get there?' she said, rubbing at the marks, all embarrassed.

'I'm wearing clean clothes,' I said, alluding to another argument we'd had earlier that day.

'I should hope so,' she answered, removing the offending item and folding it inside out to hide the stains.

On her skin, the first puckerings of gooseflesh. She shivered, wrapped her arms round herself.

I felt bad then. There was a chilly breeze blowing off the ocean, the sky darkening.

It was only going to get colder.

'No one cares if it's dirty, Dita.'

'I care.'

She shivered again.

'Put it back on,' I insisted. 'It's fine.'

My father shot me a stern look.

'Dita's quite capable of deciding whether or not she wears a jacket, Finn.'

Before I could respond, a high-pitched squeal punctured the air. A megaphone being switched on, branded with the Heritage Elm crest. Its motto too: *Learning today, leading tomorrow* . . .

They'd lent it for the speeches. Set up a coffee stand as well. The paper cups were also stamped with the school crest.

A hush fell over the crowd, *shushes* passed along like notes in class.

Detective Arnold said a few words about how nice it was to see so many people here, how he knew 'the family' appreciated it. And then he called Lu up to the makeshift platform to give her prepared speech.

'It's not right,' Dita whispered to my father. 'She should be here with us.'

I slipped a hand in hers. She squeezed it tight.

Behind the stage, the waves rushed up to the shore, petering out in a dribble. A single star pricked the firmament.

I spotted a man in a suit surveying the scene, talking into his lapel. And then someone else. Slightly removed from the crowd, the faintest of smiles on his face.

Was that the teacher from Izzy's school? The one I'd seen on her phone playing the guitar?

I tugged at my father's shirt tails to get his attention, but when I looked back, the man had gone.

'Everyone's praying so hard for you to come home safe,' Lu was saying. 'I think about you all the time. I'm heartbroken for real. Please, just let us know you're okay.'

Despite what Arnold had told us, the police had largely dismissed the idea that this was a runaway case. The blood from the graffiti at Turtle Lake had turned out to be a DNA match, though Lu was still refusing to accept there may have been foul play.

Denial, Dita said, is the first stage of grief.

'It was in *Good Housekeeping.*'

Lu came down off the stage to join us.

'Was I okay?' she asked her father in her little-girl voice.

'Huh?' he asked.

'It was beautiful, sweetie,' Mrs Underwood told her in an underwater voice, a faraway look in her eye.

The Xanax, I suppose. Hadn't Plum said she was always out of it?

Lu smiled her thanks, tucked a lock of hair behind her ears. As she did, her sleeve slipped down, revealing a three-inch gash on her arm.

Detective Arnold noticed too. Asked, 'What did you do to your arm, Lucia?'

He always called her by her full name. So did the press whenever they quoted her, something they seemed to be doing rather frequently. *A source close to the family says* . . .

'Looks like a nasty cut. How d'you get it?'

'Cut?' she repeated.

'Right there, on your arm.'

He reached out. Lu jerked back.

'Oh, that,' she said. 'I fell off my bike.'

'You need to be careful,' he said.

'I know,' she said.

160

There were more speeches, then everyone sang 'Amazing Grace'.

I once was lost, but now I'm found . . .

Mrs Underwood took a half step towards Lu's dad, who laid a hand on the small of her back.

'Hmm,' Dita murmured.

'Hmm what?' I asked.

'What? I didn't say anything.'

Someone released the lanterns. Hundreds of them began drifting out over the water. Phosphorescing in the dark.

'Ahhh . . .' went the collective whisper.

Of course, now we know how harmful lanterns are, how bad for the environment. When I think back on that night, to the glowing forms sailing off into the distance, I see doom rather than hope.

Wire frames falling into the sea. Maiming and strangling sea life.

A metaphor for what would come to pass.

NOW

Elsa Stone is on the other end of the phone, waiting for me to reply.

'What do you mean, Lu thought they were being watched?' I say.

My voice sounds strangled.

'That's what she wrote it in her diary. Says she was convinced someone else was there that night. Watching . . .'

My stomach growls. I get up to investigate what's in the fridge. Not much, it seems. Just a rather dimpled apple and a satsuma that may well be growing legs.

Stone slips another worm on the hook.

'That's not all,' she says.

I can hear cars honking on the other end of the line. A computerised voice instructs: *Turn left on St Pancras Road. The station is in two hundred feet.*

Is Google Maps directing her to King's Cross Station?

'What else?' I ask.

I wonder how much 'quid' I'll be able to draw out of her before she starts demanding the 'quo'.

'I think Dita knew,' she answers, sucking on her cigarette.

I frown, top up my vodka. Take a swallow.

'Knew what?'

She hesitates, blows out smoke. 'Knew something? Was protecting someone? I'm not exactly sure . . .'

I make a scoffing noise, say I hope her 'big exposé' has more bite. 'Or your production company will be asking for its money back.'

'It's how she reacted,' she says quickly, trying to claw back ground. 'It was . . . strange.'

The back of my neck tingles as I absorb what she's just said.

'You spoke to her?'

A hard knot of jealousy tightens in my stomach.

Dita didn't speak to me once after we left the States. Never phoned. Never wrote me back despite the mountain of letters I wrote her.

So much for her promise: *We'll talk the minute you get to England . . . I love you more than anything.*

Yeah, right.

Did she think of me after we'd gone? Did she miss me at all?

'She'll be busy,' my father said. 'A new family to look after now.'

I hated that idea as much as her ignoring my letters.

Not that I told him. By then I'd stopped telling anyone anything. Not talking about my feelings meant I could block them out. Numbing myself was so much easier than facing up to my demons.

You spoke to her?

Elsa Stone doesn't hear the jealousy, only the question.

'She was a little easier to track down than you. Kept to this side of the pond. Her name too.'

She's making a joke, trying to warm me up. I don't laugh.

'What did she say?'

What I mean is, did she mention me?

'She asked if I'd spoken to the judge.'

'The judge?'

'Your father. Judge Jackman. I got the sense maybe she was protecting him. Or . . .'

'Or what?'

'Or maybe she was scared.'

I rub the base of my skull, inhale deeply through my nose. It's hard to imagine Dita being scared of anything. Apart from Principal Smorgasbord, maybe. That ginger combover was enough to give anybody the willies.

'What would she have been scared of?' I ask.

'Or whom,' Elsa Stone suggests.

'I don't understand,' I say, but it's not quite true.

The urgency with which we left the States. The surreptitious glances between my father and Dita. The niggle I had that something was being kept from me.

Could they have been frightened of something? Or, as Stone says, someone?

Again, I think of my father's reaction to Elsa's name.

If they were frightened, did it have anything to do with her? Is that the real reason she's trying to get me to open up? To find out how much I know?

Who is Elsa Stone? What is she after?

Should I be scared too?

'I mean, it would explain the suicide,' Stone continues.

'Suicide? What suicide?'

'Dita's,' she says matter-of-factly.

The air goes very still. In my ears, the thud of my pulse. The over-amplified rhythm of my breathing.

Dita? No! Dita wouldn't . . .

My chest is tight. My muscles singing.

'God, I'm sorry,' Elsa Stone is saying. 'I just figured . . . I mean, I thought you'd have . . .'

'When?' I ask.

The word sticks, my throat suddenly desert dry.

'After I spoke to her. That's why I thought . . .'

Again, she trails off.

'Thought what?' I say. Shout almost.

'I think someone got to her,' she says. 'I think she was terrified.'

NOW

I start googling the minute I hang up with Elsa Stone, but as I type, I realise with a stab of embarrassment/horror(?) that I don't know Dita's last name.

How is that possible? Dita was practically a mother to me. She put Band-Aids on my boo-boos, fed me cookies and ice cream when I'd had a rough day. Tucked me in every night.

She knew everything about me (whether I told her or not). How is it possible I know so little about her? How can I be in the dark about something so fundamental as her last name?

I pour a vodka. Down it. Pour another.

Dita. Dead. Gone.

The finality is incomprehensible. As impossible to absorb as the idea of an infinite universe.

I love you, chick. Be good for your daddy . . .

We were at LAX, our cases loaded on the Airbus bound for London Heathrow. Hovering by the security barrier. The final goodbye.

'Come with us,' I begged. 'Please, Dita.'

My father took a deep breath to show his patience was wearing thin, said something about us missing our flight if we didn't go 'right now'.

'I *want* to miss our flight.'

'We've talked about this.'

We hadn't though. Not really. I still didn't understand why he couldn't get Dita a visa.

'I'm not going unless she comes too,' I said, jaw tight. Tears only just at bay.

Who's she? Dita would have said at any other time. *The crocodile's mother?*

'I can't do this with you,' my father said, pinching his sinuses. 'We don't have time for your nonsense, Finn.'

'It's not Finn. It's KAT!' I shouted, gripping Dita tighter round the middle.

'We can discuss your name later. Just come along. Now.'

He'd aged ten years in ten weeks. He even smelled different, as though grief had changed his internal chemistry.

'You need to go, chick,' Dita said softly, peeling my arms away.

'Not without you,' I repeated, snapping them straight back.

'You heard what your daddy said. You're going to miss your plane.'

'Good!'

She kissed my head, wiped her eyes.

'Oh, baby! It'll be okay. You'll see. We'll write all the time. Speak every single day.'

'It won't be the same.'

'No. But just think of how much you'll have to tell me.'

I considered.

'You think I might meet the Queen?'

'Not if you don't get on that plane.'

I boarded the flight but I didn't meet the Queen and I never spoke to Dita again either. My father didn't have her new number, he said, but she had ours.

'She'll call when she can.'

'She doesn't even write me back,' I whined. 'I must have sent her a hundred letters already.'

'She'll be busy,' he said. 'New family, I expect.'

All this time, I've been so focused on how losing Izzy affected my father and me. But I've never really thought about what it did to her.

I was furious with her for forgetting us. Not thinking about her was my childish way of paying her back: *If you don't care about me, I won't care about you. See how you like it!*

But of course Dita cared. I don't know why she didn't get in touch after we moved to London, but I do know she loved me and Izzy.

Turtle Lake would have destroyed her just as much as it destroyed me and my father.

Is that the real reason she killed herself? Because she couldn't live with the pain anymore? With Izzy being taken from us?

Elsa Stone reckons it's because she was afraid. But who would she be afraid of?

Isn't it more likely some journalist pitching up asking questions, raised ghosts she couldn't deal with? That Dita spent the last twenty years trying to move on and then Elsa Stone made her realise she'd never be able to? That what happened to Izzy would never let her go?

I heave myself off the sofa, glug water directly from the kitchen faucet. My mouth is arid, a road drill going inside my eye sockets.

What happened to Izzy will never let any of us go.

From the *San Diego Sun*

Vigil Held for Missing Thirteen-Year-Old Girl on South Beach, San Diego

'I know her family is really grateful for everyone's support,' her school friend, Lucia Nox, told the *Sun*. 'You never think anything like this is going to happen to someone you know. It's just surreal.'

AFTER

The day after the vigil, Detective Arnold was back at our house and Dita was back to filling his belly with treats.

'I've just made a fresh batch of brownies. Can I tempt you . . . ?'

'You can tempt *me*,' I said, reaching for the plate she was proffering.

She swatted my hand away.

'You eat any more of those, you'll be looking like one.'

'I've got a daughter your age.' Arnold smiled. 'How about you and me have a chat, Finn?'

He'd just shown me his badge, promised to show me how the siren in his car worked later too.

'A chat about what?' I said a bit too quickly. 'I've never even been to Turtle Lake.'

'You never know what clue might break this case,' he replied, stroking his large stomach as if the clue was possibly something he'd eaten for lunch. 'An overheard remark. Something you noticed that didn't quite make sense. Could be anything.'

'I'm ten,' I replied, shuffling my feet. 'No one tells me diddly-squat.'

Dita threw me a stern look, told me to mind your manners, missy.

Arnold winked at me. I grinned back. I couldn't help liking him.

'With my Milly, most of what she knows isn't what we tell her directly, if you get my drift.'

I shook my head, told him I wasn't sure I did.

He crouched down so our eyes were level. I squirmed, focused on holding his gaze. Everyone knows liars look away.

'No one's in any trouble here, Finn. We just want to find her. Okay?'

I nodded, ground my thumbnail into my fingers.

'Okay.'

I wondered what he knew. What he thought I knew.

Had Dita seen it too? Did she suspect?

'Sorry, what did you say?'

'Did your sister seem worried about anything leading up to that night?' Arnold repeated.

I glanced over at the shelf. On it, a framed photo of Izzy outside our front door, smiling at the camera on her first day at Heritage Elm. Her braces had just come off, I remember. Her uniform, too big. *Growing room*, Dita called it.

A stranger looking at that photo would have seen a happy kid. They wouldn't have seen the loneliness behind her smile. How desperately she wanted friends.

'Finn?' Detective Arnold prompted.

I tried to think back to the week before Turtle Lake, but the days all blended together. When was it she'd gone to the outlet mall with Plum? When had the girls painted their nails together on the beach towel in the backyard?

'She was crying one night,' I said. 'I heard her. Her bedroom's next to mine.'

'Crying?' Arnold said, jotting something down on his flip pad. 'About what?'

I tried to think of the snatches of conversation I'd overheard but it was like trying to carry water in your hands.

'I don't know,' I said. Shrugged. 'I guess she was just upset.'

Detective Arnold looked disappointed. The prize I'd waved under his nose had turned out to be a turkey.

'Anything else you can think of?' he asked.

'Um,' I said.

Scratched my head.

Figured I needed to give him something, and cast about for scraps.

'Um . . .'

I was just about to tell him I thought she had a crush on her biology teacher and that she'd filmed him playing his guitar when a second detective came into the kitchen and interrupted us.

'Find it?' Arnold asked her, looking up.

She shook her head. From upstairs, the sound of creaking floorboards. A door closing.

I was so busy wondering what the detective had been looking for, Ryder Grady went right out of my head.

From the AOL chat room *News Chat*

Lila091: The graffiti on the tree at Turtle lake must be a satanic ritual thing right? Wld explain why it was drawn in blood??

Sabertoothtiger: Particularly cos its HER blood . . .

Hockeyfanatic: I heard there's been stuff going on in the area 4 a while. Houses being broken into + stuff

Kareninspace: Ive heard that 2

Emma1994: U don't know that's connected to the girl tho

Hockeyfanatic: im just saying theres all this going on there so maybe it is???

Darceyy: She still cld have run away. Like maybe SHE did that graffiti to throw everyone off??

Sabertoothtiger: All the photos i've seen she looks happy

SummerRain: Hate to break it 2 u dude – but photos lie. No one post pics of themselves looking waah

From Lucia Nox's Friendster page

I miss u so much. </3 ☹ Everyone is talking about u. Where u've gone. Why . . . I keep thinking only 1 or max 2 people in the whole world know what happened 2 u. its crazy. I can't sleep for thinking about it

Advert in the *Carlsbad Ledger*

A public search party will convene
at Turtle Lake at 8 p.m. tonight.

If you would like to attend, please bring flashlights
and meet at the south-side parking area.

Snacks and bottled water will be available for volunteers.

AFTER

It was after midnight. We were back from the search at Turtle Lake. I was thrashing about in bed, unable to sleep. Unable to stop thinking about what they'd found.

Was it a coincidence, as Dita had tried to persuade me? Or proof I was right? My very worst fears realised?

I squeezed my eyes tight, clasped my hands together.

'Please, Mommy. Let me be wrong. Please make everything be okay.'

Back then, all my prayers were directed to my mother. These days, I don't pray to anyone.

Dita hadn't wanted me to join the search party.

'Not suitable,' she said. 'Kid your age.'

I tried to explain that I was very mature, everybody said so.

'It'll be too upsetting, chick,' she warned.

My father agreed with her. He always did.

'Dita's right, sweetheart.'

'No, she's not,' I said. 'And surely it's up to me to decide what I think is upsetting?'

My father told me it didn't quite work that way. My persuasive skills won out in the end though. *Wore your daddy down, more like*, Dita said with a sniff.

Whatever the reason, I joined our town at Turtle Lake that night, each of us assigned to a team headed up by a police officer. Each of us armed with flashlights and whistles and instructed to 'alert your team leader if you spot anything unusual'.

'Don't touch it,' Lieutenant King told us. 'Just blow your whistle. Understood?'

Over a hundred voices murmured, 'Yes.' Made 'Yes' sound like a storm.

'Haven't they searched the area already?' I asked as I shuffled to our starting point with my father and Dita.

'Extra eyes never hurt anybody,' Dita replied, which struck me as a non-answer.

Truth is, the search was about appeasement. The police had got a fair bit of stick for initially treating the disappearance as a runaway and losing 'precious time', as the *Ledger* put it.

Perhaps if they'd spent fewer hours at Dunkin' and more on the streets, they'd have found her by now . . .

I thought of the graffiti on the tree, felt again the now familiar sensation of guilt and fear chewing my insides.

Dita gave me a sidelong glance.

'You alright, chick? Gone a bit green about the gills.'

'I'm not a fish,' I said crossly.

I needed to learn to hide my feelings better. Last thing I wanted was her guessing what was really chewing me up.

We moved across the ground in horizontal lines, arms linked with the folk on either side of us. Heads down. Step. Stop. Look. Step again.

Beams of light swept the undergrowth. All around, the crunch of feet on forest floor.

Step. Stop. Step.

Through the pines. Past the craggy rocks. Towards the lake, its black water winking in the moonlight.

The line crept forward, ten people moving as one. No one speaking.

And then the line jolted as one of our team dropped to his knees. Blew his whistle. Three sharp bursts.

'Hey! I think I found something!'

A sort of static ripped through the air. An electric charge that set the hairs on my neck on end.

'It's Bob Murphy,' someone shouted. Yelled – 'What you got there, Bob?'

'Don't touch!' our leader called out, blew his whistle several times in quick succession. 'Stand back. Don't touch!'

He strode over to where Bob was crouching in the grass. Held his arms wide, palms open as if pushing the air out of his way.

'Stand back,' he said again. 'Nobody move. Last thing we need is a stampede.'

'What'd you find, Bob?' another person asked. 'What is it?'

'What you got, Bob?'

I was standing close enough to see the officer pick it up, examine it with his flashlight. A tiny swatch of fabric. On it, what looked like blood.

My throat closed up. Stomach plummeting to my feet.

The piece of material was no bigger than my thumbnail but I recognised it instantly.

Izzy has a shirt with the exact same pattern.

From *San Diego News Talk Radio*

Newscaster: Locals joined police officers at Turtle Lake yesterday evening in a search of the area. Bruce Altman, who coaches the Carlsbad Blue Caps softball team, was there. Can you describe the scene for us, Bruce?

Bruce Altman: Must have been near on a hundred people out last night. Thing like this happens, you want to help. Know what I mean?

Newscaster: I can only imagine what it's been like. Your community must be rocked.

Bruce Altman: It's been just awful. My kid's at Heritage Elm too.

Newscaster: They're close then? Her and the missing girl?

Bruce Altman: Well, no. But like I said, when something like this happens . . .

Newscaster: Everyone pulls together?

Bruce Altman: Right.

Newscaster: You overheard a conversation recently, didn't you? Between Judge Jackman and a police officer outside Bay Books. That right?

Bruce Altman: Yeah, that's right.

Newscaster: Can you tell us about it?

Bruce Altman: Cop was convinced the kid was playing hooky. 'We see it all the time,' he said. 'She'll be off having fun someplace, don't you worry. Turn up soon enough with her tail between her legs.'

Newscaster: Except she hasn't, has she?

Bruce Altman: No, sir. She has not. And after what was found last night, it doesn't look like that's going to happen.

AFTER

I woke late the morning after the search. The whole house was quiet. Still, like an animal caught in the headlights.

A split second of amnesia and then it came crashing back.

Bob Murphy dropping to his knees.

Three short whistle blasts.

Hey! I think I found something!

The swatch of fabric illuminated by the officer's flashlight. The unmistakable pattern of rainbows and blood spatter. The feeling of my guts being sucked out by a giant vacuum.

I'd sensed Dita stiffen beside me, heard her sharp intake of breath. But, like me, she'd said nothing. I wondered if it was for the same reason, but was too frightened to ask.

'That was Izzy's shirt, wasn't it?' I said as she tucked me in later.

She stroked my hair the way I liked. Smoothed down my comforter.

'Could be anyone's,' she answered.

'But—'

'Could be anyone's,' she repeated, more firmly this time like she was trying to convince herself.

She kissed the top of my head, switched off my lamp.

'Don't let the bed bugs bite.'

I tossed and turned, awake for hours. Dark shapes dancing on my ceiling. The bony branch outside tapping against the pane.

It wasn't *anyone's* shirt though. It was Izzy's. And whatever way I sliced it, there was only one reason I could think of why it would have blood on it.

I lay in bed the following morning, torturing myself until I could take it no longer, and went downstairs.

Dita was in the kitchen rolling out pastry, hands and apron covered in flour. She always baked when she was stressed.

'Someone's up finally,' she said as I came in. 'Give me a second and I'll fix you some eggs.'

I told her I wasn't hungry.

The nausea that had kept me company ever since that phone call from Mrs Underwood was worse than ever.

'What's going to happen?' I asked.

She looked at me quizzically, dark circles under her eyes.

'Happen?'

'Now they've found her shirt.'

She sighed heavily. *Not this again.*

'There was blood on it, Dita. Do the police think—?'

She dropped a pat of butter into a skillet, set it sizzling. Scrambled up three eggs.

I tutted.

'I said I'm not hungry.'

'Not hungry? You're a growing girl. You need to eat. Now how about some bacon to go with these?'

'Dita!'

'Trust me,' she said, plating up the eggs and setting them in front of me. 'I know what's best for you.'

I rolled my eyes.

'You always say that.'

She winked.

'Well, that's because it's true.'

The radio was on, the anchor reading the headlines.

US forces have arrested several men thought to be bodyguards of former Iraqi president Saddam Hussein following a tip-off from an informant . . .

A new study shows doctors tend to be over-optimistic when it comes to how long terminally ill cancer patients have left to live . . .

And police announce a shock development in the Turtle Lake case.

I felt my stomach heave. Gripped the edge of the counter. It was all coming out now . . .

Lieutenant Owen King told reporters this morning that Lucia Nox received a text message from the missing teen late last night, following a search at Turtle Lake during which a piece of bloodstained fabric was discovered.

The message read:

Please tell everyone to stop worrying. I'm fine. I just need some space. It was signed off with two kisses.

A text message?

A pile of rocks lifted off my shoulders. My nausea faded to nothing. I shovelled in a forkful of eggs, asked if we had any chocolate milk.

From the AOL chat room *News Chat*

SusiParker: How do we know SHE was the one sending the message??

MelWilson: It was from her fone. The cops have confirmed it. Who else wld it b?

CelinaCarver: Whoever took her??

SusiParker: U dont know someone took her . . .

CelinaCarver: You don't know they didn't . . .

Nikki Flynn: The phone was turned off straight after the text was sent

Lesley Beech: suspicious . . .

Nikki Flynn: Thats what i think

Shelly Lloyd: Mayb she doesn't want 2 be found. She said she needed space . . .

Lesley Beech: Or m/b the person who took her is the one who needs some space??? m/b this is the way to take the heat off them

Abi Nuttall: Poor kid. Hope shes ok

AFTER

The police were round at our house again later that morning. Arnold as usual and another detective whose corkscrew hair reminded me of my first-grade teacher's. She spoke to me like I was still in the first grade, too.

'Hello, Finn. I'm Detective Rebecca.'

'Isn't that a first name?'

She smiled.

'Well, aren't you smart?'

'To know Rebecca's a first name?'

Dita shot me a warning look from over by the stove, apologised for my manners. Seemed to me she was the one being rude. I glowered right back.

'Did you find out who the shirt belonged to?' I asked Detective Rebecca carefully. 'That Bob Murphy found last night,' I added when she looked confused.

She exchanged a glance with Arnold.

'What makes you think it was a shirt, Finn?'

'Did you recognise it?' Detective Arnold asked.

'She's tired. We all are,' Dita said. 'Don't know whether we're going in or out.'

Rebecca waited for her to finish then turned back to me. Repeated Arnold's question.

'Did you recognise it, Finn?'

I looked down at my feet, said no, I didn't think so.

She flicked her eyes towards Detective Arnold again, suggested we had a 'little chat'.

'Something tells me you're the sort of little girl who notices things.'

I noticed she was patronising, that's for sure.

She pulled out a chair at the kitchen table, gestured for me to sit.

'Do you want a juice or anything?'

Like this was her house. I sent Dita a telepathic message not to offer her any cookies but she was too busy jabbering to Detective Arnold to notice.

'What do you want to know?' I asked, trying to listen in on what they were discussing.

Had they tested the blood yet? Did they know whose it was? And how did a bloodstained shirt fit with the text message?

'How'd your sister seem to you?' Detective Rebecca asked me. 'Leading up to the disappearance.'

Not this again!

I shuffled in my seat, strained to hear what Arnold was telling Dita.

'Did Izzy seem like she had something on her mind, do you think?' Detective Rebecca was asking. 'Something she was keeping to herself, perhaps? A secret?'

I thought about her diary. How she'd started keeping it in a lockbox. How it wasn't in its usual hiding place.

'I don't think she had any secrets,' I said.

From the other side of the room, I heard the words 'concerns for her safety'. I strained harder to hear.

Detective Rebecca had to ask her next question twice.

'Sorry, what?' I said.

She took a deep breath, pulled the same expression Dita did when I told her I had no interest in wearing a skirt, even if it was church.

God doesn't care what I look like.

God may not, but I do. Now take off those overalls before I take them off for you.

Always so fussy about appearances!

I tried to think of something new to tell Detective Rebecca to get her off my back and allow me listen to Arnold and Dita's conversation. It might have been a good time to mention Ryder Grady, but it didn't occur to me. Instead, I told her Izzy's eating habits had got pretty bad, I guess.

'Her eating habits?'

'Nothing one minute, then stuffing herself with potato chips and cake the next. Tapeworm probably. I tried to tell Dita but she wouldn't listen. She never listens to anything I say.'

I hoped Dita might hear that, but she didn't, which rather proved my point.

Detective Rebecca and I went back and forth a little more. Her asking me questions, me asking her to repeat them. Then Arnold closed his flip pad and gave her a nod.

'Thanks for that, ma'am,' he said to Dita. 'Be good if we

could have a word with her about the missing girl now if my colleague's done.'

'Yep. We're done,' Rebecca said, a little bad-temperedly I thought.

'Alrighty,' Dita said, smoothing down her apron.

She went to the bottom of the stairs. Called up –

'Izzy, could you come down, please? The police are here. They have some more questions about Plum.'

AFTER

The night Plum had gone missing from Turtle Lake, Izzy had gone back with Lu to her place rather than the Underwoods'. Hitching a ride in a car they'd thumbed down at the side of the road and getting out for pancakes at an IHOP on the way.

'I'm so hungry I could eat a horse,' Izzy said.

'I could eat two horses,' Lu apparently replied before telling the driver to turn up the radio, then reaching for the dial and doing it herself before he could respond.

'I love Christina Aguilera. She's the best!'

They never showed up at Plum's house. Had no idea Mrs Underwood was freaking out, they said.

What, Plum didn't come home?

It was Lu who first suggested Plum might have run away. Told the police she wasn't happy.

'Her mom's always strung out on pills,' she said. 'Plum hated it there.'

I thought I remembered Plum saying something different but maybe I was wrong. Or maybe Lu was just mixed up because she was upset.

Dita said that could happen. She'd read an article about it. Dita read a lot of articles.

Magazines broaden the mind, she reckoned.

Once Izzy was home safe and Dita was satisfied where she'd been (as well as insisting she have a shower 'and give me those clothes for the wash right now, please'), she told us to get our shoes on, we were going to canvass the neighbourhood, see if anyone might have seen Plum.

Izzy made a big fuss about that, said she needed to sleep.

'I'm wiped.'

But Dita gave her short shrift. Her friend was missing, wasn't she worried about her?

Lu didn't need persuading to help find Plum. As Dita kept telling Izzy over the coming days: 'She's really throwing herself into it. You might take some pointers.'

It was Lu's idea to set up a phone tree. Lu who told Mrs Underwood she couldn't imagine how concerned she must be. And Lu who suggested making posters . . .

Never mind organising a vigil Izzy refused to even attend, and rallying the townsfolk to join the search party via her Friendster page. Another event Izzy didn't show her face at.

'It's not right,' my father had said. 'The three of us going along while she stays holed up in her bedroom.'

More or less the same thing Dita had said at the vigil: 'It's not right. She should be here with us.'

'Wouldn't hurt for you to follow Lu's example,' Dita told Izzy who was lolling about on a hammock in the backyard. The first time she'd been down from her bedroom in over a week, apart from the time a detective had asked her to give her some space please while she took 'a little look around in here'.

Izzy stretched, arching her back the way a cat might.

'I wish we had a pool.'

Dita looked at her agog, asked, 'What's wrong with you?'

Izzy asked what was wrong with wanting a pool?

'Your friend's gone missing. Anyone would have thought you'd be worried about her. Instead, you just lounge around at home all day as if you couldn't care less.'

My sister's face tightened. She pushed herself upright.

'Couldn't care less?' she snarled. 'You have no idea, do you? Has it ever occurred to you that I'm lounging around – as you put it – because I can't face going out? Can't face seeing anyone?'

She scoffed, sank back down.

'You don't get me at all. None of you do.'

'Is that so?' Dita said, eyes narrowed. 'Has it ever occurred to *you* that actions speak louder than words? You want to show you care, you better start acting like it. And wash your hair, for God's sake.'

'It's like after Abigail died,' I overheard my father tell Dita when she raised the subject of Izzy's attitude. 'Perhaps what we're seeing is another way of her clamming up. A sort of dis-association. Didn't you say denial was the first stage of grief?'

Dita's expression cleared, relieved to finally have an expla-nation that made sense.

'You think this is about stress?'

He gave a half shrug, poured himself a coffee.

'She *is* sleepwalking again . . .'

Detective Arnold started showing up more, asking questions. The longer Plum went without making any sort of contact, he said, the more likely it was that something had happened to her.

'Though officially, we're still keeping an open mind.'

He spoke more freely to my father than I suspect he would have done to Lu's dad. Professional courtesy, perhaps. Or maybe it was simply because they knew each other. Detective Arnold had been over to the house a number of times before Turtle Lake, usually late at night requesting my father sign some urgent warrant.

'Not sure I've ever been at your door during the day,' he said the first time he came about Plum.

'Troubling business,' my father answered, shaking his hand and inviting him in. 'Such a nice girl. Been a good friend to Izzy. Really got her out of her shell.'

It had been my father who'd suggested to Mrs Underwood that the time had come to call the police. My father who assured her that of the half a million children who go missing every year in America, nearly all of them are found.

'The cops know what they're doing,' he said. 'You've got to trust them.' Then later – 'Arnold's a good guy. Really smart.'

Detective Arnold asked us all sorts of things about Izzy's mood and behaviour in the run-up to the disappearance.

'The girls were close,' he said. 'If Izzy was worried about something, chances are Plum was too.'

But if Izzy had been worried about anything, she didn't tell him. Nor did she mention the row she'd had with Plum when

I'd been in the tree house or what she'd been talking about the night I'd heard her crying.

I didn't mention any of those things either. Or what I'd seen on the bathroom mirror.

'Can't shake this feeling Izzy's not being straight with us,' I overheard Arnold tell a colleague on their way out one time.

I felt my adrenaline spike.

There was a spot by the window on the landing where you could hear everything that was said in the driveway. Even whispers carried.

'What about?' I heard his colleague ask.

Arnold ran a paw over his dark hair.

'Beats me. Only thing I'm sure of is she knows more than she's letting on. Kid must keep a diary.'

'Never heard of a teenage girl who didn't.'

'What I'd give to lay my hands on it!'

'We'll just have to keep looking . . .'

Izzy wandered into the kitchen now, still in her jammies at eleven forty-five in the morning, rubbing her eyes. They were bloodshot as if she'd been crying, though she could just as easily have had a bad night. Judging by the creak on the stairs that sometimes woke me, her sleepwalking was getting worse.

She peered into the fridge, poked around. Asked where the juice was.

'Never mind the juice,' Dita snapped. 'There's been a development.'

'Have you found her?' Izzy asked Arnold, head still inside the fridge.

She located the OJ, took a swig from the carton. Wiped her mouth with the back of her hand.

Arnold watched her.

'Don't you usually ask if we've found anything new?' he said wryly.

It was the same thing every time he came to the house:

Have you found anything?

What are you thinking?

Do you have any new leads?

Izzy took another glug.

'Lu told you she ran away. She was right.'

'What makes you say that, Izzy?' Detective Rebecca asked.

'The text message, of course. The one she sent Lu.'

There was an off-note in her voice. Did she feel slighted that Plum had reached out to Lu rather than her? Old insecurities rising?

Flattered to be chosen by her, I suppose. First time she's ever been chosen by anybody . . .

'You just woke up?' Detective Arnold asked.

Then before she could answer, he turned to Dita.

'The way teenagers sleep, eh? Boy, what I'd give to catch some Zs like that!'

He had a slow Texas drawl. Left the Lone Star State because he couldn't take the heat, he said. Didn't leave his accent behind though. Or his love of barbeque.

Izzy yawned, told him yes, she'd just got up.

'And yet you already know about the text . . .'

She chugged the last of the OJ, tossed the carton in the trash.

'Lu messaged me.'

Arnold smiled. Said yes, that made sense.

'You two talk a lot, huh?'

'I've made some cookies, if y'all fancy one,' Dita told him. 'Hot out the oven.'

'I could eat a cookie,' Izzy said. 'Are they chocolate chip?'

Detective Rebecca raised an eyebrow, glanced at Arnold.

'This has been so hard on her,' Dita said, clearly embarrassed by Izzy's terrible eating habits. Only my sister could eat cookies for breakfast.

Since Plum had gone missing, her dieting had gone out the window. Along with her personal hygiene, it seemed.

Arnold said he quite understood how hard it must be for Izzy.

'If it were my friend who was missing, I'd be going out of my mind,' he told her.

'She's not missing though, is she?' Izzy repeated in a somewhat exasperated tone. 'She's run away. Like the text said.'

'You guys close?' Detective Rebecca asked.

Izzy nodded, told her Plum and Lu were her best friends. And yes, they were super close.

'We do everything together. I miss her so much. This whole thing is just surreal.'

She sounded so like Lu their answers could have been scripted.

NOW

It's terrible to admit, but when I first heard Plum had gone missing, my initial feeling was glee.

Good riddance to bad rubbish!

The longer she stayed away, the better. Dreadful girl!

But as I began to realise she might have been hurt – or worse – I was ashamed for having felt that way. And terrified about what her disappearance might mean.

Terrified to even talk about it, as if giving voice to my fears would make them come true.

I kept Izzy constantly in my peripheral vision. Lurked outside her bedroom door. Trailed after her. A superstitious sense that if I kept her in my eyeline, what I dreaded could be averted. That everything would turn out okay.

I'm at my father's care home. The elevator doors spit me out. There's an orderly by the desk filling in some paperwork. She looks up.

'Morning.'

'How is he?' I ask, trying to speak softly.

My head is thumping. I don't even remember finishing the bottle.

'Your dad's fine,' the orderly says. 'But I wonder if you could clear out that trunk of his. We really need to make some—'

'More storage space. Yes, I know. I'm sorry. I meant to do it before.'

She flashes me a smile, thanks me when really she should be calling 'bullshit'. They've been asking me to clear out that wretched trunk of his for weeks.

'I'll get you a bin bag,' she says.

Lucky me.

I knock on my father's door, obviously don't wait for a 'come in'.

'Hi Dad,' I say in a put-on cheery voice.

He's propped up on his pillows in a single bed that somehow looks smaller every time I visit. I bend down, kiss him on his papery cheek.

His eyes move up to my face in acknowledgement that I'm there. It's about all he can do without assistance.

After his stroke, I asked his doctor if he'd ever talk again. Smile even, though it had been a long time since he'd done that.

Dr Buckett shook his head, touched me lightly on my shoulder.

'We can always hope for a miracle though,' he said.

I gave up on hope a long time ago. That 'thing with feathers' can go stuff itself.

I pour my father a glass of water, help him drink. Same routine every time I come.

I should have some water too.

Or hair of the dog . . .

'My mama was an alcoholic,' says Dita's voice inside my skull.

When did I find that out? I'm not sure. I do remember it's what killed Dita's mother though. Cirrhosis, apparently. She couldn't tell night from day by the end, Dita said. Her flesh turned as yellow as a lemon.

'You don't want to end up like her,' her ghost tells me.

I'm not an alcoholic though. Booze is a coping mechanism, that's all.

'Isn't it the same thing?' she asks.

I check my watch. Half an hour then I really must leave for work. I expect Willow Rowling's already there making stupid comments about books she's only read because they sound impressive.

My father was always a big reader, same as my mother. They met at a poetry reading in San Francisco. Bonded over Byron and Barrett Browning (and the fact they both had grandparents who hailed from the same little town in England).

He has a book of poetry in the drawer of his nightstand. An anniversary gift from her. *For the poetic justice*, she wrote inside the front cover.

I read extracts to him sometimes when I visit. We both find it soothing, I think. The music of words.

'Priscilla wants me to clear out your trunk,' I tell him now, though I don't suppose he could care less.

Except he does. His eyes flicker in response. Different to the way he reacted when I mentioned Elsa Stone yesterday, but he's trying to tell me something. God knows what.

The trunk is so full, I struggle to get the lid open. Inside, it's full of boxes. Shoeboxes rammed to the brim. I remove them one by one, empty them out. Make 'keep' and 'chuck' piles like we did before leaving the States.

There are old report cards, drawings from when I was at grade school. Quiz transcripts. At the top of one: *92% – Great work, Finn!*

It's been a while since anyone described my work as great.

I open another box. Bank statements, warranties for various electrical items. Photos of my mother from before Izzy and I were born that make my eyes prick. Christmas cards . . .

And then another. This one's taped shut. The adhesive has dried out over time. It comes away easily.

There's a noise from my father's bed as I peel off the last piece. A groan, the low note of a violin.

I glance up. He's looking directly at me.

'What?' I say, which is rather pointless.

I turn back to the box, prise the lid off. And that's when I see them. Envelope after envelope, all addressed to Dita. I don't need to open them to know what's written at the bottom of each letter:

Please write back this time.

I miss you.

My chest has gone tight. I can't seem to take in enough air.

'How could you?' I croak. 'You didn't send any of them!'

But of course, he can't reply.

AFTER

'I don't see how he could have . . . ?'

Detectives Arnold and Rebecca had left. I was loitering in the hallway outside Izzy's room, eavesdropping on her phone call with Lu.

They hadn't met up once since Plum's disappearance, but the two girls were on the phone constantly – a fact Detective Arnold commented on when the police had taken my sister's cell for analysis 'in case there's anything useful on here'.

'You've logged hours' worth of calls to each other. What have you been talking about?'

Izzy looked at him as though he were stupid.

'Plum, of course,' she said.

It wasn't easy to make out what they were saying now, given I could only pick up on one side of the conversation – and even that was difficult to hear at times, Izzy's voice dropping to a whisper whenever she got to what I was sure must be the 'good bits'.

I stuck with it though, did my best to decipher whatever it was they were discussing. Spying on Izzy was nothing new.

I'd been doing it ever since she first ditched me and became friends with Plum and Lu.

What was so special about them? I'd wanted to know.

What secrets was she telling them and keeping from me?

I read her diary for much the same reason (while I could).

I never did like being shut in the dark.

'Always up in everyone's Kool-Aid,' Dita used to say.

This spying was different though. It was born out of fear rather than nosiness. Though maybe there was a bit of nosiness in it too.

I flicked my eyes towards the stairs, watching for Dita. Inched closer to Izzy's door.

'I don't get it,' she was saying. 'It doesn't make sense.'

A pause, the sound of her bed springs squeaking as she got up. The pad of her feet as she moved around the room.

'You're right. It's got to be him.'

What had to be him? And who was 'him' anyway?

Her tone changed. She became defensive.

'No, of course not. I promise.'

Then more softly.

'I miss him too.'

A slip of the tongue. She must have meant 'her'.

'Arnold thinks I'm hiding something, I can tell. I just wish I knew why . . .'

Listening to her, my muscles seemed to loosen. The pressure I'd been holding inside me for days beginning to deflate.

Had I got it wrong? Hiney over head, as Dita would have put it?

Was it all a terrible misunderstanding?

A glance over my shoulder, then I risked a quick glimpse through the keyhole.

Izzy was rummaging under the loose floorboard by her window.

'I think they've taken it.'

Then –

'He asked to see me, you know . . . ? Has he asked to see you?'

She waited for Lu to answer then said, 'Oh well. I'm sure he will soon.'

There was something in her tone that seemed to suggest she hoped the opposite, though I couldn't understand why she'd be getting competitive over Detective Arnold.

The conversation wound up and I went off to find Dita before Izzy came out and found me. She was in my father's bedroom folding laundry. My mother's nightstand was exactly as she'd left it on the day of the accident. A shrine.

Her reading glasses folded neatly away in their case. A Patricia Cornwell with a receipt sticking out the middle marking her place. A tube of lavender-scented hand cream. Even her water glass was still there, a thick skein of dust where the liquid had once been.

I liked to go in there when no one else was around. Pretend my mother had just popped out for the afternoon. That at any moment her Chevy might pull into the driveway and she'd come trotting up the stairs ready to pick up *The Body Farm* where she'd left off.

'What have you been up to?' Dita said as I ambled into the room.

Asked if I'd come to give her a hand with the folding then

straight away started banging on about the dryer eating all our socks.

Verbal diarrhoea, she'd have called it if it were me. She was often that way after Detective Arnold had been round. I wondered if she had a crush on him. It would certainly explain all the baked goods.

'Dita . . . ?'

'That's my name.'

'You think it's weird?'

'I think it's completely weird. How do great big socks just disappear into thin air?'

I shook my head, scratched the back of my calf with my toe.

'Not the socks. Izzy.'

Dita sighed like she was on the stage, asked what my poor sister was supposed to have done this time.

'She's on her phone every two seconds,' I said.

Dita scoffed, told me there was nothing new about that.

'That thing's glued to her.'

I shook my head again.

'I mean that she's *talking* on it. Before Plum, she always texted.'

'I like texting better,' Izzy had explained when Dita asked her about it one time. 'Gives me a chance to think what to say. No awkward silences.'

A rare moment of openness.

Dita set the laundry basket aside now, patted the bed for me to sit down next to her.

'When you go through a trauma, you need someone to talk

to. Doesn't matter what that person says so long as they're saying something. Makes you feel less alone. You understand?'

I told her I understood baloney muffins better. She suggested I go to my room.

'Do we really need a housekeeper?' I asked my father when he came home from court that evening.

'Yes,' he said. 'And you need to be more polite to her.'

From upstairs came the sound of Izzy's phone ringing yet again.

AFTER

The news broke as we were having dinner.

The TV was on low while we ate. Our evening meal timed to coincide with the headlines.

'What Plum's poor mother must be going through,' my father sighed.

'Must be killing her, not knowing,' Izzy agreed, shovelling in a mouthful of tater tots.

Ever since Plum had disappeared, she'd been eating like a lion, according to Dita.

Like a horse, you mean . . .

Horses don't eat nothing. Just grass.

'Must be killing you too, huh, chick?' she said now.

Always trying to get Izzy to speak about her feelings. To 'let it out'.

'Not anymore,' Izzy replied, helping herself to more ketchup. 'She'll come back when she's ready. You saw what the text message said.'

'I thought we could put up flyers,' Dita carried on as if Izzy hadn't spoken. 'The mall. Trader Joe's. Maybe the library?'

'Why?' Izzy asked, pulling a face. 'There're loads of flyers up already.'

Dita told her it wouldn't hurt to put up a few more.

'Let's see what Detective Arnold thinks. I'm sure he'll be pleased you're helping.'

A little blush settled on her cheeks as she said his name.

Dita and Arnold sitting in a tree . . .

I started to say I couldn't see why flyers would make Plum want to come home, when the headlines started up.

My father pointed the clicker at the TV, turned up the volume.

> *The leader of the 4th Infantry says his men missed the opportunity to catch Saddam's security chief in a predawn raid this morning by just twenty-four hours . . .*
>
> *And – in breaking news, Lieutenant Owen King has just announced that the text message sent from the phone of the missing Carlsbad teen is a fake . . .*

My father took his glasses off, rubbed his eyes.

'A fake? Jesus.'

'Shit,' Izzy whispered.

Dita rubbed the back of her neck, asked how they could be so sure.

'It was sent from her phone. What makes them think it's not her?'

Everyone had an opinion but me.

'I don't understand,' I said.

What I meant was, I don't want to. The fear I'd finally

managed to banish had come crashing back. I glanced at Izzy. She was staring at her plate, tater tots languishing in ketchup.

'Seems someone else might have sent that message from Plum's phone,' my father explained.

'Might have,' Dita conceded. 'But also might *not* have. I honestly can't see who else would have sent it besides Plum. It just doesn't make no sense.'

My father nodded at the screen.

'Let's listen and find out,' he said.

Television transcript from *San Diego News*

News Anchor:

In breaking news this evening, Lieutenant Owen King has told reporters that the text message sent from the phone of missing Carlsbad teen, Plum Underwood, is a hoax.

Karen Croft has the story . . .

Reporter (Karen Croft):

I'm outside the Carlsbad police station where just moments ago, Lieutenant Owen King revealed that an SMS purporting to be from Plum Underwood may actually have been faked. It is yet another startling twist in the mystery of the teen's disappearance from Turtle Lake nine days ago. The news comes as a huge blow to Plum's heartbroken family.

I was at the police press conference this evening . . .

Lieutenant Owen King:

As you are all aware, Lucia Nox – a close friend of missing teen, Plum Underwood – received an SMS following a community- and police-led search of Turtle Lake last night. The message suggested she was alive and well.

Early analysis showed that the message was sent from

the vicinity of Hidden Canyon Community Park. The park is within a one-mile radius of the missing girl's home – and inside a search zone we have been combing since her disappearance.

Analysis also confirmed that the message was sent from Plum's cell phone.

We recognise the toll Plum's disappearance has taken on her family and what this text message will have meant to them. It is therefore with great disappointment that I have to inform you, we now believe the message was forged. That is to say, we do not believe it was sent by Plum.

I have here a printout of the message if cameras would like to zoom in. And I will also read it aloud:

'Please tell everyone to stop worrying. I'm fine. I just need some space.'

It was signed off with two kisses.

As our analysts have informed me, the devil is in the detail. Or rather, the linguistics.

On examination of the messages friends received from Plum prior to her disappearance – a pattern has emerged. Plum always relied heavily on abbreviations, with words often shortened to single letters. She rarely used punctuation or apostrophes.

The SMS sent on July 25 is strikingly different. Nothing is abbreviated. There are apostrophes and the message is punctuated with periods.

Reporter (unidentified):

Mightn't that just be a reaction to stress?

Lieutenant Owen King:

I'm told if stress were a factor, you'd expect the spelling and grammar to deteriorate, not improve.

Reporter (unidentified):

To be clear, you've made up your minds about this based on the language being a little off?

Lieutenant Owen King:

The language isn't the only irregularity here, Jeff. The kisses are anomalous too. Prior to her disappearance, Plum always signed off her texts with three kisses. In this message, there are only two.

Reporter (Karen Croft):

Does this confirm to you that Plum has been taken against her will? Possibly killed?

Lieutenant Owen King:

I am unable to comment on any speculations at this time. Though I would reassure you, we are doing everything in our power to find Plum and facilitate her safe return.

AFTER

The news gave way to *Law & Order: Criminal Intent*. My father switched off the television, gave Izzy's shoulder a squeeze.

'I'm so sorry, sweetheart.'

She was picking at her cuticles, a muscle working in her jaw.

'So, the spelling was a bit different,' Dita said. 'Don't mean it weren't her.'

I glanced at my father to see if he'd correct her grammar the way he always corrected mine but of course he didn't. He never corrected Dita about anything.

Maybe he was worried about 'tipping the canoe', same as Izzy with her friends. *Place would fall apart without Dita . . .*

'They wouldn't release a statement like that if they weren't sure,' he said instead.

'Dita's right,' Izzy said, 'The language is off. Big whoopadoo.'

'I expect there are a few other things they're keeping back, darling.'

She asked what sort of things.

My father shrugged, palms up.

'Could be anything. They always hold something in reserve.'

'Isn't that illegal?' I asked.

He laughed, told me no, it was not illegal.

'They do it to rule out false confessions.'

Izzy scoffed, said that was ridiculous.

'Why would anyone confess to a crime they didn't commit?'

My father speared a piece of broccoli. Told us everyone had their reasons, he supposed.

'Though most of the time, they're just looking for their five minutes.'

'Five minutes of what?' I asked.

'Fame,' he said, dabbing his mouth with his napkin.

I pulled a face, told him that was pretty damn stupid.

'Why would anyone want to be famous for being a criminal?'

He waggled his finger. Said just because I didn't understand something, that didn't make it stupid. Although yes, he agreed. There were rather better things to aspire to than being a famous criminal.

'And mind your language, please.'

I thought about language later as I was lying in bed, the lights from passing headlamps drifting across the ceiling. The pipes creaking the way they do in old houses. Like a person rattling chains.

If Plum hadn't sent that text, who had?

Why?

And how did they have her phone?

My head went to the place it kept returning to ever since we'd first heard the news about Plum. It was the only thing that made sense. And it was all my fault.

From an appeal issued by Plum Underwood's mother

Why would someone pretend to be my daughter?

She's been missing for ten days. It's the longest I've ever gone without speaking to her. I haven't always been around as much as I should have been. I've made mistakes. But my heart is breaking not knowing where she is.

The last conversation we had, she told me, 'Life is for living, Mom.' And she was *smiling*.

I know all about the rumours going round. But Plum is not struggling with depression or looking for a way out. And she's not just seeking attention either, as some of her friends have suggested. That's not who she is.

Someone's taken her. I know they have.

Somebody's taken my little girl!

AFTER

The night my sister was taken, I was watching *Wheel of Fortune* on the couch with my father.

'Lone Ranger,' he said, calling out the answer before Lisa from Missouri could get there.

'I was just going to say that,' I told him, even though I wasn't.

It was less than twenty-four hours after Lieutenant King's press statement and just over that since Detectives Arnold and Rebecca had been to the house.

The air was hot and sticky, thick with Santa Ana dust. It got on my skin, in my mouth.

I was getting up to fetch a glass of water when I heard the sirens. Distant shrieks morphing into loud screams, a cruiser tearing up our street. Lights glanced through the living room slats, painted red and blue squares on the carpet.

The footsteps came next. The crunch on gravel. The ring on the bell.

Three hard knocks.

My father pulled a face – *What's this all about?* – pushed himself up off the couch. Went to open the front door.

I followed him, curious. Dita poked her head out of the kitchen, hands red from doing the dishes.

'What's going on?'

'Arnold?' my father said, opening up.

Dita came into the hall, drying her hands on her apron. She looked from Arnold to the two uniformed officers standing behind him. Military haircuts. Tie clips, shiny black Oxfords.

'Daddy?' I said in the same way he'd said, 'Arnold?'

Detective Arnold cleared his throat.

'Good evening, Judge.' He couldn't quite meet my father's eye. 'May we come in?'

He shuffled his feet, planted his hands on his hips then stuffed them in his pockets as though he didn't quite know what to do with them.

Next to me, Dita shuffled her feet, too. There was a light dusting of flour on the toes of her moccasins. I was suddenly very conscious of her breathing. Of mine. We both sounded as though we'd been running.

'What's this about?' my father asked.

His voice was quieter than usual. Over the next months it would settle that way, remaining forever a pitch lower than it used to be.

I slipped my hand in Dita's. On my tongue, the copper tang of coins.

Outside, a nightbird cawed. A raccoon knocked over a trash can, sent the lid skittering down the sidewalk. I jumped. Felt my heart pitter-patter.

Detective Arnold wet his lips, ran a finger inside his collar.

'What's this about?' my father said again.

Arnold's eyes slipped to the floor. He raised them slowly. Took a breath.

'We found a body, sir.'

'A body?' my father echoed.

He pressed the heel of his palm to his forehead, eyes flicking towards Dita. The blood had drained from her cheeks. There was a pulse going at her temple.

Arnold reached into his jacket pocket, removed a piece of paper. Unfolded it slowly. At the top, the Great Seal of the State of California. The Goddess of Wisdom and the Grizzly Bear.

'What's going on,' my father whispered.

'Is Izzy home?' the detective asked. 'I have a warrant for her arrest. For the murder of Plum Underwood.'

AFTER

I have a warrant for her arrest. For the murder of Plum Underwood.

The room started spinning, bright blotches of fire working in front of my eyes. Vision black at the edges. I reached out for the wall, felt the swell of bile rising up my digestive tract.

Worse than the shock though was that I'd been proved right. What I'd feared almost as soon as Plum had gone missing had been confirmed.

For the past ten days I'd been trying to persuade myself that Izzy had nothing to do with her disappearance. That she hadn't hurt her friend. That the words I'd read in the bathroom mirror meant nothing:

I hate Plum. I wish she was dead.

That they were just another example of a teen friendship in flux. Make-up one minute. Break-up the next.

Literally in this case. Before her shower, Izzy wanted Plum dead. After, she wanted to go to the mall with her.

No biggie, right?

But what about the blood on what I knew was Izzy's shirt? The scrap of material found at the search?

And how to explain the fact Izzy couldn't seem to care less that Plum was missing? That Dita had to chivvy her along to canvass the neighbours? That she seemed more interested in us getting a pool than finding her best friend.

It's why I'd been spying on her, eavesdropping on her conversations with Lu. Listening in to what Detective Arnold was telling Dita and on his conversations with his colleagues outside the house.

I was desperate to be wrong and terrified I was right.

After the search, I couldn't sleep. It was like a game of Whac-a-Mole. Every time I managed to convince myself I was worrying for nothing, a fresh piece of 'evidence' would raise its horrible head. And what could be more horrible – more damning – than Izzy's bloodstained shirt?

The text message was a momentary reprieve. The sensation of rocks lifting from my shoulders. Plum was alive, Izzy hadn't done anything after all!

All day I felt sherbet light, my whole being fizzing with relief. Until Lieutenant King came on the news that evening and told everyone there had been a mistake.

That the text was a fake.

I lay awake again.

If Plum hadn't sent the message, who had?

Why?

And how did they have her phone?

My head went to the place it kept returning. It had to be Izzy. It was the only thing that made sense and it was all my fault.

After all, if she had killed Plum, she'd done it because of me.

My father extended his hand to take the warrant from Detective Arnold.

'Izzy? Murder?' He shook his head. 'There must be some mistake . . .'

Arnold didn't answer. Just lowered his gaze, gave my father a moment to read what was written on the warrant in the same way he might have done in the past. Only now, the detective wasn't here to get my father's signature. He was here to take away his daughter.

My father's eyes rested on the name at the bottom. Another judge's signature. A friend.

'Judge Reynolds,' he said, exhaling through his mouth. 'God.'

He folded the warrant, pinched it between his thumb and forefinger. Ran them up and down the spine.

'You have probable cause?'

Arnold crossed his arms.

'The swatch of fabric found at the search had Izzy's DNA on it. And traces of Plum's blood.'

My father asked if that was it.

For the first time since Arnold and his crew had pitched up, he sounded sure of himself.

This game, he knew.

Arnold unfolded his arms, hooked his thumbs in his belt.

'We knew Izzy and Lu were keeping a secret. It's why we kept speaking to the girls. We were convinced they knew what happened to Plum but were just too scared to say. Worried about getting in trouble, we figured. Or even protecting somebody.'

He shook his head, let out a sigh.

'We never thought they might be responsible though.

Thirteen-year-old girls from good homes killing their pal? Didn't even occur to us.'

'So, what changed?' my father asked.

He sounded very calm. Measured. As though he were weighing up arguments in a courtroom.

I didn't feel calm. My insides were turning to liquid. I squeezed Dita's hand. She squeezed mine back. Both of us trembling.

Arnold rubbed his chin.

'Look, I wouldn't normally say this, but we've known each other a long time, Judge.' He took a step back, folded his arms. 'Lucia Nox came by the station this afternoon. She'd had some sort of breakdown, it seems. Couldn't take the guilt anymore. Her father brought her in to talk to us.

'He and Mrs Underwood are close, apparently. Given each other a lot of support over the years. Both have had a rough ride. Her husband left her. His wife is dying. He wanted to do the right thing by Plum's mama, he said. Said Lucia wanted that too.

'Straight away we could tell she was different. When we've spoken to her in the past, she's been . . . aloof. Bit of a smart-ass, if I'm honest.'

'And today?'

'Sat in the interview suite hugging her knees and shaking. Honestly, the kid looked terrified, Judge.'

'And what did the girl have to say for herself?' Dita interrupted in a tone that implied she wouldn't put stock in a single word Lu said.

No way she was going to believe my sister was a killer on some other kid's say-so.

Arnold ran a finger inside his collar.

'She told us everything. Admitted they stabbed Plum. Her and Izzy.'

My father gave him a hard look.

'You're arresting my daughter based on the ramblings of a thirteen-year-old you've already admitted was having a break-down?'

I gave Dita's hand another squeeze. A different squeeze than before though.

It was okay. My father was dealing with this. He'd sort this out, know just what to say.

'Lucia told us everything,' Arnold repeated. 'How they lured Plum into the trees. Where they disposed of their knives and hoodies. Even how she came by the cut on her arm.'

My father frowned.

'Cut?' he asked.

I knew what Detective Arnold was referring to though. That night at the vigil, the gash I'd seen when Lu's sleeve slipped. The one she claimed she got riding her bike.

'Plum tried to grab Lu's knife in an attempt to defend her-self,' Arnold said. 'Lucia was injured in the process.

'She told us everything she and Izzy did, sir. Every last detail.

'Only thing she won't tell us is, why.'

NOW

Why?

It's been one of those days that seems to drag on for a year. I've stamped books, sorted out the back catalogues, shelved returns – all the while thinking about the stash of letters to Dita hidden in my father's trunk.

Why didn't he send them? Why did he lie?

All the times he told me he was taking them to the post office, he was really stuffing them away in an old shoebox. Letting me think they were going unanswered, that she had forgotten about me.

Letting Dita think I'd forgotten about her.

My father had arranged for us to stay at a hotel for our first few weeks in London while he sorted out somewhere for us to live.

'Write me when you have your address,' Dita told me at the airport. 'I'll write you straight back.'

But without my letters, did she ever get our address? Is that why she didn't write?

Or did my father keep her letters to me the same way he kept mine from her?

How dare he? What right did he have?

I'm still steaming as I leave the library this evening. The sky is darkening, the sun beginning to set. Rain on the way, according to Mrs Bostock. *I can feel it in my bones . . .*

My bones feel like lead. All these years, all this silence. So many questions, they're killing me. Questions about Izzy, questions about the part I played.

And now questions about my father too.

I could demand answers till there's smoke coming out of my ears, but he'll never be able to give them to me. Not anymore.

Our grade school principal may be right. Perhaps talking is the only way to heal.

But there's no one left for me to talk to now. Dita's dead. My father's mute. Is it any wonder I spend so much time talking to myself?

I'm raking my nails over my scalp as I step outside. Jonesing for a drink. Or two. Or three. Hankering after that sweet burn, the blessed release as my brain lets go.

And that's when I see her. The woman at the bottom of the library steps.

Too tanned for March. Sun-kissed hair, perfectly cut. Watching me. Eyes glued to my face, the way a hawk watches a mouse.

I glance over my shoulder but it's just me here. I'm definitely the one in her sights.

I hesitate, then walk slowly down the library steps towards her. Her weight shifts forward on to her front foot. She stands so she's blocking my way.

As I reach the bottom step, she extends a manicured hand, the nails filed to a polished point.

I leave her hanging. She hesitates then lets the hand drop.

'Who are you?' I ask. 'Why are you here?'

But I know what she's going to say before she says it:

'Hello, Finn. I'm Elsa Stone . . .'

AFTER

Arnold left the question hanging:

Only thing she won't tell us is, why?

Why . . . ?

It's the question I've asked on repeat ever since that night. Ever since they took my sister away, hand on her head as they ducked her into the waiting cruiser. Neighbours coming out on their porches to watch the show:

Is that Izzy Jackman?

What's she doing in a cop car?

Are they arresting *her?*

Dita looked down at me, gave me a tight smile. Whispered, 'It'll be okay, chick.'

'No, it won't,' I said because I'd seen the future.

I knew how this story ended. Izzy had killed Plum. No amount of prevaricating and trying to throw Detective Arnold off the trail was going to make any difference now. Izzy was going to the slammer. I was never going to see her again. And it was all my fault.

Why had I told her that stupid lie? Why hadn't I fessed up when I had the chance?

I despaired and I felt liberated. That old poke about the other shoe finally dropping.

'Did you ever find her diary?' I started to ask Detective Arnold, before realising I was about to give myself away.

Could you get arrested for eavesdropping on private police conversations too?

'What's that, Finn?' he asked, as though noticing me for the first time.

'Nothing,' I answered, looking at the floor.

Dita rubbed my back.

'Would you call Izzy down, please?' Arnold asked. 'We need to take her in now.'

His voice was gentle. Kind. That sweet molasses drawl.

'I'll go fetch her,' Dita replied. 'She's taking a nap. This has all really taken its—'

She broke off. No point making excuses for Izzy now.

Was Izzy still sleeping? Or had the sirens woken her? Had she heard what Arnold said? Was she freaking out?

Looking back, Izzy had definitely been stressed since Turtle Lake. Binging on cookies and potato chips. Sleepwalking. Snapping at the slightest thing.

Every night she'd check my father had bolted the front door. Reminded him to set the security alarm before he went to bed. Even started keeping a night light on, just like she had after our mother died.

Signs of guilt? A mind full of scorpions?

Or something else?

My sister and Dita appeared at the top of the stairs now, hand in hand the way they used to cross the road together when Izzy was younger and still allowed herself to be guided.

She was my big sister and yet in that moment she looked so small. So fragile. Her toes turned in, her brown eyes blinking. A pink patch on her cheek from where it had been pressed against her pillow.

She looked from Arnold to the officers. Whispered:

'Daddy?'

Her voice quavered. She could have been three rather than thirteen.

Detective Arnold recited her Miranda rights.

'Izzy Jackman, you are under arrest for the murder of Plum Underwood and for the obstruction of justice. You have the right to remain silent . . .'

'Where was she?' Izzy asked when he'd finished telling her what could and would be used against her in a court of law.

Arnold frowned.

'Where was who?'

'Plum. Where did you find her?'

He glanced at the other officers, told her:

'Washington Beach.'

I'll never forget Izzy's expression then, the look of utter confusion on her face.

'Washington Beach?' she echoed.

My sister was a psychopath if the armchair psychologists on Reddit are to be believed. And everyone knows psychopaths are master manipulators. Brilliant at dissembling. But the puzzlement in Izzy's eyes that night wasn't feigned. It was real.

There's plenty I don't know, but I do know that.

And of course, it begs the question –

If she killed Plum, why didn't she know where her body was?

NOW

Hello, Finn. I'm Elsa Stone . . . It's funny, the way we build up mental pictures of people based on their voices. I pictured Elsa Stone in her mid to late thirties. Tall, for some reason. Nose in the air.

In reality, she can't be more than twenty-two. Twenty-three, tops. She's wearing ankle boots with a three-inch heel. I'm wearing flats and I'm still looking down at her.

Something about the way she's shifting the weight of her bag and fiddling with the strap suggests nerves.

Or at least, that she's not as sure of herself as she sounded on the phone.

Elsa Stone really is a poker player.

Rocking up at my place of work unannounced like this is a game too, I realise. She wanted to catch me off guard. Off balance. Get the upper hand.

Except she's the one on edge.

One arm crossed over her torso. Shoulders up. Tone a pitch too high, lisp more pronounced than usual.

Her obvious discomfort makes me feel stronger for some reason. More sure of myself.

So does her birdlike build.

'I'm sorry to doorstep you like this,' she says.

'I just thought if maybe we spoke in person . . .'

I'm tired. All I want to do is go home, put my feet up and crack open a bottle. Though I want answers too.

Maybe Elsa Stone can give them to me. Maybe she can't.

But now she's here, I may as well find out what she knows.

What have I got to lose?

So –

'There's a café down the street,' I tell her. 'I can give you half an hour . . .'

AFTER

As soon as the news got out about Izzy's arrest, people began looking for answers. Asking each other the questions they've been asking ever since:

What kind of girl murders her best friend?

A thirteen-year-old?

From a good family, her father a judge?

There must have been signs, they said. Things like this don't come out of nowhere.

Why did she do it? Was she a bad egg? Or did something happen to knock her off course?

Goodness knows how often I've wondered the same things.

Where were the signs? If I'd told my father or Dita about the video, could I have stopped it happening? What was the real reason she killed Plum?

Was it because of me? Because of what I did?

Or was it something else?

Ryder Grady? An innate evil?

They say it's a human need to understand. To impose order

on chaos. But how can I hope to ever understand what happened to Izzy? To understand what she did?

Despite having suspected it, I struggled to accept my sister was a killer. Struggled to come to terms with the fact I had never really known the person I thought I knew so well.

A sort of folklore built up around her. Everyone wanting their 'five minutes', as my father put it that time.

Kids from Heritage Elm who had never even spoken to her, holding forth for the TV cameras. Making out they had an inside track. Making up all kinds of crap.

'She used to torture cats in her garage.'

'She was obsessed with true crime.'

'She told me she was controlled by a three-thousand-year-old demon.'

She was jealous of Plum, they said. Didn't like that she was more popular with boys. She got hooked on drugs. They addled her brain.

And although parts of those stories are possibly true, they don't paint the full picture. Nor do they account for the influence of a certain older man. A biology teacher. A photography enthusiast.

A paedophile.

That would come out later, the details so shocking plenty of people refused to believe them. The Ostrich Effect, it's apparently called.

I was an ostrich too.

I went from agonising that my sister had hurt Plum, to trying to convince anyone who'd listen that the police had got it wrong.

'I've thought of something else,' I informed my father, barging into his study the afternoon after the arrest.

He was sitting behind his big oak desk, a yellow legal pad in front of him covered in scrawl legible only to him. One hand was resting on top of the telephone. The other was shielding his eyes.

They were red-rimmed. His face unshaven, becoming a beard.

'It must have been Plum's idea to go to Turtle Lake,' I said. 'She was the one who arranged the sleepover.'

He sighed heavily, pinched his sinuses.

'Just because you want a thing to be true, doesn't mean it is, sweetheart.'

I eyeballed him, stuck my hands on my hips.

'Doesn't mean it isn't either . . .'

He let out a long breath, wiped his palm across his brow.

'I've just got off the phone with Izzy's lawyer.'

'Good. Call him back. You can tell him what I just told you.'

He shook his head, explained there was no point. It was over.

'Your sister's just confessed,' he said. 'Not only has she admitted to stabbing Plum, she's also confirmed Lu's account. The whole thing was all her idea.'

From the *San Diego Sun*

Judge's Daughter Confesses to Murdering Her Best Friend

Izzy Jackman's involvement in the murder of Plum Underwood first came to light after her co-conspirator, Lucia Nox, gave herself up to Carlsbad police three days ago.

Now, Miss Jackman (daughter of Superior Court judge, Nathaniel Jackman) has given a chilling account of her role in the homicide of her best friend, in a series of taped interviews with investigators.

Jackman is currently being held at a juvenile detention centre awaiting trial to determine whether she was of 'sound mind' when she committed the crime.

AFTER

Izzy's confession changed everything.

She hadn't simply admitted to killing Plum. She seemed to want the whole world to know about it too.

'It was my idea,' she told Detective Arnold. 'All of it. It's like I always say: if you're going to do something, make sure you do it well.'

The picture of what had happened that night came into focus gradually, like one of those paint-by-numbers sets my father used to get us for Christmas.

Should keep you girls out of trouble for a while . . .

Apparently not.

We were in trouble: Dita, my father and me. None of us sleeping, hardly eating.

Every night I dreamed about Izzy, about 'the time before' when she was lonely. Trapped on the outside looking in.

How much better it would have been if she'd stayed that way!

'You're going to meet these two girls,' I told her in my dreams. 'Stay away from them. Promise me.'

236

And she would promise, but even so I knew she'd still meet Plum and Lu. That Turtle Lake would still happen.

In other dreams, I'd ask her, why? Why did you do it? Was it because of me? Because of what I said?

But each time, she'd just tap the side of her nose, tell me it was a secret.

'Tell-tale-tit. Your tongue shall be slit and all the dogs in town will have a little bit . . .'

'That song's about snitches,' I'd say, to which she'd reply, wasn't that the same thing?

I wasn't sure.

'Just be careful,' I warned. 'You think they're your friends, but they're not.'

Like she was the victim rather than the killer. I suppose in my heart, she was.

I alternately hated and mourned her, sometimes at the same time.

How could she do this to us? How could we have lost her?

Dita, never able to lose weight, dropped pounds without trying. Her size-twenty clothes hanging off her.

Meanwhile, my father would sit for hours in his chair, wringing his hands in a perpetual washing motion. Other times, he'd be filled with an almost maniacal energy. Calling up Izzy's lawyer, suggesting this strategy, that approach.

Atkinson v Scarr. What if we argued . . . ?

Have you thought about . . . ?

We were each drowning but none of us reached out to the other, as if by not acknowledging our emotions we could trick them into disappearing.

For my part, there was another reason though. I could hardly open up without admitting what I'd done. That Plum had died because of me.

A while ago, I read a book written by the daughter of a famous serial killer. She described how she'd built up a mental photo album of lasts. The last joke they shared before his arrest. Their last argument. The last time she'd said, 'I love you.'

I don't remember ever telling Izzy I loved her, though I wish I had. But like the serial killer's daughter, I also stored up a whole list of lasts.

The last movie we'd watched together (Izzy crunching loudly on Cheetos and me telling her to shut up).

The last time I heard her laugh.

Our last fight.

'God, you're such a loser.'

Why had I done it? Why had she listened?

Why couldn't I take it back?

In those early weeks, I whispered the words aloud in the stillness of my room at night. Cried into my pillow –

'I'm sorry. I'm so sorry . . .'

A desperate need to confess, to wash my hands clean.

Izzy's confession was part of the deal her lawyer facilitated with the DA's office. Plum's parents didn't simply deserve to know who killed their daughter, ADA Madden said. They deserved to know the details too. How Plum died. What she said in her final moments.

If I were her folks, I'm not sure I'd have wanted those details. The truth doesn't always set you free, though perhaps that's rich of me to say given how much of my life I've devoted to hunting it down.

A feeling I can't shake off: if I get to the bottom of it all, I'll be able to move on.

'She didn't scream,' Izzy told Detective Arnold. 'Just lay there crying for her mommy. Like *she* could save her!'

How could Plum's parents bear to hear that? How could it possibly give them closure?

Mrs Underwood organised a memorial service for Plum at the Baptist church up in Hillside. It was packed, filled with flowers apparently. People stood in the aisles and lined up outside because there weren't enough seats for them all.

It was a huge comfort, her mother told reporters afterwards. 'To feel all that love and support.'

No one loved Izzy though. No one turned out to comfort us.

Why would they? In their heads, we were to blame.

In our heads too.

AFTER

I stumbled across the footage of Izzy's confession a few years ago as I was hopping about online. Going down one mole hole after another, entire hours lost to Reddit.

A cable channel had released a true crime documentary. *Killers Uncovered*, they called it. *The Izzy Jackman Tapes.*

I still struggle to think of her that way. As a killer. To reconcile shy Izzy, scared of her shadow, with the knife-wielding maniac who stabbed her best friend twenty-one times.

I streamed the programme on my laptop, sitting up in bed with an extra blanket round my shoulders because it was December and the heating was on the fritz. A bottle of the good stuff by my side for liquid courage.

It was all there. Izzy's interrogation playing on-screen like a movie. My sister glancing at her lawyer to make sure it was okay to answer. Detective Arnold going increasingly pale as she did.

I've watched it a number of times since, not really believing what I was hearing. Or, perhaps, not wanting to. Frames from the police interview interspersed with expert opinions from the psychologists and criminologists the show-makers had gathered together, along with the narrator's own speculations.

Was Izzy Jackman mad or bad? Was she a psychopath kid or simply a troubled teen?

The same questions everyone has always asked.

'Are you filming this?' she asked Detective Arnold, eyes flicking to the camera on the wall.

He told her yes. Explained that all interrogations were recorded and that anything she said could be used in evidence at trial.

She seemed pleased by his answer. Followed up with, 'Will it be on TV?'

Arnold shook his head, said he doubted it.

She looked disappointed, asked, but might it be?

'Other people could watch it too? Hear what I have to say?' Then before he could answer – 'Do you have a hairbrush?'

'Narcissistic behaviour,' the experts on the documentary claimed. 'Attention-seeking.'

But if so, whose attention was she seeking?

'How did it happen, Izzy?' Detective Arnold asked in his soft Texas purr.

Izzy looked at her hands, at her fingers fanned out on the table in front of her. She shrugged; said sometimes you just have to prove yourself. Show you'll do whatever it takes.

'Show that to whom?'

She didn't answer, just picked at her nails. Arnold tried a different tack.

'You girls talk about it much beforehand?'

My sister looked right into the camera as though she were addressing a live studio audience rather than simply the detectives sitting opposite her.

'Oh, yes,' she said. 'We talked about it all the time. It was so hard keeping it a secret. It was a brilliant plan actually.'

'Whose plan was it?' Arnold asked.

Lu had already told the police killing Plum was all Izzy's idea, but without my sister's corroboration, they were in 'he said/she said' territory.

Her eyes flicked to the camera again. She told Arnold that the plan had been hers. Enunciated the words slowly and carefully so there could be no doubt.

Was it her idea though? Lu had been the one to call Izzy up. She was the one who'd mentioned Turtle Lake. The person who told my sister: You're going to just die Izzy Jackman.

But if that's true, why would Izzy lie about it? It hardly benefitted her to be cast as the mastermind.

'Why'd you do it, Izzy?' Detective Arnold asked. 'Why did you want to kill Plum?'

If you watch the tape carefully, you can see him lean forward at this point. A man who wanted answers as much as a conviction.

Izzy raised a shoulder, let it drop.

'We didn't want to be friends with her anymore.'

Arnold looked at her as though it were an alien sitting in front of him.

'You killed her because you didn't want to be friends with her?'

'She was spreading lies about us,' Izzy explained.

'What sort of lies?'

Her jaw tightened. She said she didn't want to say.

To this day, she's never revealed what Plum was supposed to have said or who she told the so-called lies to. And yet, a conversation comes back to me. The night I heard Izzy crying, then speaking on the phone:

But I never said that . . .

I promise. He's got to believe me . . .

Was Plum telling Ryder Grady stories about her? Is that what made her lash out the way she did?

'Couldn't you just . . . stop being friends with her?' Arnold asked.

'It wasn't as easy as that,' Izzy answered, but again she wouldn't be drawn. All she'd say was – 'A door isn't the only way out. Sometimes you got to go through the window.'

It was the sort of pretentious claptrap she was always coming out with.

The other detective in the room was a woman called Maggie Birch. Until this point she'd let Arnold do the talking. Now she piped up, told Izzy she didn't get it.

Izzy smirked, said that wasn't terribly surprising.

'Can you help me understand?' Detective Birch asked.

If she knew she'd been dissed, she didn't show it.

'Have you ever been in love?' my sister asked. 'Loved someone so much you'd die for them?'

Detectives Birch and Arnold exchanged glances.

'Did someone ask you to do this?' Birch asked gently.

The way you might approach a bear.

'If you allow lies to go unchecked, you may as well spread them yourself,' Izzy answered in a sing-song voice, as though she were reciting a favourite line from a poem.

'Who are you in love with, Izzy?' Birch tried again.

She may as well have been talking to herself.

'Are you going to put me in prison?' Izzy asked. 'Am I going to rot in there and die?'

She sounded like a child, which is of course exactly what she was. Only recently turned thirteen and still wearing a training bra.

But smart enough to have deleted the video I'd seen of Ryder on his guitar, beckoning for Izzy to come over to him.

I wonder if he told her to do it.

I wonder why I never thought to tell anyone about it. The difference it might have made if I had.

Watching the interview, remembering the video, I wondered something else.

But it's supposed to be my turn . . .

Was Plum jealous of Ryder paying attention to Izzy? (*We shouldn't always have to share.*) Is that why she started spreading lies about her? Because she saw her as a rival? Did Izzy see Plum as a rival, too?

'Did you feel bad after you killed your friend?' Detective Arnold asked later in the interrogation.

He was trying to establish whether she had remorse, one of the psychologists on the programme explained. Whether she knew the difference between right or wrong.

Izzy stuck out her lower lip.

'I figured feeling bad about it would get me nowhere,' she said. 'It's definitely easier to live without regret.'

She took a sip of soda, tucked a stray lock of hair behind her ears.

Smiled.

Article from *PsychologyNow.com*

What Creates Psychopath Kids?

Brain damage, not bad parenting, is to blame for psychopathy in children, according to a leading psychologist at Durham University in England.

Contrary to what we might like to believe, some children (like some adults) are capable of extreme cruelty. We only have to look to the notorious Turtle Lake case to see this.

But what creates these 'bad seeds'? These so-called psychopath kids who are unable to relate to others?

All too often, we blame the parents. Assume that if they had been better role models, given their children more love and attention, their offspring would have turned out better.

And while love maps are set early and parenting does play a key role in a child's moral and social development, bad parents do not necessarily create bad children.

Indeed, studies in twins have shown that environmental factors only explain to a limited degree the behaviour of psychopathic children (a term that itself raises questions).

New research reveals that the biggest contributor to violent behaviour is, in fact, the brain. Specifically, the amygdala, which is responsible for empathy and fear.

Children with psychopathic tendencies report that they rarely experience fear, which suggests amygdala dysfunction may be at the root of their condition. After all, if you don't feel fear, how do you empathise with someone who does?

AFTER

'How did you feel when you stabbed Plum?' Detective Arnold asked Izzy at another point in the interview. 'Were you afraid?'

'Afraid?' she repeated, as though she hadn't understood the question. She shook her head. 'Plum was the one who was afraid. She's the one who was crying for her mommy. She should have known the only way to live is to die.'

Birch and Arnold looked at each other. Birch interlaced her fingers, cocked her head.

'Where did you hear that, Izzy?' she asked but Izzy refused to say.

'Can you at least tell us which of you girls stabbed Plum first?'

'Both of us.'

'But who stabbed her *first*?' Arnold insisted.

The first person to act would be the leader, according to the programme's criminologist. In every criminal partnership there's always an alpha, he said. If Izzy was the mastermind, she'd also be the alpha.

Izzy threw up her hands, exasperated. The interrogation had been going on for several hours by this point.

'How am I supposed to remember that?' she exclaimed.

There was a knock at the door. The detectives excused themselves and left the room. The camera, however, was still rolling. On the tape you see Izzy stretch her arms over her head and yawn widely. Then stick out her tongue at the two-way mirror.

Her lawyer whispered something in her ear.

'Behave yourself,' I expect.

The detectives returned, noted the time for the 'benefit of the tape'.

'Lu's been talking about Ryder Grady,' Arnold told my sister, watching her closely for a reaction.

It was the first time his name had come up, though the investigators had apparently wondered for some time whether there was a third person involved. Someone influencing the girls.

Pulling the strings.

'We always had the feeling they were protecting someone,' Arnold told the programme-makers. 'Though we never dreamt it might be a teacher at their school.'

'What's Lu been saying?' Izzy asked, a flush creeping up her neck.

'We'd rather hear what you have to say.'

'Did she tell you about the necklace? Because it should have been me who won it, not Plum.'

Birch's brows rose. She caught Arnold's eye.

The police had found a chain with a heart pendant tangled in a bed of thorns near Turtle Lake. It was one of the details they'd kept from the public. A way of ruling out false confessions, as my father had explained to us.

I remembered what I'd seen written on the bathroom mirror. How I had held something back too.

'Can you describe the necklace for us, Izzy?' Detective Arnold asked.

My sister described perfectly the one they'd found.

'I ripped it off her lying neck,' Izzy told them. 'It should have been mine and she knew it.'

'What did you do to win it?' Birch asked softly.

My sister pouted, tossed her hair.

'The scouts picked me for the coronation. Do you know how much weight I lost? How hard it was? I'm crazy about that man. I didn't want to do that other stuff. He's the one I love. But sometimes you got to put your needs second, right?'

'Didn't want to do what?' Arnold asked, another quick glance in Birch's direction.

His tone was as gentle as hers had been but something in it broke the spell and Izzy clammed up.

'I'm not saying anything else.'

'Did Ryder Grady encourage you to kill Plum, Izzy?'

She clamped her lips tight, folded her arms.

Detective Birch leaned across the table, said it was okay. Izzy could let Lu tell them everything if she wanted. And Lu was certainly telling them plenty.

Izzy shifted in her seat.

'I've said everything I'm going to say. It was my idea to kill Plum. No one told me to do anything.'

'Mr Grady had no idea what you were planning?'

Izzy looked to her lawyer for help. He gestured it was alright to answer.

'Ryder didn't tell us what to do. It was all my idea. I've already said that.'

'Are you sure, Izzy? Because if this man was grooming you—'

Her lawyer sat up a little straighter. Izzy screwed up her face. Asked what grooming was.

'It's when a grown-up pretends to be your friend and then uses that friendship to manipulate you into doing things you might not otherwise want to do,' Arnold explained carefully.

The lawyer touched Izzy's arm, asked in an encouraging sort of way whether that's what happened.

'Because if so, you're a victim, Izzy.'

She shook her head, fast, from side to side.

'It was my idea. How many times do I have to tell you?'

Later on in the tape, Arnold asks how they managed to lure Plum away from the party.

Izzy smiled.

'I said, let's play hide and go seek. People who trust you are pretty gullible, you know?'

The irony is completely lost on her.

AFTER

The documentary showed more extracts from the interrogation tapes. Izzy appeared proud of what she'd done, one of the programme's 'experts' claimed. Her tone boastful.

'But also, what we see here is a child who doesn't understand the gravity of her actions,' he said. 'Nor the situation she finds herself in. The murder of Plum Underwood seems almost like a game to Izzy Jackman.'

Another psychologist dwelt on the singularity of the case. How unusual it is for children Izzy's age to kill. Especially girls.

'In fact, it's so rare for women to commit murder that even recently a highly respected FBI profiler claimed female serial killers do not exist.'

A third expert, a criminology professor from Stanford University, discussed what turns children into killers:

'The early years of a child's life are critical when it comes to developing a conscience. Without exception, child murderers have a history of neglect. Oftentimes, they come from unstable homes where they are ignored for hours at a time.'

None of that applied to Izzy though. True, we'd lost our

252

mother when she was young, but then so had I. And I've never murdered anyone.

And despite that tragedy, we had had a perfectly stable home life with plenty of love and attention. Too much attention, it felt sometimes, with Dita always in our business.

No neglect. No instability. No reason for Izzy to become a psycho killer.

How to explain her, then? How she could go from zero to anti-hero?

Only one expert suggested her behaviour might have been the result of grooming, but that was summarily dismissed, in light of her unshakeable claim that the murder was all her idea.

What *Killers Uncovered* didn't go into is what happened to Ryder. That was the subject of a whole other documentary. Two movies as well. Including a scene in a recent smash hit starring Bradley Fletcher.

Like Ryder's a celebrity or something.

Makes me sick.

Transcript from NDC documentary
Inside Ryder Grady's Ring

Voice-over:

On August 1, 2003, Ryder Thomas Grady was arrested and taken to the FBI field office in San Diego for questioning on child sexual exploitation charges. This followed comments to police made by thirteen-year-old Izzy Jackman, who had just confessed to the brutal murder of her friend, Plum Underwood.

[Image: *a mugshot of Izzy Jackman holding up a board with her name and details on it*]

Carlsbad investigators believed Mr Grady (a biology teacher at the exclusive Heritage Elm school) was grooming young girls with the promise of modelling contracts.

[Image: *the front gates of Heritage Elm School for Girls*]

They also believed he encouraged a certain amount of competition amongst the girls to strengthen his control over them. And that possibly this competition fed into the murder of Plum.

[Image: *a necklace with a heart-shaped pendant found tangled in a nest of thorns at Turtle Lake*]

The problem, however, was that despite a widespread appeal for information and the promise of anonymity, no other girls had come forward saying they were part of Grady's ring.

Everything now rested on the FBI's interviewing skills . . .

[Cut to: *clip of Ryder Grady during his interrogation. Two FBI agents wearing white shirts and black ties on one side of the table. On the other side, Ryder Grady sitting alone. Blonde hair slicked back. Hands steepled on the table in front of him. Perfectly calm*]

FBI Agent 1: Can you confirm you've been read your rights?

Ryder Grady: Yes, though I can assure you this is all a big misunderstanding.

FBI Agent 1: And to confirm, you've waived your right to an attorney?

Ryder Grady: Only guilty people need lawyers, Agent Malone.

FBI Agent 1: And you're not guilty, Mr Grady?

Ryder Grady: I'm sure I'm guilty of many things. But sex with little girls? [*Shakes head. Laughs*] Are you kidding?

FBI Agent 2: You didn't lure underage minor females to your apartment with the promise of modelling contracts?

Ryder Grady: How could I do that? I don't work for a modelling agency.

FBI Agent 1: We've been talking to Izzy Jackman, Ryder. She's gone into a lot of detail. You sure you don't want to give us your side?

Ryder Grady: Poor Izzy. She always was a troubled kid. Never quite fit in. Always so eager to please.

FBI Agent 2: Is that what made her an easy target?

Ryder Grady: You're quite right, Agent Kurt. Predators do target vulnerable kids, as I'm constantly telling my students at Heritage Elm. The only thing you should ever really trust is your gut.

Voice-over:

It turned out that as well as being a biology teacher, Ryder Grady also ran the photography club at Heritage Elm and was the head of safeguarding. As such, he was in charge of organising cyber-awareness presentations for the students and their parents. What no one realised was that he had first-hand experience of the practices he was warning against.

[Image: *Ryder Grady giving a presentation about online grooming to a packed room of seventh graders, amongst them, Plum Underwood, Izzy Jackman, and her co-conspirator, Lucia Nox*]

The FBI's interview with Ryder Grady lasted several hours. Agent Malone – one of the interrogators – has since described him as 'more slippery than an eel'.

Grady was careful. He gave nothing away, and although the two agents knew the guy was dirt, they had no way to prove it.

Time was running out. And then Grady tripped up.

FBI Agent 2: Have you ever taken class A drugs, Mr Grady?

Ryder Grady: And risk losing my job? No, of course not.

Voice-over:

The FBI couldn't make the child exploitation charges stick. But a team had managed to get a search warrant and been to his apartment to retrieve any relevant evidence. Possibly Grady had been tipped off, possibly he was cautious.

For whatever reason, his computer had been removed and there were no photographs of any sort. What they did find, however, were small amounts of LSD along with a two-inch roach. Drugs they suspected he plied teenagers with as part of his grooming activities.

[Image: *a small sheet of blotting paper stamped with pink hearts*]

Ryder Grady had been careful but he hadn't been careful enough.

He told Special Agent Kurt he had never taken class A drugs. And he'd been caught in the lie.

Lying to an FBI agent is a federal crime. A person can be found innocent of a more serious charge and yet still find themselves in the clink for telling fibs. A fact Dick Cheney's former advisor, 'Scooter' Libby, would discover just a few years later.

Ryder Grady learned his lesson on August 2, 2003.

In prison, he would go on to brag to his cellmate that he had a ring of 'nymphets' who would do anything for him.

[Cut to: *clip of Ryder Grady's cellmate. Large bearded man in an orange jumpsuit sitting on a plastic chair, his left ankle resting on his right knee*]

Cellmate: He says to me: There's this big murder case. Two girls stabbing their best friend. Everyone thinks they know what happened, but they are so far off the mark, man, they're shooting at something else altogether.

You don't mean that business at Turtle Lake? I say, and he says, in this proud sort of way: Yes, that's the one.

You know why they did it, don't you? he asks.

No, I say.

And then he grins and prods his chest. Says: You're looking right at him.

Voice-over:

That was Ryder Grady's second mistake: trusting a con. Just

hours later, his cellmate was cutting himself a deal with the feds. His end of the bargain? To get more information out of Grady.

[Cut to: *clip of Special Agent Bill Malone under studio lights*]

FBI Agent 1: Grady's cellmate did good. Fished out enough rope to hang the creep with.

That bastard is exactly where he deserves and he'll be there for a long time.

NOW

I fish a Sweet'N Low out of the sachet holder, tear off the corner. Tip the granules into my cup.

Elsa Stone and I are sitting across from each other in the Brew House Café (cheesy name, excellent coffee) when it hits me: I know this woman.

Yet I also know for a fact I've never met Elsa Stone before.

How could I have?

I was ten when we upped sticks and moved to London. She would have been a toddler – at most – then and I don't remember a single toddler from those days.

She can't be from here either.

Elsa Stone is too young to have been at high school at the same time as me. And I can count on one hand (with a few fingers chopped off) how many people I've met since dropping out.

I've worked hard at not having friends.

Her face is so familiar though . . .

The shape of it. The eyes. Even her mannerisms are familiar.

The way she touches her hair. How she looks down when she speaks.

It doesn't make sense. How can I be so sure I know someone I've never met?

I watch as she brings her coffee cup to her lips, little finger crooked. She sips. Sets it back in the saucer, rotating it in both hands. Warms them against the porcelain.

'So cold out,' she says. 'It's seventy degrees in San Diego.'

She's from back home, then. If I do know her, that must be where from.

Where my father knows her from too, I realise with a start.

My father, whose eyes widened in shock when I mentioned her name. My father, whose eyes don't react to anything.

So, who is this woman? Why am I so certain I've seen her before?

What is she really doing here?

AFTER

My father was in his study with Izzy's lawyer, Karl Kihm – pronounced 'Kim' (*The 'h' is silent. Same way I like my clients*). The two of them were discussing trial strategy. They'd been at it since lunch. It was now twenty after five in the evening and Dita was in the kitchen fixing dinner.

Izzy may have confessed to killing Plum, but there would still be a trial to determine her punishment, my father had explained to me.

'So, she might not go to jail?'

He shook his head sadly.

'She'll be locked up, whatever happens. Question is, where . . .'

The key question would be whether she was suffering from a mental disease or defect, and therefore whether or not she should be held criminally responsible.

'You mean if she's crazy,' I asked.

'Ill, not crazy,' he corrected. 'To get your sister the help she needs, we need to convince a jury she's not of sound mind.'

'So, you do mean crazy . . .'

He tried again to explain.

What he didn't mention was the effect Ryder Grady might have had on Izzy's mental state. At this point, the pervert hadn't yet bragged to his cellmate, although both the police and Mr Kihm had their suspicions about what had been going on at his apartment.

Just suspicions though, nothing concrete since Izzy and Lu were keeping schtum (despite what Arnold implied to my sister about Lu giving them all the dirt).

'A pity,' Karl Kihm said. 'If only the girls would testify that they'd been groomed, it might result in a lesser sentence.'

But even if they did, was grooming enough to explain why they'd crossed the line into murder?

What could Grady possibly have said that could have compelled them to stab their best friend? Twenty-one times.

Or do I only think that way because I wasn't under his spell like she was? Because I didn't look into his demon eyes and see a god?

I edged closer to the door. Mr Kihm was speaking. Even when it was just him and my father, he used his courtroom voice. Must give his wife quite a headache.

'How do you rate her chances, Karl?' my father asked.

I put my eye to the keyhole, watched Karl Kihm run the tips of his fingers over his gelled hair.

'All we need for reasonable doubt is another way of looking at things,' he said. 'It all comes down to who tells the best story. Us or the DA. I'll argue folie à deux. Madness shared by two.

'Izzy and her friend became obsessed with the idea Plum was spreading lies about them. Two girls who'd previously been outsiders were paranoid about becoming outsiders again. It caused them to spiral, to lose touch with reality.'

'You think that's what happened?' my father asked.

Karl Kihm smiled. Displayed a lot of teeth.

'It's what I'm going to say happened. And it doesn't hurt that Izzy's a nice-looking kid.'

My father asked what that had to do with 'the price of fish'.

The lawyer's smile broadened. He had a gold incisor that I thought made him look like Jack Sparrow in *Pirates of the Caribbean*. He had Sparrow's beard too, a thick line of dark hair tracing his pointy jaw.

'Jurors are suckers for a pretty face, same as the rest of us,' he explained. 'There have been studies. Attractive people are let off more often than' – he paused to think of a PC term, settled on – 'less attractive people.

'I'm not saying it'll be easy, Judge. ADA Madden will argue the crime was premeditated so Izzy knew exactly what she was doing. That this was a murder born out of jealousy, pure and simple.'

'Jealousy?' my father asked.

The lawyer ticked the reasons off on his manicured fingers.

'He'll say Izzy was jealous Grady gave a necklace to Plum rather than her. Jealous that Plum held the dominant position in the friendship group. He might even argue Izzy was jealous the girl still has a mother.'

My father rubbed his eyes, murmured, 'Jesus. There's evidence of that? That she was envious of Plum's relationship with Mrs Underwood?'

Karl Kihm blew his lips. *Evidence, who cares about evidence?*

'There's nothing concrete, per se. But enough for the prosecution to float the idea. Often that's all you need. An attorney's job is to paint a good picture. Give the jury enough to colour between the lines.'

'I thought this was all about them not wanting to be friends with Plum anymore. Isn't that what the girls told Arnold?'

Karl Kihm raised an eyebrow. *Don't be so naïve*, his eyebrow said.

'Murder is never about one thing, sir. Least of all the motive the perpetrators give. And jealousy always plays well in a courtroom. People can relate to it.'

My father murmured, 'Jesus' again.

Kihm patted his shoulder.

'Don't look so worried, Judge. Like I told you, it's all about how we present the facts. And I assure you, I'm an excellent storyteller . . .'

Article from *Court Insider*

A court in Carlsbad, California, has today heard how two teenage girls who carried out a savage plot to murder their best friend may have been affected by 'folie à deux' – a psychiatric syndrome that translates as 'the madness of two'.

In what is described by defence attorney Karl Kihm as a 'rare form of psychosis', Elizabeth Jackman and Lucia Nox (both on trial for the homicide of thirteen-year-old Plum Underwood) became paranoid that the victim was spreading lies about them.

The defendants were emotionally vulnerable, Mr Kihm said. Elizabeth Jackman because she lost her mother at a 'tender age' and Lucia Nox because her own mother is terminally ill.

'For children, the lines between fiction and reality can become quite blurred,' Mr Kihm told the jury during his opening statement.

'As such, when Elizabeth Jackman and Lucia Nox

stabbed Miss Underwood, they failed to grasp the gravity of their actions.'

Folie à deux was identified by French psychiatrists Charles Lasègue and Jean-Pierre Falret in the 19th century. Most common in romantic partnerships, it can also occur between siblings and close friends.

AFTER

It was October 15, 2003.

The day the Staten Island Ferry collided with a pier, killing eleven people and injuring seventy more. That Colin Powell was accused of misleading the world about Saddam's weapons of mass destruction.

And Karl Kihm made his closing arguments at Izzy's trial.

'I can't go,' I told my father.

My stomach was churning. My chest seizing up. I just wanted to stay in bed with the covers pulled up over my head. To pretend today wasn't happening.

My father wanted me to hustle.

'We don't have time for this, Finn. We have to be at the courthouse by eight.'

The elephant clock on my nightstand showed seven thirty-five.

'I'm not going,' I repeated.

'Yes, you are. Now get dressed.'

Up till then, I'd been to court every day. Mr Kihm had been

very clear how important it was that we all showed up to support Izzy. '*It's all about creating the right semiotics* . . .'

But the thought of going today and hearing the verdict made me want to hurl.

My father didn't ask why I didn't want to go, but even if he had, I'm not sure I could have explained the dread which had kept me awake all night. The suffocating fear we were about to lose Izzy.

Was it worse than when I suspected her of hurting Plum? I'm not sure. That fear had felt pretty suffocating too. But at least there was hope then that things might turn out okay.

I'd tried to remain hopeful during the trial, scanning the jurors' faces for signs they were sympathetic towards my sister. Sending them ESP messages that she was a good person really. Willing Mr Kihm to come up with the magic words that would get her off.

But today we were at the end of the hope road. After the jury went off into their little room to deliberate, there would be nothing else any of us could do to help Izzy. No more rabbits left to pull out of hats. No more clever party tricks.

It was hard enough watching her being led away in chains at the end of every day. But to think she might be kept in them. That she might have to live in a cell, locked away for hours at a time. Bars on the window. Guards pacing about outside.

That if it weren't for me, she'd be at home swinging in her hammock or eating Pringles in front of the TV. That if it weren't for me, she'd never have wanted to kill Plum in the first place.

I was still charitably inclined towards her at that point. Still shouldered the blame for what had happened.

Later, that would change.

Later I would start to hate her. Refuse to see her for different reasons.

When it came to court, I could refuse to go all I liked but ultimately I didn't have a choice in the matter.

'Shoes on in five minutes or no television for a week.'

'It's not fair . . .'

'Life's not fair. Now let's hustle!'

Dita rode up front in the Oldsmobile fiddling with the handle of her purse and sniffing loudly. My father said nothing, a robot at the wheel. I sat in the back staring out the window and making deals with a god I would soon stop believing in.

Please God, let Mr Kihm find something to show that the police got it wrong . . .

I'll never hide my broccoli under my potatoes ever again if you make it all okay . . .

I don't think I'd really absorbed what my father had told me: that she'd be incarcerated whatever happened.

If we don't hit any red lights, Izzy will come home . . .

If I see another scrub jay, Mr Kihm will win . . .

The radio was on. I don't know why. You'd have thought we'd have had enough of the news.

Defence closing arguments are expected today in the trial of Elizabeth Jackman. Miss Jackman has pleaded guilty to being a party to the homicide of her best friend, Plum Underwood, and could now face decades behind bars . . .

'She didn't do it,' I said as my father shut it off.

Dita reached her arm back through the gap between the seats and squeezed my knee.

'It'll be okay, chick. I got you.'

I pushed her hand away, repeated that Izzy was innocent.

'Why else was she so confused when she heard where Plum's body was?

My father sighed, turned on to 11th Street.

'We've been through this,' he said, patience thin. 'Your sister was in shock. Of course she seemed confused.'

I kicked at his seat, told him he never listened. That I'd warned him and Dita about Plum and Lu.

'You didn't listen to that either . . .'

We pulled up outside the courthouse. The street was teeming with news trucks and reporters. A thick crowd on the sidewalk several feet deep. Sightseers who'd camped out all night for a 'decent spot' according to *Good Morning San Diego*.

They turned as one as we approached the building. Shook their placards. Hissed like we were the guilty ones.

The cameras started clicking. The newshounds scenting blood. I wondered how many of them had called the house, how they'd got hold of our number:

I'm so-and-so from such-and-such paper. May I have a moment of your time?

We'd had letters in the mail too. Lined pages ripped from notebooks giving off the tang of sad motels and stale cigarettes.

I'd be very grateful if you'd speak to me. The Times is of course willing to pay . . .

And now they were at it again. What was wrong with these people?

Judge Jackman, how did you miss the signs?

Sir, can you honestly say your daughter didn't know exactly what she was doing?

My father put his hand on my back steering me forward. Repeated the same words over and over:

'No comment. No comment . . .'

AFTER

'I feel sick,' I told Dita as we took our seats inside the court-room.

'You and me both, chick,' she whispered.

Izzy and Lu were sitting at the defence table. Izzy looked like she'd come straight from class. Her hair was tied back in a ponytail. She was wearing a white button-down shirt and baby-blue V-neck. Karl Kihm's 'semiotics'.

You saw what Winona Ryder did with that little headband?

It's why I'd been forced into a skirt, though surely no one gave a hoot what I was wearing.

Lu clearly hadn't got the memo. She was in a baggy Bugs Bunny sweatshirt and loose cargo pants. She'd really ballooned since I'd last seen her. Her face gerbil-esque, skin lit with a sweaty sheen.

'What've they been feeding her?' I whispered to Dita.

Judge Mortimer appeared before she could tell me to hush and worry about myself. The court rose, then settled back in their seats.

You could sense everyone in the gallery pulling themselves

up straight. Waiting for the show to begin. A raisin-faced woman was staring at me. I glowered back. Anywhere else, I'd have stuck out my tongue.

'Is the defence ready to proceed?'

Karl Kihm stood, straightened his jacket. Told the judge, 'Yes, Your Honour,' in his big booming voice.

He came out from behind the table, puffed out his chest. Addressed the jury, hands tugging at his lapels.

'Good morning, ladies and gentlemen. I would like to start by thanking you all on behalf of the defence for giving up your time to be here as citizens of the great state of California.'

He strode alongside the box, came to a stop in front of the foreman. Smiled like they were old friends.

'Here we are, at the end of our journey . . .'

The jury retired just before lunch.

'I'll call you when it looks like they're coming back in if you want to go get a bite to eat,' Mr Kihm said to my father, who told him there was no need, we were staying put.

I wonder if he felt as I did that it would be bad luck to leave. Or maybe he just didn't have the energy to face the mob outside.

We could have gone and sat with Izzy in the family room but she'd been very clear she wanted to be alone.

Outside, the bell tower chimed the hours. One, two, three o'clock. At four, Mr Kihm came hurrying to find us, the thin soles of his brogues clacking on the polished wood floor.

'They've reached a verdict,' he said in an out-of-breath voice.

My father raised an eyebrow, a non-verbal question.

'Could go either way,' Kihm responded.

'Please God, please God . . .' I whispered.

People trickled back into the courtroom, took their seats. The judge mounted the podium.

'All rise! This court is now in session. The Honourable Harold Mortimer presiding.'

When I think back on what came next, I recall it the way you recall a dream. In snatches and out of focus. My memory a kaleidoscope.

The jury filing in.

Judge Mortimer asking them if they'd reached a verdict.

The foreman saying, yes, they had. And yes, it was unanimous.

I heard the words: 'guilty' and 'criminally responsible'. My father's sharp intake of breath. Dita gasping. And after that, nothing except the thunder thud of my heart.

'But she was so confused,' I whispered as the room emptied out, the three of us still sitting there. Frozen.

Dita put an arm round me, pulled me close.

'None of us were expecting this, chick.'

It wasn't what I'd meant.

AFTER

Twenty years later, the confusion on Izzy's face when Detective Arnold told her where they'd found Plum's body still makes no sense. If she killed her friend, why didn't she know where she'd left her corpse?

And if she didn't kill her, why say she did?

It always comes back to that. The circle I can't square.

We're here outside the Bell Tower Courthouse, where just moments ago, the daughter of a Superior Court judge was sentenced to twenty-five years to life in prison for the murder of her best friend . . .

The jury's verdict didn't simply condemn Izzy. It condemned us too. As the news headlines the following day showed:

Judge Jackman's Daughter, a Killer . . .

From the Suburbs to the Slammer:
Judge's Daughter Goes Down

What Do You Think of Capital Punishment Now, Judge Jackman?

'I can't show my face in this town,' my father said, staring into his coffee cup.

Coffee he'd poured an hour ago and still hadn't touched. Flecks swimming on the surface where before there had been steam.

'Because everyone hates you?' I asked.

He shook his head, told me no. *Because I hate myself.*

I hated myself too but I didn't say so. Didn't say much of anything. Though there were plenty of people who wanted me to . . .

The press was back outside the house with their cameras and recorders and big furry microphones after the sentencing. Wolves waiting to pounce the moment we showed ourselves.

Judge Jackman, can we talk to you?

Finn, how do you feel . . . ?

Just a minute of your time . . .

My sister was more famous than Paris Hilton. Her picture was on the cover of *People* magazine, *Baby-Faced Killer* splashed across the top. *Newsweek* carried a double-page write-up. A well-known publisher contacted my father asking if he'd write his side.

'A dad's story, is how we'd pitch it. Your relationship with Izzy. The making of a monster.'

My father slammed the phone down, pulled the lead out the wall when they kept calling back.

'You need to prepare yourself for the attention,' Karl Kihm had warned us after we left court for the last time. 'The media is going to start showing up, ringing the house, even more than with the arrest. It's up to you whether you want to speak to them and what you want to say. Though my advice would be, speak to no one. Say nothing.'

If only other people were saying nothing.

I didn't know what was worse: that the whole world was talking about Izzy, or that everyone at school would be talking about me.

'You sure she doesn't need some more time off, Judge?' my school principal, Mrs Langley, asked

My father's response was the same as when she suggested Izzy see a therapist all that time ago.

'What Finn needs is to get back to a normal routine. She'll be in tomorrow morning.'

'I understand,' Mrs Langley answered, although her tone suggested otherwise. 'I'll make sure the counsellor sits down with her first thing.'

My father tightened his lips.

'Finn is not ill. I don't want people treating her like there's something wrong with her.'

'But there *is* something wrong, Judge Jackman. The child has been through a trauma. She needs to talk to someone who can listen and guide her through it.'

My father thanked her for her concern but assured her we were dealing with this in our own way. And then he hung up.

'She get a kickback or something?' he muttered.

He never asked me if I wanted to see the counsellor. I might have said okay, if he had. But chances are I wouldn't have. It's not as though I've been to see a therapist since.

I could talk till I'm blue in the backside, as Dita would have said, but it wouldn't change anything. Izzy would still be in prison. Plum would still be dead. And it would all still be my fault.

My first day back at school, I was ambushed walking down our street. A reporter from the *Record*. Dick, his name was. Dick suited him.

He grabbed my arm, bent his face so close to mine I could smell the bacon he'd eaten for breakfast.

'I'll give you a hundred bucks to talk to me.'

I told him to get off, twisted my arm in a bid to break free. He gripped tighter. My skin began to throb.

'Just think of all the candy you can buy with a hundred bucks, kid.'

The other reporters called out to him:

'Leave her alone, buddy.'

'That's not cool, pal.'

It sounded like they were on my side but I suspect they were just worried Dicky Boy was going to get an exclusive.

I stamped hard on his foot and managed to wrestle away, leaving him hopping about like Steve Martin in *Cheaper by the Dozen*, which would come out later that year.

'Why, you little . . .'

I probably imagined it but I remember applause.

It wasn't just the streets that were treacherous. School was sniper territory too

I was tripped in the hallways. Spitballed in class. Even stuffed into a locker one time.

Kids I'd been friends with gave me the silent treatment. No one would partner with me in PE or sit with me at lunch.

Play-date invitations dried up. I was left off birthday party lists, no matter that the rest of the class was invited.

I started to hate Izzy. It was alright for her. She didn't have to deal with any of this crap in prison.

Why did we have to suffer because of something she'd done?

Being her sister sucked.

It wasn't much better being her dad.

I'll never forget my father's face when he came back from visiting her at juvie. His skin grey, the way a T-shirt gets when it's been through the wash too many times. His eyelids red and puffy.

'They wouldn't even let me hug her,' he said, putting his head in his hands. 'I teared up, right in front of her.' He sank into his easy chair, poured a large glass of port. Drank it down like water.

I watched, asked what she'd said.

Izzy would have hated him crying. It was a sign of weakness, she used to tell me.

'Never show them you're hurt, Finn.'

My father misinterpreted my question though. Said Izzy had asked why he'd come.

'I told her I was there because I loved her. That she was still my little girl, whatever she'd done. You know how she responded to that?'

'That you shouldn't love her? That she doesn't deserve it?'

He looked horrified.

'What a thing to suggest!'

I thought it was a perfectly reasonable thing to suggest but simply said –

'Well, what then?'

'She said she doesn't want me to come back.'

'Ever?'

'Reckons it's bad for her image, me being a judge.'

She was a murderer. What did she think that did for our image?

I asked if he'd given her a ticking-off. It would serve her right. I'd been wedgied twice that day.

'I don't think you *should* go back, Daddy. She needs to learn a lesson.'

He told me I needed to be more compassionate, that it wasn't her fault, although clearly it was. She was the one who'd stabbed her best friend.

'Your sister obviously feels deeply ashamed. But she doesn't need to feel ashamed in front of me.'

'She said she was ashamed?'

'She didn't have to,' he said, claimed he knew instinctively.

I wasn't buying it. When had Izzy ever felt ashamed about anything? Even when she broke my snow globe, it was somehow on me.

He went back to the detention centre several times after that. On the fifth occasion, he wasn't allowed through the door. He returned home in a daze. Told us –

'My visiting rights have been revoked.'

I asked what that meant, irritated that Izzy was calling the shots. I hadn't committed any crime, yet I wasn't even allowed to stay up past eight o'clock.

'The guard told me I'm not on the list. "I'm her daddy," I said. "Of course I'm on the list."'

'But he just put his hands up, said: "Only the messenger, buddy. She don't want to see you, there's nothing I can do."'

My father wrote a string of letters to my sister, but the result was always a big fat nothing. Until one day, Izzy finally wrote him back:

What part of 'leave me alone' don't you understand? she said. *I don't want to talk to you.*

It wasn't the guilty verdict that killed him. It was that.

AFTER

Unlike my father, I didn't try to visit my sister at Pinewood – a youth correctional facility about fifty miles from LA.

I was mad at her. She'd ruined my life, taken everything good in it and crumpled it up. Morphed me into the pariah she had once been.

I was mad at myself too, of course. At Dita and my father as well. If only they'd listened to me, Izzy's friendship with Plum and Lu could have been cut down before it had a chance to turn deadly. And if I hadn't lied, she wouldn't have started to hate Plum, fantasised about killing her.

The anger broiled inside me, effervescing in my veins. I was a rattling pot, a kettle ready to scream. Not that I did.

Maybe Mrs Langley was right, maybe it would have been better if I had expressed what I was feeling. Lifted the lid a bit.

Instead, I turned inwards, put a stopper in it as Dita might have said.

I forgot how to speak without first running the words through in my head. Lost the ability to stand in a room without wondering what to do with my hands. Where to look. How to smile in a way that didn't come across like a grimace.

I was hated for being Izzy's sister. And in time I came to hate myself for the same reason. To be ashamed of my blood and of my name.

Izzy and I were born from the same seed. If there was a monster in her DNA, was there one in mine too?

I'm sure Dita would have found a way to make me feel better if I'd opened up to her. She always knew just what to say.

But I never told her how I was feeling. And for the first time, she didn't guess.

I wasn't the only one fencing demons. We were each caught up in our own private battles, none of us in a position to go rescuing anyone else.

It might sound strange then that although I had no intention of visiting Izzy, the possibility of doing so was the card I played in a last-ditch attempt to stop my father uprooting us to England.

'What if Izzy changes her mind?' I asked him.

'Changes her mind about what?'

He was sitting in his easy chair by the fireplace, staring at his hands. *The Times* rested on his lap unopened. An untouched coffee mug at his side.

'You can't visit her if we're in London.'

He looked up, eyes glistening. Told me he could be on the moon and he'd still find a way to visit her if she wanted to see him.

'How's she supposed to tell you? She only knows our address here.'

'I write to her every week,' he sighed. 'All she has to do is write back.'

But she never did write to him and he never saw her again. Nor have I.

NOW

'I'm so pleased you changed your mind,' Elsa Stone says.

She sets her coffee cup to the side, takes a cardboard folder with 'Turtle Lake' written across the front out of her bag. Lays it on the table between us. Glances up to make sure I'm paying attention.

And that's when it clicks.

It's like one of those Magic Eye puzzles. You can't see the picture if you're looking too hard. There's a pun in there, of course, given Elsa's eyes are the clue.

It's the brown ring around the blue iris. Not only distinctive. Incredibly rare.

Heterochromia, my father said it was called. A hereditary condition that occurs in less than one per cent of the population.

Lu had it.

And so does Elsa Stone.

I wonder if lisps are passed on genetically too, as he once told me. Another thing Elsa and Lu have in common.

Two for two. Or three for three, if you count some of Ms

Stone's mannerisms, which are dead ringers for my sister's friend. The way she fiddles with her hair, particularly.

What are the odds?

My heart skitters as I put it together, mind flashing on that last day in court. Lu sitting at the defence table in her baggy Bugs Bunny sweatshirt and loose cargo pants. Me asking Dita, 'What've they been feeding her?'

She'd always been such a little thing but she'd ballooned since I'd last seen her. How puffy her face looked! Like a gerbil, I thought at the time.

And with that, another memory comes: the three musketeers out in the yard. Lu chowing down a Snickers bar. Plum watching disapprovingly.

'You really going to eat all that?'

Lu lowered the candy bar.

'I don't know what's wrong with me,' she said sadly. 'I can't stop guzzling chocolate.'

A teenage girl putting on weight and craving chocolate needn't add up to anything. But factor in the paedo creep, Ryder Grady, along with the brown ring around Elsa Stone's irises – Elsa's age too – and the idea forming in my head is hard to refute.

Did the police do a DNA test? Did it bolster the testimony of Ryder's cellmate? Prove statutory rape?

And what about that Google search? How I couldn't find a single reference to Elsa Stone.

She told me it was because she was 'more what you call "behind the scenes"' but is there another reason?

'Are you even a journalist?' I ask.

She flushes, blinks rapidly.

'What?'

I suppose it's a bit of a non sequitur.

I repeat the question

'I told you,' she says, speaking fast. 'I'm working on an exposé about Turtle Lake. For a big TV company. We start shooting next week.'

People give too many details when they lie. I read that somewhere. Also, that they touch their faces, which Elsa Stone is now doing.

Self-soothing, it's called. Only psychopaths are comfortable telling fibs.

'Is this really about Izzy?' I ask. 'Or your mother?'

Elsa Stone's mouth flaps open. She stutters, searches for the right words.

I don't know if she is a journalist. But I do know she's Lu's daughter. A baby Lu must have been carrying when she was on trial.

And when she murdered her best friend.

NOW

'I'm right, aren't I?' I say to Elsa Stone. 'Lu is your mother.'

The flush that settles on her face makes her look younger than I'd first thought. I suppose she must be if she's Lu's kid. Twenty at most.

She looks down at her hands, at the cardboard folder they are resting on.

'How did you know?' she asks.

Do I detect relief in her voice?

Keeping up a façade is tiring. I should know.

'Your eyes,' I say. 'They're the spitting image. You talk like her too. Your lisp.'

Is that rude? Is a lisp something you're not supposed to comment on?

Elsa Stone seems pleased though.

'Huh . . . ' She smiles to herself, twirls her hair. 'I never knew that.'

'Really?'

My brow crinkles.

I realise Lu wouldn't have been able to keep her baby in

jail. I also know from a prisoners' rights campaign my father spearheaded that she was likely shackled while giving birth. Not because she posed any inherent risk, but because up until only a few years ago, it was protocol.

'It's dehumanising,' I heard him tell a colleague. Judge Reynolds. The man who would later sign Izzy's arrest warrant. 'The test of a civilised society is how well it treats its weakest members.'

Lu couldn't have kept her baby but her father could have brought Elsa with him when he went to visit Lu.

In which case, how come she doesn't know her mom had a lisp?

I say as much.

'My mother's parents didn't want me,' she answers fiddling with her teaspoon. 'Mrs Nox was bed-bound. Raising a little kid on his own was too much for Lu's dad apparently.' She wets her lips, meets my eyes. 'I never met my Lu. All I have is her diary.'

Sympathy tugs, but it's all I can offer her.

'So go visit. I guarantee Lu knows more about that night than I do.'

Elsa's shoulders round. Her neck droops like a plant in need of a drink.

'I can't visit her,' she whispers.

'I realise it might be awkward but—'

She interrupts me, voice barely audible.

'Lu's dead,' she says

'Dead?'

How did I not know? The hours I've spent scouring the

internet, and yet I missed that? What else have I missed? What else has passed me by?

'It was kept out of the press,' Elsa Stone explains. 'Bakersfield hushed it up.' Clarifies: 'That's where she was staying.'

Staying. Like it was the Hilton rather than a maximum-security facility.

Izzy and Lu were sent to different detention centres from day one. So they'd be as isolated as possible, I expect. The public's appetite was definitely for punishment rather than rehabilitation.

Make those monsters suffer . . .

'I don't understand,' I say, because I just can't wrap my head around it. 'How did she die?'

She tells me another inmate stabbed her with a shank in the laundry room while she was folding jumpsuits.

'Guard was there at the time. Not ideal for prison PR. Hence the hush-up . . .'

'Always about appearances,' I mutter, thinking of Dita's campaign to get me out of overalls and Karl Kihm banging on about headbands semiotics.

There's a moment's pause, then Elsa Stone tells me she's sorry about Dita's suicide. 'Her passing' she calls it.

'Your family was good to me.'

My mouth opens and closes. *We are not a salmon, Finn . . .*

'You knew my family?'

'Indirectly,' she explains. 'Your father helped keep my existence out of the press. And of course, I would never have ended up with the Stones if it weren't for him.'

I furrow my brow. Ask why.

'He arranged for them to foster me. My dad – my adoptive dad – was a circuit judge. He was friends with yours. Golf buddies. They played together at the club in Aviara.'

I remember it. We used to go there for Sunday brunch. The dessert buffet covered two tables.

'Lu's parents didn't want me,' she continues. Fiddles with her spoon again. 'As well as the practical issues, they couldn't bear the constant reminder of what their daughter had done, her father said. Didn't want to have to look at "that man's eyes" every day.

'Until now, I assumed I must have Ryder Grady eyes.' She inhales deeply, lets it out. 'Lu's father can't have even looked at me.'

I send her a tight smile. Yet another life that paedophile destroyed.

How many lives? How many lies?

Elsa touches her hair in a way that is pure Lu. Sends me hurtling down the decades.

'I didn't find out till a year ago who I really was. That I'm a killer's daughter.'

She's speaking in a rush now, the words tumbling out.

'Nothing prepares you for discovering a thing like that. My world tipped. Everything I thought I knew was a fabrication. I went into a depression, started smoking weed. Drinking too much. Days curled up on my bed in a ball.

'In the end, I went to this therapist, who helped me see I could either accept who my birth parents were and face the pain, or else just stay stuck in this dark place forever.

'"You've got to decide," she said, "if you're ready to put the work in."

'We talked and talked – so many sessions! – and in the end, I came to terms with where I'd come from. Realised it's not your blood that determines your fate. It's the choices you make.'

She gives me a shy smile.

'Does that sound corny?'

I shake my head. Tell her no, it doesn't.

'I still need answers though,' she says. 'I need to understand what really happened at Turtle Lake. Because I'm telling you: something does not add up about that night.'

I say I get it. Think: my father knew.

Knew Lu was pregnant. Must have suspected she was carrying Ryder Grady's child. Knew who might give it a good home.

Izzy took a life and he gave a life back. Gave the woman sitting in front of me a second chance.

No wonder he reacted when I mentioned her name. After all this time, it must have seemed as though I was summoning a ghost.

From *Insider.com*

Frightening: Thousands of Unreported Deaths in US Jails

The justice system has no interest in inmates, according to Congresswoman Leila Cabot.

She described prisons as 'human trash cans' and went on Twitter to say:

Jails are being used as garbage bins for the mentally ill. This is unacceptable. Inmates are people. We need to treat them that way.

She cited thousands of in-custody deaths that go unreported year on year to illustrate her point, while an investigation by the television station MJT found that women account for nearly seventeen per cent of all in-custody deaths – which is nearly double their share of the total prison population.

NOW

'Lu died in prison,' Elsa Stone says. 'Her death was buried because it didn't look good for the Department of Corrections.'

She opens her hands, a gesture of supplication.

'I need to know if that's the only thing that got buried. Because what I've learned strongly suggests there's more to her story – their story – than what we've been told.'

Maybe she does know something . . .

It all comes down to who tells the best story. Us or the DA.

The jury bought the District Attorney's version of events, but was the prosecution's take the whole truth?

Or did something else happen that night?

Something that would explain why Izzy didn't seem to know where Plum's body was.

How two thirteen-year-old girls were able to get to a disposal site over thirty miles away – let alone carry a body any real distance.

The identity of the person Lu thought was watching them.

The famous prosecutor, Vincent Bugliosi, once said people

see what they expect to see, not what's right in front of them. Is that what I've been doing? Seeing but not looking?

Is there another explanation for what happened at Turtle Lake? Or do I just want there to be?

I rub my occipital, take a breath.

'Have you really uncovered new information?' I ask Elsa Stone, aware it's not a question I can take back because what I'm really saying is, I'm ready to listen.

To talk.

'Yes,' she says, and there's no artifice in her voice, no avoiding eye contact.

Even so, I'm sceptical. Of course I am. From what she's told me, Elsa Stone has only been looking into Turtle Lake for a year. She didn't even know Lu, never mind Izzy or Plum.

But maybe that distance has enabled her to see what I haven't been able to. Again, I think of Magic Eye puzzles, how you have to step back for the picture to come into focus.

My research has always had an agenda.

I want to believe Izzy was falsely convicted, that she didn't kill Plum. Because that way, I can convince myself I wasn't guilty either. That I played no part in a girl's death. That I needn't be ashamed for not letting on about my suspicions Izzy was involved in her disappearance. That I could have given her mother closure sooner.

But has that bias blinded me? Is it why Elsa Stone has found clues I missed?

Though if she's willing to tell me what those clues are, does it matter that she found them first?

Her eyes are on me. Eyes that are so like Lu's it's as though I'm looking straight at her.

And with that thought, another comes nipping at its heels.

I know what it feels like to live in the dark.

I know what it's like to be tormented by uncertainty. To hunger for answers the way a starving person hungers for food.

Maybe Elsa Stone knows things I don't. Maybe she can help me. Maybe she can't.

But that doesn't mean I shouldn't try to help her. Fill in the blanks.

For the first time in twenty years, I'm ready to open up.

NOW

Tea lights in mosaic holders throw flickering patterns up the café walls. There's a Nat King Cole track playing on the stereo: 'Let There be Love'. A woman breastfeeding a baby a few tables over. The baby is covered with a shawl. The mother is eating carrot cake.

'They weren't close, you know,' Elsa says, gaze flitting in their direction.

'Who weren't?'

'Plum and her mom. It was in that book. I forget the title. One of the cops wrote it.'

I know the book she's talking about, though the name eludes me too. It was co-authored by a Carlsbad detective who worked on the case and an investigative journalist who sounds like she wishes she had. It was also an immediate *New York Times* bestseller.

Twenty years on and people are still fascinated by Turtle Lake.

Intrigued by what would drive two seemingly normal girls to stab their best friend twenty-one times.

I bought the book, lured by the promise of 'unknown details', though the only detail I hadn't known was that Plum and her mother didn't get on well.

The authors picked holes in the prosecution's argument that Izzy was jealous of Plum's relationship with her mother. A key motive in the murder, ADA Madden claimed at trial.

But Izzy Jackman had nothing to be jealous of. Neighbors regularly heard doors slamming at the Underwoods' home near Poinsettia Park and Plum and her mother yelling at each other. On more than one occasion, they overheard Plum tell her mother she hated her. That it was 'my life/my business'.

I'm not sure it makes any difference whether Plum and Mrs Underwood got on or not. The fact she simply had a mother would have been enough to stir Izzy's jealousy. That comment at grade school on my first day: *I hate seeing them all with their mommies . . .*

I hated it too. Felt my loss more keenly with other kids and their mothers around.

'That's not your new information, is it?' I ask Elsa Stone.

I'll feel rather cheated if it is.

She shakes her head, wets her lips.

'No. What I've found out is much more' – she searches for the right word – 'revelatory.'

I feel myself tilting forward, tell her to go on.

'You know what the BAU is?' she asks. 'The FBI's Behavioral Analysis Unit . . .'

'Of course,' I say, by which I mean, I've watched *Criminal Minds*. 'It's all about psychology, right? Profiling.'

She nods. *Right.*

'Profiling's how Bundy got caught. The Unabomber. Loads of killers. No one understands the way murderers think like the FBI.'

I twist my coffee cup on its saucer, ask what this has got to do with Turtle Lake.

'I've got in touch with someone,' she says, fingers stroking the edge of her cardboard folder. 'A criminologist. Retired agent from the BAU. Works as a private investigator now.'

She starts telling me what a great guy he is. How you'd imagine it'd be daunting to speak to someone like that, but how, actually, he couldn't have been nicer.

'Just charming. A real gentleman, you know? He—'

My eyes go to her folder.

'What did he say?' I interrupt.

She looks down at the folder too, then back up. Interlaces her hands on top of it, bends forward at the waist.

Tells me –

'He doesn't believe Izzy and Lu killed Plum.'

NOW

Over the years, there have been plenty of people who've suggested my sister is innocent, that she and Lu didn't kill Plum. But they've all been crackpots. Conspiracy theorists. Forum fanatics. Dudes who live in their mothers' basements eating cold beans out of the can.

An ex-FBI agent, though. From the Behavioral Analysis Unit. That's a whole other animal.

Don't get your hopes up, I tell myself.

But it's too late. The adrenaline is already prickling.

Because what if Elsa Stone has the numbers? What if this guy is right?

I cradle my coffee cup to keep my hands from shaking.

'What makes him think they're not the murderers?' I ask.

'The stabbing wasn't what killed Plum,' Elsa says with something of a flourish.

I feel my shoulders slump, the bitter tang of disappointment on my tongue.

Of course, this was too good to be true.

'That's hardly news,' I say. 'The cause of death was suffocation.'

Mud in her throat, specifically.

Izzy and Lu held Plum down, ADA Madden told the jury in his opening statement. Pushed her face into the dirt while they stabbed her, possibly so no one would hear her screams.

That's who these girls are. Ruthless and calculating. Not mentally disordered, as Mr Kihm over at the defence table would have you believe . . .

Elsa Stone gives me a look. Is she smiling?

'Exactly,' she says. 'Plum was stabbed but the actual cause of death was suffocation.'

I really don't see where she's going with this. I scratch my head, tell her as much,

'Bill explained stabbing and asphyxiating are two very different ways to kill a person.'

'Bill's your FBI guy?'

She nods impatiently. *Keep up . . .*

'They have a saying at the BAU apparently – "what and why show you who". It's from *Mindhunter.*'

'That show on Netflix?'

'It's a book too.'

She takes a sip of her coffee, tucks a lock of her perfectly cut hair behind her ear.

'He told me the way a person kills speaks to their psyche. For instance, I don't know . . . someone unconfident might sneak up on their victim. Clock them from behind or whatnot. A blitz attack, he called it. Whereas someone socially confident might approach them in a bar and lure them away.'

I massage the back of my neck. I'm still not following.

'So?' I say.

'Like Bill said: stabbing and asphyxiating are two very different methods of killing. As such, they suggest different profiles. Different perpetrators.'

'He's saying Izzy or Lu stabbed Plum and then the other suffocated her? That still makes one of them the killer, Elsa.'

She shakes her head, breathes in like I'm being dense.

Maybe I am.

'Both girls stabbed her. We know that. They confessed, remember? Plus, two knives were found in the lake.'

In Izzy's case, the paring knife Dita used to cut up peaches for her famous cobbler.

'The number of stab wounds on Plum's body is what Bill calls "overkill". Excessive force, he described it as. An expression of pent-up rage.'

'What about asphyxiation?' I ask.

'Indicates a completely different profile. Strangulation is personal but holding a victim's face down is cold. It's not about rage. It's about getting the job done.'

'What about what Madden said?' I ask. 'Couldn't they have held her down while they stabbed her?'

She opens the cardboard folder, takes out what looks like a report. Passes it across.

'Read it for yourself. It's all in here. But to answer your question, no. He doesn't agree with Madden or the profiler who worked the case at the time. Behavioural science has come a long way since then, apparently.

'And having the wherewithal to press someone's face into the ground to prevent them screaming is out of character with such a frenzied knife attack.'

'One act was calm and rational. The other was pure emotion.'
She points out a line in the report:

Like oil and water, logic and emotion do not mix.

She slides the report across. I use the flashlight on my phone to read it.

Everything Elsa has told me is in there. And it's signed off by an ex-FBI agent. A real-life Aaron Hotchner.

I reach the end. Look up. Heart going at a thousand beats a minute.

'Lu was right,' Elsa says, watching me. 'Someone else was there that night. And that person killed Plum.'

NOW

Is it possible? Might Izzy really be innocent after all? My most fervent prayers answered?

My brain pours cold water on that one pretty quickly.

Because maybe my sister didn't actually kill Plum, but that doesn't mean she didn't try to. And as far as the US justice system is concerned, it makes her just as guilty as if she actually took her life.

'And not only that,' I say to Elsa Stone. 'We're still no closer to finding out what really happened at Turtle Lake. Who the mysterious third person was. Why they murdered her.'

She takes Bill's report back, tucks it away in the folder. Tells me, 'This is where you come in.'

'Where I come in?'

'We have the lines. Now we need you to colour them in.'

Her words conjure up Karl Kihm: *An attorney's job is to paint a good picture. Give the jury enough to colour between the lines.*

'I wish I could add some colour,' I say. 'But frankly, I think you might know more about Turtle Lake than I do.'

She shakes her head. Says she expects I know more than I think I do.

'The body, for example.'

'The body?' I repeat.

I'm starting to sound like a parrot.

'I couldn't understand how two thirteen-year-old girls could have moved it to a beach thirty miles away. Not unless they had help.'

The prosecution had their theory, of course – some tale about hitchhiking and a suitcase. A witness claimed to have seen a Ford pick-up pull over and give two girls a ride. But a driver had never come forward to corroborate the account and frankly it never rang true for me.

Izzy and Lu pitched up at a party with a human size bag? Or they left Plum's body while they went home to fetch one? Rode all the way to Washington Beach in a stranger's vehicle with a corpse rattling around in the trunk?

No, I'm not buying it.

Elsa taps the folder with the long nail on her index finger.

'Finally, there's another explanation.'

I frown, ask: 'What's that?'

'They didn't move the body. The real killer did.'

I concede that yes, that is possible.

'Think hard,' she says. 'You ever notice anyone hanging around the house? Hear the girls talking about anyone?'

I shrug.

'Only Ryder Grady.'

She shakes her head.

'Can't be him. Remember how he boasted to that guy he shared a cell with?'

I think about the documentary I watched a while back. The (very long) biography I ploughed through.

His girls would do anything for him, he bragged to his cell-mate – the one who would go on to snitch on Grady later, getting him the extra jail time he deserved.

'You know why they did it, don't you?' he said.

He was talking about Turtle Lake.

His cellmate said no. Grady responded by pointing at him-self.

'You're looking right at him,' he said.

A big grin on his face.

Elsa Stone is right. From what Grady said, he can't have been Plum's killer. Otherwise, he wouldn't he have said: You know why *they* did it?

And if he had finished the job he'd hardly have boasted about what Izzy and Lu had supposedly done for him.

He knew about it – he may even have been there – but he didn't commit the act.

'He was careful too,' Elsa tells me as we bat this about. 'Getting rid of his computer was smart. And how he conducted himself in his interrogation. His answers were clever, con-trolled. Almost like he was playing a game.'

'Not the sort to get his hands dirty,' I say, thinking back to one of the first things Elsa said to me.

'Definitely not,' she agrees.

'You must remember something else,' she presses. 'Someone else. Think, Finn. You were around then, I wasn't.'

I wish I had an answer for her but I don't.

'What about another member of Grady's group? One of the other girls?'

I shake my head, tell her no.

'I just don't see it. They were all under fifteen. It wouldn't have been any easier for one of them to move the body. And even if it was one of the other girls, that doesn't tell us who.'

'Back to square one.' Elsa sighs.

I grind the heel of my hand into my temple, feel a weight settle on my shoulders.

Because we're so far back from square one, we're not even on the board.

I finally have an answer. And I still have no answer.

Someone else killed Plum.

But I have no idea who – and no way of finding out.

NOW

I come to on the couch in my living room with no memory of how I got there. Though my arid mouth and pounding head give a clue – as does the empty Smirnoff bottle lying on its side on the floor. A dark puddle darkens the carpet. Gives off boozy fumes.

Damn waste.

I go to right the bottle, but my arm doesn't move. I'm made of lead. Everything hurts. Everything is pointless.

There's a sour smell, like gone-off milk. A snail trail of dried vomit down my shirt front. On the couch cushions too. Nice.

Get up, says my brain. *The state of you.*

I want to get up but I can't. Body and brain in disconnect.

Morning sunshine filters through the slats in the blinds, painting prison bars on the walls. I close my eyes to block it out. The light is an intrusion. And it's hurting my head.

I sleep on and off, a fitful, fevered sleep, so that when I wake it's as though I haven't slept at all.

My phone's been ringing. Several missed calls from old Bostock. Now she's texting: *Where are you, Kate?*

Kat, not Kate. Silly cow.

But I'm the silly cow, not her. Because my name's not Kat either.

Hours trickle by. The sky begins to darken.

At some point, I manage to heave myself up, grab another bottle out the pantry. And then one more for luck.

I take them upstairs, crawl into bed in yesterday's clothes. Drink.

Time passes. Blackness creeping in at the edge of my vision. Dizziness. Cold sweats. A chaser to make them go away.

The days meld together until I'm down to the emergency fifth I keep in my nightstand. My body calms even as I'm uncapping it. I take a slug. The vertigo subsides. With it, the barrage of thoughts, the knowledge of never knowing.

I forget all about Izzy and about Grady and about how I'll never be sure what really happened that night. Never know who really killed Plum. Never know why.

And then the booze bliss fades and it all comes back. A fresh wave pulling me under.

I have the urge to cry but I can't. My eyes are dry. Lousy body, good for nothing.

At some point, a woman's voice calls from outside:

'Kat? Are you there?'

'Fuck off,' I growl.

Or maybe I don't. Maybe I just think the words. Talking is such effort.

I roll on to my other side. Shutter my eyes.

Give in to the darkness.

NOW

Wednesday? Thursday?

Who knows . . .

I'm on my hands and knees rifling through the cabinet under my bathroom sink. Panic courses through me. My body on fire.

Where is it? It's got to be here. I know it is . . .

I pull out packets of sanitary pads, cosmetic bags, talcum powder. Toss them on to the floor. Grab another armful. Toilet paper, shampoo bottles, boxes of Dove soap . . .

Where is it?

My vodka stash is wiped out. But there's alcohol in cough syrup. I'm sure I read that somewhere. Only I can't find the damn bottle.

Box of Band-Aids, bottles of sunscreen, a tube of Colgate . . . and then, there at the back . . . thank you, Lord!

My whole being loosens, relief a warm bath.

My fingers close around the Benylin, uncap it, bring it to my thirsty lips. I tip my head back. The tiniest trickle dribbles out.

The tears come then. I hurl the bottle at the wall. Scream from the pit of myself.

An animal howl. The cry of a wolf.

Maybe it's the sound, a literal wake-up call. Or perhaps it's the sight of the broken glass all over my bathroom floor. The sticky splatter coating the tiles. Physical indicators of just how far I've fallen.

Rock bottom is a bathroom that looks like a bombsite.

I sit there amongst the wreckage, shards on my thighs. A thick smell of cherry on the air, and the onion smell of days-old sweat.

What am I doing?

What have I become?

How have I let things get this bad?

The tears are different now. Shame rather than frustration. Disgust at myself.

I can't carry on like this. I won't. And for the first time, I actually mean it.

I'm done with drinking.

I get up, splash cold water on my face. Stare at myself in the mirror.

'What do you look like?'

My skin is pale and puffy. There are panda circles under my eyes. A breakout on my chin.

I brush my teeth. Change my filthy shirt. Go downstairs to fetch a cloth and a dustpan. Clean up then clean off . . .

I've got the shakes. Nerves jangling. A scalpel driving through my brain.

Good, I think. *Remember this . . .*

The envelope lands on the doormat as I reach the last step: large. Manila. Thick.

I check my watch. Bit late for the postman, isn't it?

I pick up the envelope, feel the weight of it, and only then do I register the name on the front. Not Kat, but my old name: Finn Jackman. Written in a hand I recognise but can't immediately place.

My first thought, of course, is Elsa Stone.

We haven't spoken since that evening in the café. I don't suppose we'll speak again.

Strange, but the thought makes me sad. I should have taken her number. It always came up as withheld when she called me.

I resisted talking to her, put up a good fight, but when I finally let my walls down, I found I quite liked sharing.

I've never spoken like that with anyone about Turtle Lake. It felt good. And also oddly reassuring to know I wasn't the only one struggling. That someone else was in the same leaky boat.

I turn the envelope over, wondering if there's a return address. Perhaps this is a parting gift before she heads back to the States. Evidence she's compiled, maybe? Printouts like the ones stacked up all over my house.

Towers of them thick with dust that I can't bring myself to throw away just in case there's a clue in there I've missed.

Is she still outside? Maybe I can catch her.

I open the front door. An unfamiliar feeling of wanting to talk. To connect with someone who feels the same way I do. Who understands.

I look left and right, scanning the street. There's no sign of her though.

Weird. Where did she disappear to?

I'm about to shut the door when I see him. A man getting into a Ford Focus with a rusted fender. Looking over his shoulder at me. The only person on the street.

Alcohol gives you courage when you're drinking. It makes you stupid when you've stopped.

Stupid and aggressive and a bit paranoid too.

'Did you put that letter through my door?' I say, marching up to him. 'Who are you? How do you know my name?'

He twists his torso so that he's facing me. One foot in, the other foot out of his car.

'Just the delivery boy,' he says, then smiles because he's forty at least.

Hardly a boy.

I rub my arms, shiver. It's cold out here and I've got nothing on my feet.

'Delivery from who?' I say.

In my head, my father's voice: *Whom, not who . . .*

The man shrugs, folds his body into the driver's seat.

Starts the engine.

'Only one way to find out . . .' he says.

NOW

Who sent the envelope? How do they know who I am?

How did they find me?

Almost exactly the same questions I asked myself when Elsa Stone called me up that first time. The same nagging fear too. My animal brain telling me I'm in danger. That the jig's up.

As so often over the last few days, my mind goes to Turtle Lake. To the mystery third person. Can I really be so sure it wasn't Ryder Grady?

What if he *was* there that night? What if he sent the text message too? A message the police didn't believe came from Plum because the language didn't chime with the way teenagers write.

So, written by an adult? An adult like him?

Grady is in prison. But he must have contacts on the outside. Fellow degenerates who photographed 'his girls', and plenty more besides. Degenerates he's never named.

'I want you ladies to show my man here a lot of love tonight,' he apparently told Izzy and the others. 'He's in magazines. He'll make you famous. Be nice to him now . . .'

Has one of them tracked me down? Did they track Dita down too?

Was Elsa Stone right? Was Dita afraid of someone? Were they threatening her?

I'm staring at the spot the Ford Focus has just vacated, putting off opening the envelope that's waiting for me inside. Scared of what it might contain.

Of who it might be from.

I take a deep breath, fill my lungs with the cold March air.

Rip off the Band-Aid, chick . . .

I'm turning back towards the house when—

'Oh SHIT!'

My hands go to my mouth, my stomach to my feet.

How could I? I ran out without putting the door on the latch and now it's slammed shut. Trapped me out here in the cold with no keys and no shoes.

When I first moved on to the street, my neighbour, Mrs Gupta, told me there was a community WhatsApp thread and did I want her to add me in? I turned her down the same way I turned down her offer to keep my spare key.

Are you sure? Never know when you might get locked out, yaar.

Well, quite . . .

There's literally no one I can ask for help. No one who knows me apart from Mrs G, and judging by her empty driveway, she's not home.

If I'd bothered to go to a single one of the coffee mornings she organised or joined the Area Watch, the neighbours might invite me in now. Put the kettle on while I call a locksmith.

But who's going to open the door to a complete stranger? To

a woman in bare feet who hasn't washed for days? Who, looks like a tramp.

I know I wouldn't.

I look up at my house. Wish I were MacGyver. Or had at least opened a window.

I'm not MacGyver though, just a drunk without a friend in the world.

I sink down on the stoop, bury my head in my hands. Shiver like I'm high.

And that's how she finds me.

I don't hear her Volvo pull up or the pad of her approaching footsteps.

Only her voice as she says –

'Praise be, she lives!'

NOW

I look up at the sound of her voice and wipe my eyes quickly.

'Willow?' I mumble, embarrassed to be caught in such a state. 'What are you doing here?'

'I was worried,' she says. 'You going AWOL like that. I told Mrs B I'd swing by again on my way in, check for signs of life . . .'

So, it was her outside the house that day. I think about how I ignored her, went back to sleep.

'Still kicking,' I tell her, force a smile.

'Was beginning to think I might have to call the police . . .'

The word 'police' makes my muscles tense. Has done ever since Arnold and his men took Izzy away that night.

Willow tilts her head.

'Are you okay?' she asks.

I shrug, tell her: 'Yeah, I'm fine.'

My default response. Then I laugh, because I'm so obviously not fine.

'It's been a rough few days,' I admit.

Not coming up with some excuse? Who am I? It isn't like I can't think on my feet, even if I'm not wearing shoes.

Willow gives me one of the tight smiles I remember from after my mother died.

Poor little lamb . . .

I hated those smiles, but for some reason, I don't mind it on her. Willow's smile doesn't look like pity. It looks like empathy. And when she asks if I want to 'talk about it', I find that maybe I do.

'Any chance you could phone a locksmith for me first? I managed to shut myself out. Would hate to miss the call from Mensa.'

She grins. Tells me, of course. Pulls out her mobile and removes her jacket.

'Put this on. You must be freezing.'

It's such a kind gesture, it makes my eyes prick. I didn't have a single comforting thing to say to her at school, yet here she is, comforting me.

Reminding me what it means to be human.

'I do remember you,' I tell her. 'I don't know why I said I didn't.'

She shrugs. *Water under the bridge . . .*

'It was a long time ago. But not so long I don't remember what rough days are like.'

I tell her I'm sorry, that I wish I'd been there for her. And it's true, I do. I wish I'd been less focused on myself, better able to see what was going on around me. That I wasn't the only one hurting.

'I'm fine now,' she says. 'That's what matters. Got my grandma to thank.'

'Your grandma?' I repeat.

'She realised what was going on at home, got me out of there and moved me in with her. Fattened me up with her homemade chicken soup. Medicine, she called it. Introduced me to Chekhov and *Murder She Wrote*. Every Saturday night, we watched Jessica Fletcher tucked up together on the couch with a big bowl of Doritos. But not the spicy ones because they gave her heartburn.

'That lady changed my life. I used to be so bottled up before.' She laughs. 'And yet now, as you see, you can't shut me up!'

I laugh with her. It feels good.

She's been scrolling on her phone for locksmiths.

'Bingo!' she says, showing me the screen. 'This one's got one of those pizza promises: here in fifteen minutes or money off.'

At the top of the website is a slogan:

Help is just a phone call away . . .

It strikes me that this might be the first time I've accepted help from anyone since we lost Izzy.

NOW

'There you go, love,' the locksmith says, opening the front door as if this is his house and he's inviting *me* in. 'Bet you had a nasty fright, eh?'

I'm not his 'love' and I suspect the bigger fright is whatever's waiting for me in the envelope on the doormat, but I stitch on a smile, ask how much I owe. Keep my snarky comments to myself.

Willow has been waiting with me. She follows my gaze, eyes landing on the letter. On the name written across the front: *Finn Jackman.*

Turtle Lake is one of the most notorious crimes of the century. There's no way she won't have heard of it. And I'd put money on her having heard of Finn Jackman too. It's certainly more memorable than Jane Doe.

I wait for the inevitable question, the one I got asked all the time after Izzy's arrest:

Aren't you that girl's sister? The girl who . . . ?

But Willow Rowling doesn't mention Izzy, just asks if I need anything before she heads off.

'You know what Mrs Bostock's like – a real bee in her bun about being late . . .'

I'm about to correct her – *you mean bonnet?* – when I realise she's making a joke. Old Bostock wears her nasty hair tied in a knot at the back of her head. Same style every day. Same cardigan too. Neither suit her.

I think back to Dita's malapropisms, how I was always correcting them. Perhaps she was joking too and I just didn't get it.

Maybe it's thinking about Dita, the sucker punch that gets me every time I do. Maybe it's because Willow's been decent enough not to pry. Or maybe it's just because I'm so sick of hiding, of pretending to be someone I'm not.

Whatever the reason, I hear myself say, 'I changed my name when I was ten. It used to be Finn. Izzy Jackman's my sister. The Turtle Lake killer.'

I wait for the horror to show on Willow's face. The revulsion she won't be able to disguise.

But instead, she just nods as if I've mentioned something nice I've got planned for the weekend.

'Times I'd like to change my name too,' she says.

'Because of what happened to you?'

She laughs, shakes her head.

'Because Willow Rowling is a really shit name.'

A warm feeling spreads inside my chest. A feeling Willow and I might become friends after all. That maybe someone might actually like me despite knowing who I am.

Is that even possible?

'Any message for the boss?' she asks, hand on the latch, preparing to leave.

'Tell her I'll be in tomorrow,' I say. 'And that I'm sorry I couldn't call but I'm better now.'

She does a finger salute, tells me: roger that. Then apologises for being cheesy.

'I've watched way too much *Homeland*.'

I close the front door behind her. Then I take a steadying breath, sit on the stairs and open the envelope that's been waiting for me this whole time.

NOW

In my ears a ringing and the horse hooves of my galloping heart.

The letter is from Dita. That's why I recognised the handwriting on the front of the envelope. The cursive from Post-it notes dotted around the kitchen in Carlsbad. On recipe cards and shopping lists and in my school reading-record book.

How could I not have realised immediately it was her writing? It feels like a betrayal, that I've let myself forget.

She begins: *Chickadee* . . .

My chest stabs. The endearment conjures up my childhood the way a song conjures up old feelings.

It evokes nostalgia and loss. And the deepest love.

I pinch my sinuses to stop the tears coming but my eyes prick anyway.

How did she track me down? A PI? Is that who the guy outside was?

I trace her handwriting with the tip of my index finger.

Dita! At last . . .

And yet, thanks to Elsa Stone's little visit to her, I'll never be able to reply. Never be able to tell her how much I still miss her. Never hear her voice again.

I inhale deeply, hands cupped over my nose and mouth. And then, I start to read . . .

Chickadee,

A journalist came to see me today. The truth is coming out. There's no way to stop it. But I need you to hear it from me first.

And not to blame him.

The journalist must be Elsa. But what truth is she talking about? Why wouldn't she want it coming out? Who mustn't I blame?

Was Elsa Stone right? Was she protecting someone?

Withdrawal is disorientating. I'm struggling to focus, my body screaming for a drink. But I'm not falling into that hole again. That snake pit.

I take another breath. Continue reading.

This is my story.

Yours too, I suppose . . .

Her story – our story – starts with Plum and Lu, she says. Those girls were trouble right from the start. She could smell it a mile away. Plum especially. That need she had to always be the centre of everything, the constant attention-seeking.

You remember how she'd never sit at a table? How she always insisted on standing up to eat? Like she was on the stage. Look at me!

Izzy was different around them. Finally out of her shell, Dita says. She had worried about her for so long, Dita couldn't remember a time she wasn't worried. Didn't understand why my sister was so awkward around people. Why she found it so difficult to make friends. A sweet girl like her . . . people should be lining up to be her pal.

'Leave her be,' my father advised. 'It's something she needs to figure out for herself. You can't run her life for her, Dita.'

And then Izzy started at Heritage Elm and befriended 'that Plum and Lu' and everything changed. Dita was torn. Izzy finally had friends, but Dita didn't like them one bit. Plum especially was no good, so entitled.

Calling me the help, indeed!

Worse, though, was the hold she had over my sister. Izzy would have jumped out of a plane if Plum told her to, wouldn't have been able to do it fast enough.

Copied everything that little girl said, do you remember? Even started dressing like her, speaking the way she did . . .

Dita spoke to my father. The judge was smart. He'd know what to do. And he had answers, of course, but those answers did nothing to reassure her.

'The main thing is she's fitting in,' he said. 'Izzy's no fool. If these girls aren't right for her, she'll see that and find someone else who is.'

But what if she didn't?

Dita knew I felt the same way but she didn't want me getting anxious. That was her job, not mine.

Lu and Plum came over to pick Izzy up the night of the party at Turtle Lake. Not that Dita immediately realised that's where they were going. Of course, she didn't! Boys and alcohol? She'd never have given Izzy permission to go somewhere like that.

If she hadn't happened to overhear the girls talking about sneaking out, she'd have believed they really were just having a sleepover at Plum's.

'We're going to watch *Sweet Home Alabama*,' Izzy had told her. 'Plum's cleaned the store out of gummy worms!'

How could Izzy lie to her that way? Looked her right in the eye too!

She was all ready to storm into her bedroom, let my sister know she'd been found out. But then she had a better idea. She'd sneak out too, catch her in the act. Teach her a lesson about lying. Teach my father a lesson too about not listening to her.

It was time for him to wake up and smell the toast. All that talk about letting Izzy run her own life! She was only thirteen . . .

As Dita tippy-toed down the stairs later that night, she heard my father stir. Heard him get up out of bed and open his door. He always slept 'like a dead person'. So what was he doing awake now?

Quickly-quietly, quietly, she opened the front door. Pulled it shut gently behind her. Placed her feet carefully on the gravel so as not to make a sound.

The Oldsmobile wouldn't start. She glanced back at the house, tried the ignition again. My father's shadow moved across the glass above the front door.

What was he doing? Why was he downstairs?

The engine spluttered, came to life. Dita hit the gas.

She didn't know the way to Turtle Lake; drove with one hand on the wheel and the other holding a map. For a crazy moment, she thought my father was tailing her. Headlamps following in the dark.

But she was being stupid. Wasn't she?

Paranoid because, really, she should have told him what she was up to. Only what if he'd tried to stop her?

No, it was better to do this her way. So much easier. Better for everyone.

She arrived at Turtle Lake. Pulled over. Cut the engine.

The place was heaving. *Like flies on leftovers.*

A bonfire. Kids dancing. Swigging beer.

Hundreds of them!

How was she ever going to find Izzy?

What if she was too late and a nasty high school boy was already having his way with her?

Izzy, so desperate to be liked. She'd be plasticine in their hands.

And oh Lord, what if she was drinking? Just a few sips can damage your brain at her age. Get you addicted. Make you do things you shouldn't.

Dita should never have let it get this far. She should have said 'no' to her going out when she had the chance. Should have put her 'shoes down' hard, grounded Izzy for lying then and there.

Why had she tried to be clever? Why hadn't she just called her out?

Where was she?

What if . . . ?

A male moving near the trees caught her eye. A spike of adrenaline shot through her veins. Her first mad thought was that it was my father. But this man was blonde. And when had the judge ever worn a leather jacket?

She shook her head. Told herself to focus. Her imagination was getting the better of her. So busy worrying how my father would react if he knew what she was doing, she was seeing him everywhere.

Keep alive, she told herself, and that's when she spotted her.

My sister disappearing into a cluster of cottonwoods with Plum and Lu.

Lu was leading the way, beckoning to the other two to keep up. Brushing the brambles aside with a big stick.

What were they up to?

Why were they going somewhere so secluded?

Was it some illicit voulez-vous?

Oh dear, oh dear, oh dear . . .

Dita hurried to catch up to them, stumbling over roots and half-buried rocks. By the time she got there, it was already happening.

Curiosity kills the kitten, they say. Only there were no kittens there that night. Only angry cats . . .

It was dark. At first it just seemed like a game, until she heard the scream. The way it tore the air.

Plum was on the ground, curled in a ball, protecting her head with her arms.

'Why?' she whimpered.

The breeze carried an iron tang. It got in Dita's mouth so she could taste it.

She was hidden in the undergrowth, frozen in shock. All she could do was watch.

A frenzy of movement. The flash of metal. Then the two girls standing over Plum.

'Liar!' Izzy hissed, reaching down.

She tore something off Plum's neck, hurled it into the undergrowth.

Lu kicked Plum in the ribs.

'Skank,' she said. 'Homewrecker.'

Dita must have made a noise, though she was still unable to speak or move.

As if I was in a movie and someone had pressed pause . . .

'There's someone here,' Lu whispered.

'You're being paranoid,' Izzy replied, though she didn't sound too sure.

Lu tugged her arm.

'Let's get out of here!'

They ran off giggling as if they were playing ding-dong-ditch. As if they hadn't just stabbed their best friend twenty-one times.

A moan broke the spell. Unfroze Dita.

She says she doesn't remember going over to Plum, just kneeling in the dirt beside her. Seeing the blood. The way it pooled out of her on to the ground. So much blood it made her flesh creep. She'd always been squeamish.

Yet despite everything, she didn't believe the evidence of her own eyes.

Izzy couldn't have done this. Not her sweet girl!

On autopilot, she went to take off her jacket, thinking to stem the bleeding. Though where to start?

Thank goodness for the dark, the way it turned the blood black. Made it easier to pretend it wasn't blood at all.

'It's okay,' Dita whispered. 'You're okay.'

Plum grabbed her wrist, nails digging into Dita's flesh. Eyes flashing wide.

'The . . . help . . . Izzy . . . Lu . . .' she stammered, a gurgling in her throat. 'Call police . . .'

You told me once you were Cassandra. Do you remember that, chick? A Trojan horse you said was cursed to see the future and never be believed. *But suddenly I was the one who could see the future. Could see what Plum Underwood would do if she lived.*

It wasn't a conscious decision. Just pure maternal instinct. Pure love.

I didn't even realise I was holding her face into the ground until she stopped struggling. Went limp like she was a raggedy doll . . .

Dita became a lion. Her mind sharp as if she'd drunk a whole flask of coffee and washed it down with Red Bull.

She drove the Oldsmobile into the trees, loaded Plum into the trunk. Wrapped her in the plastic sheets that were still there from the new coffee table she'd recently picked up from IKEA. Took the roundabout route away from the lake so the partygoers wouldn't spot her, though frankly they were so out of it they wouldn't have known what they were looking at if they had.

The amount of beer in that place, it was like a brewery . . .

She'd scrub the car out when she got home, use Lysol and the new scouring pads she'd bought to clean the oven. Burn them after. Maybe get the vehicle valeted while she was at it. Never hurts to be thorough.

Already she was making plans, realising she'd had no choice but to finish what Izzy had started. What else could she do? What else could she have done?

Because what if Plum had made it out alive? What if she had gone to the police and reported Izzy?

Dita couldn't have allowed that. Couldn't let that little madam ruin *my sister's life.*

Didn't I always say I'd do anything for you girls . . . ?

NOW

I pause, press my fingertips against my eyes until I see stars dance.

Dita killed Plum? No, it's impossible! The letter's a fake, just like that text message. Someone must be setting her up.

And yet the handwriting is unmistakably Dita's. The same cursive I remember from the shopping lists stuck up on the fridge in Carlsbad –

Applesauce . . .

Pasta . . .

Brownie mix (Trader Joe's) . . .

But if someone was threatening her? Could they have forced her to write this letter?

Jesus, what if she didn't kill herself at all . . . ?

What if . . .

What if . . . ?

I'm grasping though. Reaching, my father would have said if we were in his court. *Jury, disregard that . . .* Because there's too much in here that only Dita could have known. Not least what she was always telling us: *I'd do anything for you girls . . .*

How she was more of a mother than a housekeeper to us.

That I hated Plum and Lu too.

Memories swarm, black as crows.

Dita plying Detective Arnold with baked goods. Me thinking she had a crush on him, singing that stupid K-I-S-S-I-N-G song whenever she mentioned his name.

Dita and Arnold sitting in a tree . . .

But what if she didn't have the hots for him?

What if she was just buttering him up?

Her heart may well have fluttered each time he stopped by, though perhaps not for the reason I thought.

And how about the posters she insisted Izzy stick up around town?

Let's see what Detective Arnold thinks. I'm sure he'll be pleased you're helping.

Always trying to impress Arnold. Always trying to put Izzy in a good light.

How blind I've been! How stupid!

Another crow lands. Another memory.

The night of the vigil.

'That chocolate on your sleeve?' I asked, pleased to have a chance to get my own back for some slight earlier. 'I thought you were dieting.'

'How'd that get there?' she said, rubbing at the marks, removing the jacket when the stains wouldn't come off.

On her skin, the first puckerings of gooseflesh. She shivered, wrapped her arms round herself.

I felt bad then. There was a chilly breeze blowing off the ocean, the sky darkening.

'No one cares if it's dirty, Dita.'

'I care,' she said.

Shivered again.

But what if it was never about the jacket being dirty? What if the stains weren't chocolate?

She talks about Plum grabbing her wrist. Is that what the stains were from?

A dying girl's blood?

I'm hot and cold, both at once. Bile rising up my digestive tract.

I've loved Dita my whole life. Loved a murderer.

There are four pages left of her letter.

I pick it up again, my hands trembling.

Read on.

NOW

I sometimes ask myself whether I'd have done it if I'd known what else I'd have to do. The toll it would take. I think, no way, Andre. But the truth is, of course I would have.

That's what love is, Finn. You'll do anything.

I remember when Dita first came to live with us, how she'd told us her mother was sick and how she'd stayed in Green River to look after her even though the place bored her to tears.

'Family's all you got,' she said. 'You do everything you can to take care of them.'

I never considered that might extend to murder.

She was worried about Izzy after Turtle Lake, she says. It was like my sister hadn't absorbed the seriousness of what she'd done. The way she'd mooch about on the hammock in our backyard wishing we had a pool. Tut when Detective Arnold questioned her about Plum. Tell him: 'You've asked me that already.'

She was so blasé I could almost believe she hadn't stabbed Plum at all.

It wasn't just Izzy's state of mind that worried Dita though. It was the constant fear she was going to trip up and give herself away. That's why she had to get rid of her diary, she says. Izzy was keeping it in a lockbox by that point (Dita hadn't been able to read it for months) but a combination code would be no match for Arnold and his team. Goodness knows how much Izzy had written down. Rope that could end up hanging her.

I was on high alert all the time. It was exhausting.

Dita did everything she could think of to keep the 'foxes at bay'. She posted rumours in chat rooms that quickly took off. Anything that took the heat off Izzy and directed it elsewhere.

'Plum had taken an overdose' was one rumour she was particularly proud of. Another was that she was having trouble at home. Her most ambitious story, though, was that Plum had joined a sex ring.

It was more on the money than she realised.

The night of the search at Turtle Lake, she intended to plant 'evidence' that suggested Plum had simply run away. A phone charger, since no one seemed able to believe a teenage girl would play hooky without taking one. She knew I'd be close by, was angsting about how to sneak it out of her bag without me or anyone else noticing.

That's the real reason I didn't want you coming along, chick. But of course, you were stubborn. Refused to be left out as per usual.

Even so, she might have managed it had Bob Murphy not gone and found that torn scrap of Izzy's shirt first.

I was thrown a boomerang there.

No matter, she had Plum's phone.

I'm not sure why I kept hold of it, but I sure was glad I had. I used it to message Lu, figured it would take the sting out of what Bob happened upon at the search.

She hadn't factored in the police's linguistics analysis team though. Or the science:

Bodies float.

NOW

The truth always comes out, she says.

I had no idea the body would wash up like that. Once I'd tipped her off the pier, I figured that was that. Home dry, if you'll pardon the pun . . .

My father came to find Dita after Detective Arnold had led Izzy away. My sister in cuffs, frogmarched to the waiting cruiser.

The moment all my nightmares became real.

'We need to talk,' he said.

'My heart's broken,' Dita told him, mopped her eye with the corner of her apron.

He looked at her, eyes narrowed.

'But you weren't surprised.'

'Sir?'

She furrowed her brow, played dumb. But my father wasn't a fool. His job was reading people (even if he was no good at reading his own daughter).

'I was knocked for six when Arnold handed me that warrant,'

he said, a watchful expression on his face. 'But you . . . you were expecting it.'

Dita stammered. What could she say? What should she say?

My father's hair was sticking up in tufts like he'd been tugging at it. His shoulders sagged.

'Please, Dita. You've got to tell me what you know. I can't help her if you keep me in the dark.'

Dita says part of her was relieved to finally open up. There were times she couldn't sleep, the burden of her secret weighed on her so heavily.

So, I told him everything . . .

She took a half step towards him as she wound up, half expecting a hug even though they'd never hugged before. Relief, gratitude. An acknowledgement that they were in this together. Something.

But he stayed completely still. Body rigid, eyes blinking.

'This whole time?' he whispered. 'You said nothing?'

He ran his palm across his forehead. Stared at her in disbelief.

'Izzy's a daughter to me,' Dita told him. 'What else could I do?'

My father spoke again. Such sadness in his voice.

'She's not your daughter, Dita. She's mine. I trusted you. You should have come to me.'

I'm your family, Finn . . .

I never understood the hardness that set over his face when he said that to me. But it makes sense now. He must have been reliving the conversation with Dita. She says she relived it a thousand times too. The way he told her, 'You need to leave.'

'Leave?'

Her throat caught. She couldn't leave. Izzy and I were her babies. Her everything.

But my father wouldn't listen.

'Think of Finn,' she begged him. 'What's in store the next few months. She needs me. She needs—'

My father sighed, moistened his lips.

'You're right,' he said. 'Finn does need you now. Maybe more than ever.'

Dita's heart lifted, praise the Lord and hallelujah!

'You won't regret it, sir!' She only just managed to restrain herself from throwing her arms round his neck. 'I promise not to keep a single thing from you ever again.'

'You realise it's just for the time being?'

The hallelujahs withered.

'Just for the time being?'

'I trusted you,' my father replied, the same sad note as before. 'I trusted you . . .'

I think about how he said he couldn't get Dita a visa to come to England with us. And how he couldn't meet my gaze as he said it.

He obviously never even tried. At last, I know why.

Dita's letter draws to a close. She tells me what he said to her, the day he announced we were leaving California:

I'm an officer of the court. I broke my oath by keeping quiet. Folk are right, what they're saying about me. I am guilty. They just don't know why.

For so long, I've resented my father for leaving Dita behind.

But as her words sink in, that resentment begins to dissipate the way the sun would burn through the morning mist back home.

At the beginning of her letter, Dita told me not to blame him. She says it again at the end:

Don't blame your daddy, chick.

But what am I not supposed to blame him for?

For making me leave California? Or for not revealing what really happened at Turtle Lake?

I don't blame him for either, not now I know why. Though I do wish he'd said something. Maybe not when I was ten, but when I was older at least.

He should have told me the real reason Dita didn't come with us to London. And why he hadn't mailed my letters. I wish too that he'd told me why he was so sad all the time. Maybe I could have helped him if he had.

Maybe we could have helped each other.

I reach the end of Dita's confession, tears blotting the ink.

It's all coming out now. The journalist says there's new evidence that proves what really happened at Turtle Lake. That Izzy and Lu didn't kill Plum. That someone else did.

I'm too old for jail, chick. If they lock me up, I'll never get out. Never see Washington Beach again. Never hear the mockingbirds sing.

Which is why I have to go this way. And why I needed you to hear the truth from me first.

I love you, chick.

Forgive me, please.

Dita

NOW

I sit, staring at the pages in my hand. The words blurred and swimming.

How did I not guess? How did I miss what was right in front of me?

Looking back, the clues were everywhere, right down to Dita's hinky grammar whenever she spoke to Arnold. A sure indicator of discomfort.

And yet, despite her lengthy confession, I can still hardly believe it. The woman who stroked my hair until I fell back asleep after a nightmare is the same woman who held a girl's face down in the dirt until she stopped breathing. Pressed with such force, her throat filled with earth.

What else could I have done?

It's the cornerstone of every true crime documentary I've ever watched: *none of us knows what we're capable of until we're pushed . . .*

Does violence make us monsters? Or human?

After my sister was arrested, my guilt was all-consuming. I knew I was partly to blame for what happened to Plum, that my lie set events rolling. And that not saying anything about

Ryder Grady allowed things to go as far as they did. Added to that, the world treated me like I was guilty too, simply by virtue of the fact I was related to Izzy.

Because I was part of the breaking news. News broadcast all round the world, a story still being discussed in internet chat rooms twenty years later.

The guilt I'm feeling now comes from a different place though. It comes from having loved a killer and failing to see that's what she was.

I loved Izzy too. But my love for Dita was different. She was my protector. My rock.

My father's words: *I trusted you . . .*

The person who looked after me, a taker of life.

A cold sweat spreads over my skin as I begin to accept that's what Dita was. A murderer. One who acted in cold blood. Who cleaned up calmly after herself.

My father knew, yet he said nothing. He didn't report Dita, didn't tell Plum's parents how their daughter really died.

Izzy would have gone to prison regardless of whether or not she were responsible for the 'fatal blow'. She and Lu stabbed her twenty-one times. They were guilty of homicide even if Plum didn't die by their hands.

Telling the police about Dita wouldn't have saved Izzy. But my father was right, he was an officer of the court. He had a duty to uphold the law.

To make sure justice was done.

The world's full of folk who think . . . they're better than everyone else . . . But in a court of law, everyone has to abide by the same rules.

No wonder he hated himself.

I never fitted in here, never tried to. Worked hard at keeping my accent and my Americanisms. Refused to spell the way the British do or use the metric system. An outsider in every way possible.

My classmates went home at the end of every day to their 2.4 families. I lived alone with my old man because my sister was in jail and my mother was dead.

An alien in both senses of the word..

My father didn't fit in either. To be fair, he was hardly the gregarious sort back home, preferring his port and slippers to evenings out with friends. *There's no company like a good book* . . .

But after we moved to London, he retreated even further into himself, until all that was left was a shell that would tell me 'good morning' and 'goodnight' and not much else.

He'd lined up work at University College London before we arrived, a teaching post in the law faculty. I don't remember him going in though. Perhaps he lost the job, but there was always food in the fridge (mostly pizza and microwave meals).

I never asked how work was going. Never really thought about it. By then I was as lost as he was, my gaze turned inwards as his was. Fixed on the past. Life paused the moment Judge Mortimer banged his gavel and we lost Izzy.

My letters to Dita were my only outlet, though it's not much of a conversation when the other person doesn't write you back.

Hundreds of letters and not a single reply. In the end, I gave up, unaware of the Faustian pact of silence she'd made with my father.

One that ultimately damned them both.

NOW

It's like surveying your street after a tornado. Wreckage strewn everywhere. The familiar made strange. Unsure where to put your feet.

Dita asked for forgiveness but is forgiveness mine to give?

All the way through her letter, she says she killed Plum to protect Izzy, that she acted out of love. But was love the only thing driving her?

Or was she also fuelled by hate?

Dita wasn't just a housekeeper. She was our family, whatever my father may have said later. But to Plum, she was only ever 'the help'. A hired hand whom she treated as such – and made a point of doing so.

That night after dinner, for instance:

My sister and Lu had taken their plates over to the side, but Plum had left hers on the table, knife and fork splayed like dead soldiers, for Dita to clean up.

'What did your last servant die of?' Dita called after her.

From the corridor came Plum's voice, a stage whisper designed for Dita to hear:

'What does she think she gets paid for . . . ?'

I remember the look on Dita's face. Hurt, I thought at the time, but it could just as easily have been rage.

'Entitled little madam,' she muttered under her breath.

Plum didn't only disrespect Dita though, she rivalled her too. Before she befriended Izzy, Dita's influence over my sister was total. Even my father deferred to her.

If Dita says it's okay, it's fine by me . . .

But then Little Miss Plum came along and everything changed. As Dita says, Izzy didn't just want to be like her, she wanted to *be* her too. Ryder Grady would eventually take over the strings, but until Izzy fell in with him, Plum was the one who made her dance. Dita's control lost for good, her authority turned to dust.

The evening Plum announced she was a vegetarian, is an example. Izzy and Lu quickly followed suit. Dita put her foot down, wasted her breath.

'No one has the right to tell you what to put in your body,' Plum told Izzy.

My sister lowered her fork, said to Dita, 'You don't get to tell me what I do and don't eat.'

Plum rewarded her with a smile.

Dita wasn't smiling though.

When she smothered Plum, was she only thinking of protecting Izzy? Or was she remembering those occasions as well? Did a part of her want to teach a lesson to the 'entitled little madam'? A lesson she would take too far.

Calling me the help, indeed!

As I struggle to make sense of it all, another question rears up:

If Dita really wanted to protect my sister, why not tell the police it was her who killed Plum?

I twist my hair into a rope, let it drop.

Why didn't Dita take the fall?

Why didn't she confess twenty years ago?

Why didn't she come forward when it might have made a difference?

It gets me wondering how much she really told my father. Because while I can believe he wouldn't have ratted on her for protecting Izzy (sending the text from Plum's phone, watching out for her with Arnold . . .) I just can't accept that he'd have kept schtum if he'd known she'd committed actual murder.

A Superior Court judge. A man who'd made it his life's work to uphold the law . . .

It simply doesn't ring true.

At the beginning of her letter, Dita told me she wanted me to hear the truth from her.

But has she told it to me? The whole truth and nothing but . . . ?

I finally have the answers I've longed for.

I know why Izzy was so confused when Detective Arnold told her where Plum's body had been found. And I know who really killed her best friend.

But there are some things I'll never know. Some things I'll never be able to ask:

What haven't you told me, Dita?

What did she tell you, Daddy?

Did you do it because of what I said, Izzy? And because of what I didn't say?

I'm pacing up and down the hallway when the doorbell rings. I put my eye to the spyhole and open up. Smile.

'You're back!' I say.

NOW

Willow Rowling is on the doorstep, sheltering under an umbrella that's come unstuck from its spokes.

Same could be said about me, I suppose . . .

'Just checking in,' she says. 'Making sure you're okay.'

'I'm fine,' I lie.

So many lies, I've started to forget what's real and what's dissembling.

She takes in my unwashed hair, my still bare feet.

'Do you still want to talk?' She puts a hand up. *Wait.* 'Before you answer . . .'

She rummages in her overlarge shoulder bag. Brown leather, fringed with tassels. My mother had a similar one.

'I come bearing gifts . . .'

She produces a massive bar of Dairy Milk.

'Chocolate makes everything better.'

The tears come in a torrent, gushing down my face like I'm Niagara Falls rather than a grown woman who should know how to behave. I apologise, sniff loudly. Wipe my nose on the back of my hand in a way Dita would certainly not have called ladylike.

'I'm so sorry. I—'

Willow draws me into a hug. My body is stiff at first, but then I relax into her embrace. The wretched tears start up again.

'Sorry,' I say again.

God, what's wrong with me?

'Hey,' she says, rubbing my back. 'You've got nothing to be sorry for.'

Except I do. And I start to tell her why. Mouth before brain, my father would have said. Dita probably too.

'It was a case that shocked the nation, rocked our town to its roots. Put it on the map for all the wrong reasons . . .'

I talk and talk, a lock opening. Water finally flowing free (along with my stupid tears). And with the words, I start to feel free too. Find, at last, I can breathe.

We end up in my living room; me curled up in the corner of the couch, Willow perched beside me. Listening without interrupting. Feeding me chocolate. Murmuring 'It's okay' and 'I understand' in the right places.

When you go through a trauma, you need someone to talk to. Doesn't matter what that person says so long as they're saying something. Makes you feel less alone . . .

I reach the end of the story, meet her eyes. Vocalise my earlier thought:

'Dita asked for forgiveness but is forgiveness mine to give?'

Willow puts a hand on my arm.

'Perhaps the person you really need to forgive is yourself . . .'

I shake my head.

'I watched that video on Izzy's phone. I saw her by the ice

349

cream truck with Ryder Grady. But I didn't say a word to Dita or my dad. Not even when I found out he was a teacher at her school. If I'd spoken up, if I'd said something in time . . .'

She smiles sadly.

'I used to say the same thing to my grandma. If only I'd told someone about my dad. If only I hadn't waited for things to get as bad as they did . . .'

'You understand, then . . .'

'I understand this wasn't your fault.'

I shake my head again. She doesn't get it. How could she?

'You know many ten-year-olds?' Willow asks, breaking off another strip of chocolate and passing it to me before snapping off one for herself.

'Huh?'

Don't say, 'Huh?' Say, 'Pardon.'

'You're putting it all on yourself, Finn. But you were just a kid.'

It takes me a beat to realise she's called me by my real name. Another to realise I like it.

'I should have said something. I should have made them listen. At least made them see Plum and Lu were bad news.'

'You tried.'

'I should have tried harder.'

Willow shakes her head, lets out a breath.

'You can't force someone to listen. If you could, there'd be no addicts in this world. No broken hearts.'

'What about the charm bracelet?' I ask.

She frowns.

'What about it?'

'Plum didn't take it, I did. I figured if my sister thought she'd pinched it, she wouldn't want to be friends with her anymore. And I was pissed she'd called me pathetic.'

The furrows on Willow's forehead deepen.

'Don't you see?' I explain. 'It's the real reason Izzy stabbed Plum. You don't know how much that bracelet meant to her.'

Willow gives my hand a squeeze.

'Your sister didn't stab her friend over a bracelet, Finn. She stabbed her because Plum was stirring shit about her to Ryder Grady, a man she was literally obsessed with. You said so yourself.'

'Is that the real reason though?' I ask. 'Or is the charm bracelet what set it all off? What made her hate Plum in the first place?'

Willow gives me a look, eyebrow at half mast.

'There's only one way to find out.'

'What's that?' I ask.

'By talking to your sister, of course,' she says.

NOW

The plane touches down at LAX as I'm finishing my morning coffee. No hangover to chase, though my hands are quaking as if I've spent all night on the sauce.

The letter from Little Rock Prison arrived on Tuesday, two weeks after I collected my first sobriety chip. I've been going to meetings every day.

They take place at a church on Pilgrim's Green; one I've walked past I don't know how many times on my way to the library.

On the board that first time, a quotation that could have been speaking directly to me:

Matthew 7:7–8 . . . knock and the door will be opened to you. For everyone who asks receives.

Yet even so, I struggled to go in, despite how much I wanted (still want) to get better. I was wrong – alcohol isn't a crutch, it's a curse. For me, at any rate.

I don't know how long I was standing outside those big wooden doors. Shifting from one foot to the other, gnawing my lips.

A woman came up behind me, a fellow American. Skin the colour of rosewood, grey cotton-wool hair.

'It gets easier,' she said. 'I promise.'

Her eyes were kind.

I tried to smile.

'What happens?' I asked, meaning 'I have no idea what to expect.'

She understood. We didn't just have the States in common.

'We take it in turns to tell our truth, talk about the worst things in our lives. And somehow it helps. Makes you realise you're not alone.' She smiled. 'Though I guess it's different for everyone.'

She opened the door, stepped aside to let me in.

'I have to, don't I?' I said, more to myself than to her.

'Only when you're ready, honey.'

I wet my lips, told her:

'I am ready.'

Followed her inside.

There was a trestle table set up in the hall. A plate of short-bread cookies. A big box of Krispy Kreme original glaze. A flask of coffee.

A man in a navy cardigan came over and shook my hand. Told me he was the chair and that his name was Arthur.

'I'm new,' I said. 'Is that okay?'

He smiled the same way the woman outside had.

'More than okay . . . and welcome. You're with family now.'

We sat in a circle on plastic bucket seats that squeaked whenever you shifted position. Some people were in suits, others in sweatpants. Businessmen and folk on benefits. Young and old.

'It doesn't matter who you are, if alcohol is costing you more than money, you have a place at our table,' Arthur told me.

'No one drinks the way we do because they like it,' an Asian lady said, telling a story about how her daughter, who'd stopped speaking to her at the height of her illness, had now reached out.

'Recovery isn't deciding to quit your addiction. It's about recognising what's causing it.'

There were murmurings of agreement. I was surprised to find my eyes welling. Still more surprised when I agreed yes, okay. I'd speak.

'My name's Finn. I drink to drown my guilt. I don't know any other way. But I want to stop.'

I didn't mention the letter I'd written to my sister after speaking to Willow or that I was going to get on a plane and visit her after twenty years of pretending we weren't related.

Now, as I disembark the aircraft, there's a sickly feeling in my stomach. My muscles have turned to liquid. I've been trapped inside this metal tube for eleven hours but suddenly I don't want to leave it. I want to hide under my seat. To stay there until the plane taxis back up the runway and peels away from the ground.

Will I even recognise Izzy? Will I know what to say?

The flight attendants are standing by the doors, lipsticked smiles fixed to their faces.

'Thank you for flying with us.'

'Goodbye now.'

'Cheerio . . .'

I go through passport control in a sort of daze. Pick up a rental from Enterprise.

'I forgot American cars are so big,' I say to the clerk.

Everything seems bigger here. Like I'm a foreigner, rather than coming home.

I'd planned to go to my hotel first, freshen up. Maybe take a nap if there was time. But instead, I find myself entering 'Little Rock Prison' rather than 'Holiday Inn' into the satnav.

My father's motto:

Best way to finish something is to start it . . .

I used to ask him what he'd do if Izzy changed her mind and said she wanted to see him.

'Catch the first flight,' he answered every time.

Only she never did change her mind. And now I'm the one coming back.

It feels wrong visiting her without him.

But right that you're doing it, his voice says inside my head.

Head west on World Way, the satnav instructs. *You will arrive at your destination in an hour.*

NOW

The flat farmland stretches out on all sides as I draw close to the jail. A patchwork of yellow-green fields punctuated with high-to-the-sky fencing and coiled snakes of barbed wire.

This is what Izzy sees when she looks out. If she looks out.

Her only view since graduating juvie.

I pass the towers. More fencing. More barbed wire. They've planted flowers on the 'public' side. Purple seaside daisies, red salvia and aloe vera. Somehow it only makes the place seem bleaker.

I pull up to the barrier, give my name to the guy in the booth. Wait while he checks my passport. I'm trembling, hope he doesn't notice, and am immediately cross with myself for caring.

He glances at my photo, back at me. Hands me a visitor pass.

'You'll need to fill this in. You understand it's a felony to bring any weapons or illegal drugs on to prison grounds?'

I nod. He waits for me to say it.

'I understand.'

'You also understand a visual inspection of the inside of your vehicle is allowed at any time you're on prison grounds?'

He's a robot, reciting his lines by rote. Not unlike the way Izzy recited what must have been Ryder's.

I tell him yes. I understand.

'All visitors and their possessions must be searched before visiting a prisoner.'

'Okay.'

He waits again until I tell him: yes, I understand.

Hands me back my passport. Directs me to the parking lot. Tells me to make my way through to the processing centre.

'Thank you,' I say.

He doesn't answer.

I park in the visitor section, cut the engine. Sit there for a long moment staring out the windscreen. Vision blurred. Heart smacking against my ribs.

I'm going to see Izzy. And I'm pretty sure I'm going to be sick.

'What am I doing here?' I say aloud, grinding the heels of my hands into my temples.

It's what I should have done a long time ago though.

A deep breath. A mental shakedown. *Pull it together, Jackman.*

To take my mind off the hurricane in my head, I run over the checklist the prison sent.

Items a visitor may bring . . . Attire restrictions . . .

I pause at 'no excess jewelry'.

Think of the charm bracelet I pinched. How I framed Plum. Burned the house down.

How many lies did we tell that summer? How many liars?

I get out and stretch. My back stiff from sitting so long.

A deep breath and then I start to walk. One day at a time, they say in AA.

One foot at a time, I think.

There are other visitors waiting in line. I shuffle forward, fill in my pass. Give it to the woman behind the desk when I reach the front. She takes it from me, enters my details into a computer.

Writes something on it. Hands it back.

'This is your key to get in and out of the prison. You'll need to surrender it to a member of staff while you're in the visitor room. It'll be returned to you when you leave.'

She runs through the long list of items I'm not allowed to bring in. Asks if I have any of them 'on your person'.

It's as bad as airport security, an analogy I'm well placed to make, having been through it twice in the last twenty-four hours.

'Go through the metal detector.' She waves me over. 'You're in Visitor Room 3.'

I'm expecting one of those little glass cubicles with a phone on the wall like I've seen in movies, but instead I'm escorted into a largish room with twenty tables and chairs arranged in lines.

'Over there,' my chaperone tells me, pointing to a spot at the far end of the room.

The tabletop is sticky. The room smells of stale cigarette smoke despite the big 'No Smoking' sign on the wall.

There are five corrections officers standing by; another sits behind a podium, fingers interlaced. In each corner of the ceiling is a surveillance camera. I think of Izzy looking up at the camera during her interrogation, asking for a hairbrush. Asking if she was going to be on TV.

She seemed so grown-up to me at the time, but watching the tapes now, I see she was really just a child. A kid who sucked her thumb at night when there was no one around to remind her it would give her crooked teeth.

I sit on my hands. I don't want the first thing she notices about me to be how much I'm shaking.

Ten, fifteen minutes go by. I start to think maybe she's not coming.

Then the door opens.

And Izzy files in.

NOW

The person being led over to my table is a woman. The Izzy I knew was a thirteen-year-old girl.

I should have been prepared. But I'm not.

My sister is a stranger.

Her once sun-kissed hair is now the colour of dirty dishwater. Her eyes dull in the way of stones.

Visibly ground down by the years.

I expect she sees me the same way.

What hits me the hardest though is her orange jumpsuit. The last time I saw her was at court in her baby blue sweater and white button-down shirt.

Her eyes are lowered as the corrections officer removes her cuffs.

'Hands on the table,' he barks. 'Any inappropriate touching and the visit will be terminated.' He rattles off a list of examples of what's deemed inappropriate. 'No feeding each other. No touching each other's faces. No adjusting each other's clothing.'

The old Izzy would have made a snarky comment. *But sex*

is okay? Izzy 2.0 says nothing. Keeps her head down. I expect she's learned to.

'There are books and board games if you want them. Your visitor is allowed to buy you a snack from the vending machine. You can't touch the machine though. Or handle the money. Do so, the visit will be terminated and you'll be subject to discipline. You understand, inmate?'

Inmate? God.

Izzy nods.

'Yes, sir.'

I haven't heard her voice in twenty years. Like her face, it's unrecognisable. The spirit squeezed right out of it.

What have they done to her?

'It's your responsibility to clean up your area afterwards. Books or games need to be returned to their proper place. Trash cleared away. You may share a brief hug or kiss with your visitor at the end of the visit.'

It occurs to me this may be the first time she's been told this. That I'm the first person to come and see her in twenty years.

A pressure builds behind my eyes. I bite down hard on my tongue, determined not to cry.

Izzy sits, lays her hands flat on the table. Finally raises her eyes.

'You came,' she whispers.

'I'm sorry it wasn't sooner,' I say.

NOW

At first, it's a conversation between strangers, both of us feeling our way.

We skirt the real issue, keep the chat light. Izzy's favourite bagel chips. That I work in a library now. The cost of commissary.

All the while, I'm conscious that the clock is ticking. If I'm going to say what I came here to say, I need to spit it out.

Put up or shut up.

I run my bottom lip through my teeth, pick at my nails.

'What is it?' Izzy asks.

The Izzy from twenty years ago, the Izzy I knew as well as myself. Or thought I did.

'It was me, not Plum,' I say.

She frowns, asks, what was me?

'I took your charm bracelet. Not her. I was stupid. Jealous. I'm so sorry.'

A smile stretches across Izzy's face.

'What's funny,' I ask a little crossly.

'I knew it was you, Finn. You've always been a crap liar.'

'But—'

She puts her hands up. *Okay, you got me.*

'Alright, I found it in your room.'

'You went through my stuff?'

She shrugs, the one-shoulder shrug I remember so well.

'You went through mine enough.'

I'm about to make some retort, then I stop myself. We're not kids anymore, and she's right. I snooped through her things all the time. Instead, I ask why she didn't say anything.

She shrugs again, tells me it's so long ago she doesn't remember.

'Expect I didn't want to give you the satisfaction. And I took it back so . . .'

She trails off. Shrugs again. *No biggie . . .*

I didn't know she'd taken it back. Never even checked it was still where I'd hidden it.

'Why are you telling me now?' she asks.

'I thought that's why you killed Plum,' I say, my voice going quiet.

Her eyebrow shoots up.

'Because I thought she stole my bracelet?' An almost perfect rendition of what Willow said. 'What kind of psycho do you think I am?' She gives a sad laugh. 'Actually, maybe don't answer that.'

I fiddle with my cuffs, work my jaw.

Izzy tilts her head.

'There's something else, isn't there? Is it Dad . . . ?'

Where to start? I hunt for the right words, end up just blurting it out.

'You didn't kill Plum. It wasn't you.'

Izzy looks at me, lips parting.

'You know?' she says.

I tell her about the letter Dita sent. How she went to Turtle Lake, followed Izzy and Lu into the trees. How she finished the job they started.

It's not until I wind up, that I register what Izzy said: *You know?*

'She already told you, didn't she?' I ask.

I'm not sure what I feel. Surprised? Disappointed? Envious?

All these years, while I waited in vain for letters from Dita, was she busy visiting Izzy? Her favourite, despite what she always claimed about not having one.

But Izzy shakes her head, tells me no. She had no idea Dita did that. That Dita's never been to see her, though not for want of trying.

'Makes sense it was her though.'

I pull a face, ask what makes her say that. Dita killing Plum still barely makes sense to me and I've had over two weeks to get used to the idea.

Izzy gives me a look, like it's the most obvious thing in the world.

'Washington Beach? I mean, come on! She'd go there any chance she got.'

We reminisce for a few minutes. The seals Dita used to take us to watch. The walks along the pier. The ice cream afterwards.

Dita was great at outings. Great at killing too, apparently.

Again, it takes me a beat.

'So, what did you mean when you said, "You know?"'

'Huh?'

'After I told you didn't kill Plum.'

She scratches the back of her neck with her index finger. Says:

'I dunno.'

She's playing dumb, though. I can see it in her eyes. The way she won't meet mine. My father was the same, couldn't look at you if he was fudging.

I've travelled five and a half thousand miles. I didn't come all this way to be bullshitted. I say as much.

She glances over her shoulder as if worried about being overheard. Then, in a low voice:

'I didn't kill Plum.'

I let out a breath, exasperated.

'I know. I just told *you* that.'

She shakes her head like I'm being stupid. *You're such a bonehead, Finn . . .*

'I mean, I didn't stab her.'

I stare at her, ask if this is some kind of joke.

She scoffs, tells me it wouldn't be a very funny one if it were.

I rub my temples.

'I don't understand. You confessed. Told the police the whole thing was your idea. I saw the tapes, Izzy. And the bloodstains on that swatch of material from your shirt.'

She scratches at a bite on her wrist, tells me she was right there when Lu knifed Plum. No wonder her shirt got blood on it.

I tell her I don't get it.

365

'Why say you did it if you didn't?'

I think of Elsa Stone. She's called me twice since getting back to California, gave me her number so I can call her. It's a funny old relationship. Bitter sweet. If it weren't for Elsa, Dita would still be alive. And if it weren't for Elsa, I'd still be in the dark.

Certainly I wouldn't be here talking to Izzy.

'Did they play a trick on you?' I ask my sister. 'Is that why you confessed?'

There was a case in Iceland in the seventies, Elsa told me. Six suspects confessing to a crime they didn't commit because interrogators somehow managed to undermine their memories of what really happened.

Is that what happened with Izzy? Or was she being threatened? Though if so, by whom?

She laughs; it's hollow.

'No one was threatening me, Finn. If you recall, I was the one giving people nightmares back then. Not the other way round.'

'What, then? Why would you say you stabbed her if you didn't?'

The tips of her ears go pink, the way they used to when she was a child. She looks at the table, at her hands. Anywhere that isn't my face.

'I wanted to impress him. Wanted him to know how far I'd go to prove my love.'

'Arnold?' I ask, though I know she means Ryder.

It makes her laugh, properly this time.

'Honestly, I'd have thought that was more Dita's schtick,' she says.

'Wasn't just me who thought that, then?'

Izzy scoffs.

'All those brownies, I mean . . .'

She trails off. A beat passes when we say nothing and then I ask:

'Do you still love Ryder?'

She shakes her head

'Not anymore. And if I could take back Turtle Lake, I would. In a heartbeat. I wanted Plum dead. I agreed to Lu's plan. But when it came to it, I just couldn't go through with it.'

'It was really all Lu?' I ask. 'The plan? Twenty-one stab wounds? All by herself?' I let out a long breath, rub my eyes. 'Jesus.'

'She had more reason than me, I guess.'

I raise a brow. An unspoken question.

'Plum's mom was having it off with her dad,' Izzy explains. 'While Lu's mother lay dying in bed. "You'd think she'd know better," Lu said. "After what her husband did with that Hooters waitress."'

I think back to the night at the vigil. Mrs Underwood taking a half step towards Lu's father. Him touching her lightly on the back. Dita murmuring 'Hmm' in a knowing sort of way.

To what she said about Lu kicking Plum in the ribs as she lay bleeding on the ground. Calling her a skank. A homewrecker.

'I get she was angry,' I say. 'But why go after Plum? Surely Mrs Underwood was the one she hated.'

'Oh, she hated her too. But Plum was an easier target. And attacking her was a way of hurting her mom too, I suppose.'

I nod. *I suppose . . .*

'So, who do we talk to?' I ask. 'I'll sort out a lawyer. We've got Dita's written confession and if there's a way to show you didn't stab Plum . . .'

Izzy sits up straight in her chair, face suddenly closing up.

'I can't tell anyone,' she says.

I stare at her in disbelief, ask why on earth not.

'We'll hire an investigator. There's got to be a way to prove you didn't do it.'

'You're not listening, Finn.'

The same accusation I used to throw at my father and Dita.

'You're not making any sense,' I retort.

'I'm up for parole next year. If I start kicking up a fuss about being innocent, how do you think that'll play out?'

I raise an eyebrow.

'I don't know, like maybe you are . . .'

She presses her lips together, shakes her head. *Bzzz. Wrong answer.*

'I've been around the block long enough to know how this game works, Finn. No remorse means no parole. And a person who can't accept their guilt is definitely not going to get early release.'

I let what she says settle.

'A year?'

She nods.

'A year.'

'Okay, then.'

Under the table, I rest my ankle against hers, feel the tick of her pulse beat against mine –

The sister I lost. The sister I've found.

ONE YEAR LATER

'Morning, Finn . . .'

'Lovely flowers you got there, Finn . . .'

Twenty years is a long time to wear a mask. I'm still getting used to people calling me by my real name, to introducing myself as Finn Jackman. To owning my past and casting off my guilt.

Mrs Langley was right. So too the woman I met on my first day at AA.

It does help to talk. Like Willow says: once you start, it's hard to stop.

I used to be so afraid of how people would respond to me if they found out who I was. So worried about becoming an outsider, I ended up becoming one.

I felt ashamed of being related to Izzy, was convinced that if there was a demon in her blood, there must be one in mine too. That I shared the blame for what happened at Turtle Lake.

Visiting my sister, owning up to my lie, changed everything.

Face the pain or stay in the dark place, Elsa Stone's therapist told her. I still have my bad days, days when I crave the sweet oblivion of liquid numbness, but I'm getting there. Learning how to live.

Izzy is learning too.

She was granted parole last week and given permission to travel to London to visit our father. I watched her walk out of Little Rock Prison, blinking in the sunshine. A mole underground so long she was unused to the light.

I had to send clothes for her to wear. Civvies, they call them. The ones she'd worn at her trial being very many sizes too small. The jeans I got her were the wrong size too, but at least they weren't made for a child.

Now, we're walking up the corridor of my father's care home together.

'Which room is he in?' Izzy asks.

I've already told her. She's nervous, I expect. I'm a little nervous too.

'What if he doesn't want to see me?'

She's asked that already too. I tell her what he used to say to me –

'If he'd thought you wanted to see him, he'd have jumped on the first flight to LAX. Hired a space rocket if he had to.'

'Okay,' she says, takes a deep breath.

I slip a hand in hers.

'Okay.'

I knock on his door, don't wait for him to say, 'Come in.'

He hasn't said anything for over a decade. Can't even control his facial muscles.

But as Izzy walks into the room, his dead eyes light up. His broken face lifts into a smile.

And then a miracle. My father says her name.

'Izzy . . .'

To anyone else, it might sound like an expulsion of air. A sound trick or whatever the audio equivalent of 'trick of the light' might be. But I know it's not air and it's not a trick.

I'm not just hearing what I want to hear.

My father is finally talking.

Izzy goes to his bed and drops to her knees. Holds his hand in both of hers, brings it to her lips.

'I'm home, Daddy,' she says.

And it's true. This may not be California.

But we are finally home.

ACKNOWLEDGEMENTS

I am so grateful to you, my readers, for trusting me with your time and for sitting back and letting me tell you a story. Being able to call myself a writer has always felt like a privilege and I wouldn't have that privilege without you.

I am also hugely privileged to have David Headley (aka The World's Greatest Agent) as my champion. Two years ago, he signed me on the back of an idea (it would later become *Truly, Darkly, Deeply* but then it didn't even have a title). I will always be grateful for his belief in me and for placing me with my wonderful editor, Stef Bierwerth.

Thank you, Stef, for your patience as we chipped *All the Little Liars* into shape. For your eagle-eyed insight and for encouraging me to stretch myself and be brave. This is a better book because of you.

Thank you also to the Quercus team (especially Joe, Kat, Madeleine, Dave, Lipfon, Hannah and Bethan) who helped *Truly, Darkly, Deeply* become a *Sunday Times* bestseller, Theakston's Old Peculier Crime Novel of the Year longlistee and Richard & Judy pick (still pinching myself!) and for everything you do to help me reach new heights and new audiences.

And thank you to my agency, DHH, for your support and for bringing my books to other territories (and even the screen!). Special thanks to Helen Edwards, Emily Hayward-Whitlock and Emily Glenister. You rock!

These guys rock too: My friends (special call out to the *Criminal Minds* posse and Linda-Jane Buckle who could win any of the world's best cheerleader and advice-giver awards hands down).

My Crime Time FM podcast co-hosts, Paul Burke and Barry Forshaw. Nobody knows more about crime fiction than these guys or expresses it so well!

And to my family who put up with me banging on about my books and occasionally even read them: my parents, Carolyn and Martin. My brother and sister, David and Henrietta. My father- and sister-in-law, Richard and Lynsey and my nephews, Jake and Harry (senders of shelfies and super cool humans). My sons, Max and Joey, whom I love to heaven and back. Charlie, the most beautiful retriever in the world (no, I'm not biased) and Tim – my husband and my best friend.

Which brings the circle back to you!

I really hope you've enjoyed *All the Little Liars*, do let me know by tweeting @VictoriaSelman.

One of the best things about being a writer is getting to meet readers. I post details of upcoming events and appearances on my website where you can also sign up to my newsletter: www.victoriaselmanauthor.com for sneak previews and giveaways.

And to be the first to hear about upcoming releases, follow me on Amazon or check out my author pages on Waterstones.com or Bookshop.org.

Hope to tell you another story again soon!

Victoria x